FULL SLAB DEAD

An Un-Cozy Un-Culinary Josie Tucker Mystery

EM Kaplan

BLACK
CROW
BOOKS

ISBN: 1548119784
ISBN-13: 978-1548119782

FOR MY AUSTIN FRIENDS

Amy & Matt;
Lois & Buddy;
Laura the Stick Lizard Lady;
and my friends from BMC.

CONTENTS

MANY THANKS TO

Megan Harris, editor
Katherine Cruz, editor
The Josie Tucker VIPs

Part 1: Spark

Listen to the sizzle of a steak hitting a hot grill. The sound is as magical as the unexpected spark of chemistry on a first date.

Imagine the first person to turn a slab of gory meat on a spit over a fire. Can you hear the pop and hiss of juice as it hits the hot coals? Cro-Magnon man wants food. His daughter adds a handful of roots and a parsley garnish.

From a charred, fuzzy mammoth shank, we flash over to a glistening roasted pig, buried in leaves and savory smoke. The flame of history forms a filet mignon, perfectly pink, until it cycles back to a blood-red beef tartar. The evolution of cooking, the sublimation of a recipe, grows complex and intricate in the blink of an eye, as quick as a flying spark, roaring into an inferno.

—Josie Tucker, *Will Blog for Food*

CHAPTER 1

Thunder rolled outside Ruby's Gen-U-wine Texas Bar-B-Q Shack as Josie shook the water drops off her denim jacket. Through the speaker, Stevie Ray Vaughan wailed from the great beyond about the floods keeping him from his baby down in Texas. The downpour pounded on the corrugated tin roof overhead. The restaurant door slammed shut in a gust of rainy, smoky, barbecue-scented air as she squinted at the menu board above the counter.

"Do you want a full slab or a half? Itty-bitty thing like you could make a fool out of me by tucking away a full slab of baby backs. That's why I never try to guess a person's order," the woman behind the chest-high counter said and made a *pshaw* noise with her puckered, hot-pink lips.

Josie hesitated like a deer caught in the headlights of a Ford F-250. Good thing the lunch rush was over and no one was goading her with impatient throat-clearing and watch-checking. Did she—Josie Tucker, food blogger extraordinaire and slave to her cranky stomach—want a full two pounds of fall-off-the-bone rib meat drenched in tangy fire-red barbecue sauce? Her eyes said yes, but her gut said, *Are you out of your ever-lovin' mind?*

She was two-for-two in eating at the local Austin barbecue places for her blog while her boyfriend, Drew, was at a Geriatrics medical conference in town. Two places in two days. Their hotel room mini-fridge was already packed with yesterday's leftover containers of brisket, chicken, and ribs—and she suspected her over-taxed stomach had as little space left in it as well. She'd already felt a warning tremor from her midsection on the drive over to Ruby's.

And yet...

3

"Well, now I feel like you've thrown down the gauntlet," she told the woman, whose name tag said *Georgia*. "And I'm not known to back down from a challenge."

When the woman saw her reading her badge, she grinned with glossy white teeth. "Yeah, that's my name although I'm a native, born and bred. Guess my mama thought the grass was greener over in the Peach State. But guess what? Eighty-three years old and she still hasn't ever left Texas."

"Not even for a day trip?" Josie's mind was slightly boggled. In the past two years, she'd been back and forth from Boston to the western United States twice—and she wasn't counting a stupid Vegas trip she would forever regret. If she could erase it from her memory bank, that would be *super*.

"A day trip? Even if you start in the morning, you could drive all day and still be in Texas when the sun went down, I tell you what. You pack up your bags for a big adventure and you end up in Lubbock or somewheres. So if you really want to leave this state, you've got to plan ahead, if you know what I'm saying." She fluttered her fingers as if shooing away the thought. "But that's neither here nor there. I interrupted you while you were making the decision of a lifetime with your ribs. What's it gonna be?"

Josie decided to come clean. "The truth of the matter is, I had barbecue yesterday. I'm going to have it today and then again tomorrow." That statement, spoken aloud, made Josie want to double over in submission and lay prostrate on the nearest flat surface. Even the trendy stamped concrete floor under her gray Chuck Taylor low-tops would do. After lunch, her stomach was going to hate her. Even more than usual.

What else is new.

"Three days in a row? You got some kind of slow, drawn-out death wish for your arteries? Because as much as I love me some good old fashioned brisket and ribs, that's a lot of red meat for one woman. Unless you're from out of town, because then it makes perfect sense. Taking a tour of the sights, tasting the local fare. So where're y'all from?"

Having correctly ferreted out Josie's non-native status, Georgia propped her meaty elbow on the tall countertop and rested her chin in her hand. Her hot-pink fingernails matched her lipstick, which Josie found to be an impressive, yet personally foreign expression of femininity.

Georgia's question was simple enough, but Josie didn't know how to answer it. She'd been born in Massachusetts and lived there currently in an apartment near Fenway Park with Drew, but her heart was stuck in Arizona where she'd spent her formative teenage years after her dad had died.

"Boston," she said, finally settling on an answer, though it didn't feel exactly right. She sometimes still felt as displaced as a tumbleweed on Boylston Street. "I'm doing a food tour of Austin-area barbecue places for my blog. I was at The Mineral Lick yesterday and I'll go to Smiley's tomorrow. Then to Off The Bone later in the week."

If her belly could take it. *So far, so good.*

Until this week, her notoriously testy digestive system had been quiet since her brief stay on a college campus a couple months ago. During that trip, she'd more or less fasted—not because she'd thought it might clear up her stomach problems, but because the food wasn't fit for human consumption. Plying her tum-tum with spicy, tomato-based sauces every day of this vacation was no doubt hastening the inevitable.

Never mind the Very Important Question—which called for all caps—she was preparing to ask Drew. Yes, *that question.* Her standard MO was avoidance on that front. But this was just a *simple* vacation. No dead brides. No stalkers. No recurring nightmares. No crazy plots in which she could get embroiled. She was just here to eat excessive amounts of animal flesh, take a few pictures for her blog, and otherwise enjoy the week with Drew.

"Some of the barbecue places in this area have an intertwined history, did you know that?" Georgia asked. When Josie shook her head, the woman plowed ahead, tossing out tidbits of gossip like hand grenades. "My uncle, Conrad Ruby, who owns this place, is also the uncle of Billy Blake. Now, Billy is the sad-sack owner of Smiley's and the least smiley person you'd ever want to know. Conrad—who may or may not have been directly related to Jack Ruby, the nightclub owner who took down that blackguard, Oswald, who shot America's one true king, John Fitzgerald Kennedy—used to co-own Smiley's with his cousin back in the 80's. Those two boys had a big falling out, and Conrad went off to start his own place, *this* place, Ruby's Gen-U-wine. Since then, their rivalry has been epic, the stuff of history books. Well, local history books, at least.

"When Conrad sponsored a local softball team, Billy sponsored their biggest competitors. When Billy phoned in a donation to the local Shriners' telethon, Conrad called them up and beat the amount by a dollar. It just went on and on over the years. Never got very ugly, though. Just little things to show they were annoyed with each other.

"The big exception to our barbecue relations is Off The Bone. They're not any part of this Shakespearean tale. Off The Bone is relatively new, just eight or ten years old. A young couple from the Carolinas—ACC region, if you're a sports fan. Hook 'em horns, by the way—opened that place, and they have the nerve to serve Carolina vinegar sauce on their menu. Landsakes, that's just evil. The rumor is, she's actually a *vegetarian* at home."

Josie blinked, as if clearing her vision would straighten out the details in this barbecue pitmaster family tree. She needed a spreadsheet...or a flowchart. *No. Absolutely not.* Though she could feel herself getting sucked in, she didn't want to hear any of this drama. She was here to find out what kind of dry rub they used on their ribs and if they used mustard or oil to get the rub to adhere to the meat. In Memphis, for instance, she knew they tended not to use barbecue sauce on their ribs—just to enjoy the crust or "bark" of spices on the meat. But Texans were pretty much married to their sweet, spicy tomato-based sauce. She hoped—

"And have you heard Smiley's is haunted?"

Dog-gone it. Against her will, her interest was piqued. She wanted to know more, but she could resist temptation, right? *Wrong.*

"Haunted? As in...inhabited by ghosts?" She tried and failed to keep the Archie Bunker skepticism out of her voice. None of the websites or tourist info about Smiley's had mentioned ghosts or anything supernatural. Keeping the naysayer out of her tone was harder than tamping down her interest in *why* people would think it was haunted.

Georgia whipped her head around and yelled toward to the kitchen, "Manny, come mind the counter. I got some educatin' to do for my new friend."

Here's where I should run screaming, right?

Josie plunked her denim-clad butt down on a metal bench that looked like it had once been a bleacher seat. The table in front of it was wooden and heavily scarred with names, lop-sided lovers' hearts, and cheers for something called the Hutto Hippos. She couldn't imagine they'd be a school mascot in these parts—hippos were from Africa, not Austin—but what did she know?

Georgia slid a plastic oval basket lined with wax paper in front of her. It was filled with the most delectable looking half slab of ribs Josie had seen in…well, the last 24 hours. She dug her phone out of her pocket to take a couple of artsy, angled photos for her blog. Although she wasn't the best photographer, she could add on an Instagram filter with the best of 'em.

Now all she needed was a little peace and quiet to enjoy her lunch, to savor the flavors and let her world-class taste buds—which was The Times' description of her, not her own—do their magic so she could translate the whole experience into pithy words for her readers. After a few rapid-fire clicks, she set down her phone and leaned over the basket of ribs, inhaling deeply. She had discovered some subtle but important differences in the local barbecue lexicon and was developing a theory that she wanted to further—

Georgia lowered her substantial weight on the bench opposite Josie, jostling the table. In her hand was a cardboard Shiner Bock six-pack, which wasn't full of beer bottles but yellow and red squeeze bottles. Each condiment bottle held one of Ruby's barbecue sauces to put on her ribs or…white bread? Josie frowned at the stack of slices on the side of her order.

"Wonder Bread," Georgia explained. "An American tradition. The best thing since, well, sliced bread. Soaks up the grease in your gullet like nothing else. White and fluffy, just like the first loaf that came off the assembly line in the 1920s."

All right, so I have a lunch companion. I'm okay with that. She's part of the local flavor. I'll get her picture. That exquisite manicure alone deserves a spotlight.

Josie searched the table for a fork or a knife to hack apart her ribs, which was only a half-slab of them, she was relieved to note as she ran her hand down her poor concave stomach. Her tank was not up to snuff in terms of its normal capacity, but she forged onward. No utensils in sight. The only thing she found on the table was a centerpiece of utilitarian brown paper towels. The big roll didn't have tear perforations, as if it had been intended for a restroom dispenser but brought out to mop up the dining room clientele instead.

"You just go ahead and dig on in. Don't let my gabbing stop you." Georgia nodded to the steaming slab of meat in the nested wax paper in front of Josie.

As if. Nothing was getting between Josie and her food.

She picked up the charred end of the last rib on the slab with two fingers...and came away with a bare bone as the tender meat fell onto the wax paper in a succulent heap. Drool pooled in her mouth. She didn't know whether to stick her face directly into the basket like it was a trough or prolong her anticipation by pulling away another bone. If she did it again, she could watch the meat fall off and imagine how it would melt on her tongue. Very little chewing required.

With a vague, apologetic thought to the other patrons who might be embarrassed witnessing her private moment, she stuffed a bunch of it into her mouth. Sweet, sour, bitter, salty, and savory—five of the basic taste sensations—stampeded across her tongue. How could one bite encompass all of those kinds of flavor? Josie felt her grumpy, black heart crack open a just a little, thanks to the heavenly ambrosia sliding its way into her stomach.

"In about 1982, Billy Blake left his family ranch outside of Waco to go to college up at SMU in Dallas. All of them Blakes were Baylor graduates, so there was a little bit of a kerfuffle with him going away from home." Georgia interrupted herself, grasping a squeeze bottle out of the caddy with her plump fingers and pushing it toward Josie. "Try this one if you got a sweet tooth. It's my favorite, but I'm not biased or anything."

Josie was already on her next bite of baby backs, but she squirted a dab of the sweet sauce on her plate. Then she added a dollop of each of the other sauces in the caddy on her wax paper, making an array of them from sweet to blow-the-top-of-your-head-off. Her plate became a chili and tomato-based artist's palette. She was going to perform due diligence even though she already suspected garrulous Georgia's favorite flavor would be hers as well.

"So anyway, Billy did his bachelor's degree, and just like his family feared, he didn't come home afterward. It might not seem like a big distance to some folks. From here to Dallas is only a couple hundred miles with Waco smack dab between, but for people used to keeping their loved ones close, it's a very big deal."

The majority of Josie's family was either dead, trapped in the la-la-land of dementia, or far away in Arizona, yet she nodded. Despite her early isolation, Josie had managed to find a group of close-knit friends, a boss who gave her free reign to write her food blog remotely, and even a benefactor-slash-puppetmaster, Greta Williams, who popped in and out of her life at the oddest times. It seemed to Josie that no matter how far away she was, the ties to certain people stayed just as strong as the connections to those close by.

She took another mouthful and came away with nearly all of the meat, biting off more than she could chew. Literally, this time.

"That's some good stuff right there." Georgia grinned through her pink lipstick. "But getting back to Billy, the worst thing those Blakes could have imagined came true. He fell in love with a girl in the Big D."

When Josie raised an eyebrow, Georgia said, "Girl, not that D. I'm talking about the 'Big D' as in Dallas. I know what it means when the kids say it with their urban slang, but I'm not referring to a fella's privates. I'm talking about the city of Dallas. Because while Billy was up there at college, he got engaged to a big city girl named Mary Clare, one of them socialites. This was the late 1980's by then, so think raccoon eyeliner and Aqua Net. Big blonde hair." She gestured like she had a swarm of bees circling her head. "The works, if you know what I'm saying."

"She really must have caught Billy's eye," Josie said. She hoped she didn't sound sarcastic. Different time, different beauty standards. Plus, they were in Texas, after all. Everything was bigger. Especially 1980's hair.

"Oh, she was a beauty, no doubt about it. Along came the 90's and her hair calmed down. When that Marie Osmond slapped-cheeks look and glossy lips went away, you could really tell just how gorgeous she was. You know, stripped clean of all that paint."

The irony did not escape Josie that Georgia herself seemed to be an avid fan of hot pink cosmetics. If Josie had to name that particular shade, she'd call it BBQ Barbie in honor of her new acquaintance.

"So how did they end up in Austin running a barbecue restaurant?" Josie tore a wad of paper towels off the roll and swabbed her face. She probably wasn't getting all the mess off her face, just smearing it around more. But the flavor had made the mess totally worth it.

Georgia gave a rueful shake of her head. "All the cockamamie things people do for love... Billy didn't want to live in Dallas. Mary Clare didn't want to live out in the country by his people. So they settled here, bought a piece of land in the Bee Caves area west of Austin—this was before the town was overrun with tech companies and millionaires. Mary Clare had a stack of her own money, so the place they got was darn near palatial. I haven't been there myself, but it's been featured in a couple of architectural type magazines. You know, the ones where the couches are white and fluffy and not fit for the backsides of normal human beings."

Josie pushed back from her plate, belatedly realizing she'd Hoovered all the meat off the bones faster than a back alley street dog. She took a couple of shallow breaths to test the vindictiveness of her stomach, but it seemed to be holding steady. Spice was good for the tongue, but not always the best thing for her testy tank. Luckily, she didn't feel any abdominal lurches or weird pressure, so she settled back on her old bleacher seat for the rest of the saga about the local barbecue dynasty.

"What about the ghost?"

"Getting to that," Georgia assured her. "See, Billy wasn't the type to sit around and do nothing. He had a Business degree and a good knowledge of ranching. With some family recipes, he and his cousin, Levar, opened up Smiley's. And they did real well—it's still doing great despite the, you know, murder rumors. But 'round about 1995 or so, Mary Clare disappeared."

CHAPTER 2

"She went missing?"

In Josie's experience, a person didn't just dissipate like a puff of smoke. Usually there was violence, often fueled by one of the seven deadly sins. Lust. Pride. Envy. Avarice. Anger. Not usually gluttony or sloth, though. Those two sins were the more stay at home, play bongos, and smoke pot kinds of trespasses—not against others, but "against ourselves" kind of transgressions and self-harm.

"Vanished. Into thin air," Georgia said with a dramatic snap of her fuchsia-tipped fingers. "But the prevailing rumor has it that Billy killed her right there at the smokehouse."

In the restaurant? That was horrible and…kind of gross. But people often got passionate about their food—herself included. Why wouldn't there be a crossover into love gone sour? It was natural. It was also just so *unsanitary*.

"Why would he kill his wife?"

Josie was careful to reserve judgment as to whether this story might be the seedy tale of romance gone wrong. After all, there was gossip, and then there was gossip rooted in truth. Often a person couldn't tell one from the other without the benefit of hindsight.

Or getting clonked on the head with a shovel in the Arizona desert. Talk about a wakeup call. Josie hoped to avoid such violent epiphanies in the future. Some people had brain cells to spare, but she'd needed every last one of them to get out of the dumbass situations she'd gotten herself into previously. And there was no telling what the future held.

"She wanted to leave him to go back to Dallas, but he wasn't having any part of that. He loved her so much that he wouldn't let her go. Here's where the stories diverge. Some people say he shot her with an antique pistol. Others think he strangled her. You know, strangling is a sure sign that it's a crime of passion, when the killer gets all up-close and personal, right up in the victim's business."

Josie was intrigued but skeptical. Rumor and innuendo didn't amount to much when it came to solving old, mothballed mysteries. Hearsay didn't light the fires and stir the pots of cold cases. Not like a good old fashioned confession, anyway. And if Mary Clare's body had never been discovered, that made it a million times harder to solve. And yet...maybe she could help.

"What about the police—did they get involved?"

"Oh yeah they did. There were billboards and flyers. Her face was on every telephone pole and highway from Amarillo to Brownsville. The family hired some private detective fellow, but all he did was harass poor Billy near to death. Suspicion fell on Levar, too, but nothing came of that either. All it did was break up their relationship—they couldn't work together anymore after that. Levar went down to San Antonio right after Mary Clare vanished. He got a job at some fancy nightclub or hotel, and the two cousins aren't speaking anymore.

"Now remember, in the mid-90's, not everyone was all wired up with technology. Not everyone had a cell phone or GPS or what have you. All seriousness aside, Texans are not exactly early adopters when it comes to technology. I mean, Austin is different. It's the Silicon Prairie, as they say, but when you get farther out into the boondocks, you still have your people who are afraid of fax machines."

Josie suspected she might have an increased heart rate if she were confronted with one as well, never mind changing the ink for her printer. Her cell phone still gave her the cold sweats when it did something she wasn't expecting, like take a picture of a murderer without her knowing it.

Waitaminute, did Georgia just say "all seriousness aside"?

Josie's mind went off into lala-land for a minute, thinking about Georgia's crazy wordplay, thanks to her full belly and a distinct need for caffeine.

Georgia is the Texan equivalent of the great Reverend Spooner. Or is that Mrs. Malaprop? I think that's using the wrong word in place of another, like having a short stack of panic cakes for breakfast. But a spoonerism is accidentally saying "lack of pies" instead of a "pack of lies." Or a "pretty fart smeller" instead of a "pretty smart feller."

Focus, Josie, focus.

"And, like a lot of us, Mary Clare was a cash or check kind of lady, so no AMEX or Visa card to trace. If she had wanted to empty her bank account and go to Mexico and disappear, she darn well could have. Her mama may want to imagine she's living out her life eating mangoes on the beach, just for peace of mind. But *we all know* she didn't do that."

Josie had begun to fray a section of brown paper towel between her fingers. She creased it like an accordion, worrying it into smaller and smaller folds. All of her silly word pondering and mental gymnastics were a lame attempt to avoid the issue. Her nosy little self, that interior instinctive part of her brain that longed to insert itself into other people's problems, was waking up. Nothing like a good puzzle to make her focus on something other than her stomach, bad dreams, and other issues, like, oh, intermittent panic attacks…

"You know this how? Because of the ghost?"

As if a spiritual sighting was proof of murder. Casper CSI. Bloody Mary, the vanishing hitchhiker, the Flying Dutchman, and the creepy twins from *The Shining* all banding together to form a supernatural Our Gang? *Yeah, right.*

"Yes, ma'am."

Josie was not an expert on paranormal matters. She wasn't sure if she could call herself imminently qualified on anything. Talking, thinking, and writing *about food* was instinctive as breathing…as was meddling in other people's business. But ghosts and things that went bump in the night? She didn't believe in them.

Sure, a lot of cultures—from charismatic Christians who spoke in tongues and could be possessed by holy spirits, to the East Asian practice of honoring ancestors through altars and offerings like paper money and oranges—believed in voices and beings from the afterlife. She believed in karma, but not coincidence. Good luck and *definitely* bad luck. But did she believe in ghosts? *Meh.* The jury was still out. In fact, the hypothetical jury was so far out, they were having smokes and smoothies at a diner five miles away from the courthouse.

"Why do people think Smiley's is haunted?"

Thunder boomed, and Georgia leaned closer, smashing her abundant bosom on the table, her garish lips mesmerizing Josie. The sky grew darker, throwing her face into shadow. She looked like Vincent Price thanks to the bright overhead hanging pendant lights made from brown glass Shiner bottles with the bottoms sliced off.

"First, there are the strange noises. Crying and fussing, like a weeping woman. And they only happen when Billy is not there."

Woman done wrong. Check.

"Then there's the walls. Water has been known to leak down the walls—but it's not rainwater or a broken air conditioner. It's been serviced again and again by professional plumbers and HVAC guys. There's no damage to the roof or walls. And here's the kicker: it tastes like saltwater—like tears."

Dripping bodily fluids. Check. And if Georgia mentions anything about blood or barf or hands caught in garbage disposals, I'm outta here.

"Waitaminute. Someone tasted it?" Josie made an *eww* face. That was disgusting. Why would a person go around tasting strange liquids dripping down the walls? Frankly, someone's mother had done a terrible job.

"Ghost hunters have been through the place. They tested everything." *Including licking foreign substances off walls, apparently.* "I don't remember what else they found. Ectoplasm or what-have-you. They had the little machines with the lights and the beeping noises. Full-blown, 100 percent Ghostbusters. Experts or expert scammers. Six dozen in one, half in the other, if you ask me."

Josie frowned, mentally trying to catch her flailing comprehension and falling flat, like tripping on the sidewalk and face-planting. She backtracked and replayed Georgia's phrasing. *Six in one, half-dozen in the other?* Maybe Josie had just misheard her.

Is this a Texas thing? Or a Georgia thing?

"What do *you* think about all this?" she asked Georgia.

"Well, being is how Billy is a relation of mine, though not by blood, I can say with a clear conscience I think he did it. He's got a face like a murderer, and I've seen him have fits of temper—well, not me directly. I haven't witnessed it, but I've heard about it from his employees. I know a couple of them have actually quit over it. I think he flat-out scared them."

"Really?"

Enter suspect number one.

"During a bad electrical storm, we had a city-wide power outage one year. Just about every block of the city was in the dark. His whole freezer of meat spoiled because someone had forgotten to get gas for the back-up generator. When Billy found out about it, he went on the rampage. He had a big shipment of bread and pies that he destroyed, smashing them like he was the Hulk. Strawberry pie torn apart and splattered everywhere like it was a slaughterhouse. Everyone went running until he cooled off, which wasn't for several hours. Or so the story goes."

Mr. Barbecue Blake had anger management issues? Josie was personally familiar with self-control issues—her big mouth often got her in trouble and she had trouble not eating things she was supposed to avoid. She was aware of people with a tendency toward deviousness, like her benefactor, Greta Williams. However, she hadn't been around many men with anger problems. Drew was so even-keeled it took a great effort on her part to rile him up. She didn't mean to do it, but managed to on a regular basis anyway. She'd never been attracted to bad boys with mean streaks and anger issues. Because she was a petite person who was intimidated by big men, she shivered now thinking about Billy Blake.

"Yep," Georgia said. "That's why I think he did it. Because of his raging temper."

CHAPTER 3

The wide-open Austin skies cleared up and unveiled a flamboyant pink November sunset that took away Josie's breath—and her need for a jacket. She was intrigued enough by the ghost tale that she wanted to hop on the road and seek out Smiley's BBQ right away, but her newfound buddy Georgia had warned her against it.

"Avoid the roads this time of day. I-35, Mo-Pac, 360. Avoid everything. It's all bad. Just go back to where you're staying and park your car for a while. Get out and walk when the rain stops. We've got over two million people in this area now, and it ain't getting any better. We're not the sleepy, 'Keepin'-It-Weird' town we used to be. It's hard to find a hippie these days. They're buried under high tech fiber optic wire and refugees from California. So you'd best not risk any road rage situations if you don't have to."

Josie took Georgia's word for it—as well as her phone number, when it was pressed on her, to text the woman later if she had questions about "barbecue, Billy Blake, or life"—and returned downtown to the high-rise glass hotel where she and Drew were staying for the week. Maybe she could find other people who would talk with her about Billy Blake. She parked her rented Hyundai in the underground lot beneath the hotel and rode the elevator up to the lobby. She was on a mission...of sorts. She had a secondary, hidden agenda for coming on this trip with Drew, and it wasn't to stick her nose into someone else's business and get herself in trouble. Again.

She checked the time on her phone. Drew had a cocktail hour to mingle with other physicians and medical people attending the conference. He'd probably been back to the hotel and left while she was gone. She was invited to join him as a plus-one every night this week, but she'd agreed, in her typical asocial manner, to attend just one night later in the week. Prolonged exposure to crowds, especially ones who said things like "titrate the dosage" or "retest in three weeks," gave her the hives. The good news was, her boyfriend already knew this about her and didn't seem to mind.

Just one of the many reasons he's the perfect guy. He puts up with me.

Life with her wasn't exactly a cup of tea. She knew she was lucky to have him, and she was realistic about toning down her foibles so she didn't eventually drive him away. At least, that was the plan. Some couples refused to let each other into the bathroom. She felt the same about her weird mental states. *No one* needed to know the exact amount of her Crazy with a capital C.

Instead of returning to the room, she changed directions and headed out the hotel's front doors, peering up at the building above her as she exited. The entire front was encased in glass, but totally transparent so she could see the steel struts and tresses that comprised its skeleton. That's what she needed to emulate in her life and relationship with Drew—transparency. Well, to a certain extent. At least the good stuff, the useful things. Better communication. She needed to attempt to have one of those *Always Kiss Me Before Bedtime* relationships that were the stuff of self-help articles and mass-produced wall hangings in big box stores.

Yeah, right. Never mind that those wall words made her slightly nauseated.

She found herself on Cesar Chavez Street, in walking distance of the state capitol building in one direction and, in the other, the Colorado River and something called "the bat bridge" under which the fuzzy creatures of the night congregated en masse. Spiky glass buildings intermingled with quaint, older brick structures. Willie Nelson Boulevard sprawled not too far from the monument to Confederate soldiers. A cluster of tie-dye wearing protesters stood across the street from a pair of tie-wearing missionaries.

"Look where you're going, pretty lady." A bicycle whizzed by just as Josie was about to cross the street.

"Oh, sorry…" She turned her head in time to catch cork high heels wedges pedal past, above which were scrawny legs attached to pale, flat butt cheeks in a pink thong bikini bottom. Josie wished her gaze hadn't followed the legs up, but her eyes were on that train wreck of a journey, and she hadn't been able to stop them at the torso, which was twisted toward her. A silver sequined bikini top stretched across a flat sun-weathered chest. Above that, a toothless grin beamed out at her from behind a stained gray beard.

"...sir," she finally finished.

The bikini man waved at her and disappeared down the street. She blinked. Had she really seen him? Maybe her eyes were deceiving her. She shivered. It was downright balmy compared to the East Coast, but it was no bikini weather.

Isn't he freezing to death?

"Okay, then." Josie stepped off the curb, this time looking both ways first, just in case a pink elephant parade happened to be lurching up the boulevard as well.

Across the street, she ducked into what she'd thought was a jeweler's, but in fact was a bead shop. While it wasn't what she expected, she was immediately entranced by the rows and rows of beads and baubles. Crystal, wood, glass, in different shapes and hues. This place would be a field day for a crow. And, wow, this place had good lighting, because everything sparkled.

"Hi. Were you looking to sign up for a class today?" a woman asked her. Earrings made up from thousands of microscopic beads dangled from the woman's earlobes all the way to her shoulders. Equally ornate beaded cuffs encircled her wrists, and a stick pin with a beaded lizard perched on her shirt collar.

"Ah, no. I'm from out of town. Taking a tour of the local barbecue places for my blog."

"Awesome. Have you been to Smiley's?" Apparently blogging was no big deal in this town. Maybe these were Josie's people.

"It's on my list. I think I'll go there tomorrow."

"They have the best beans."

"Really? You're not a meat eater?"

"Oh, don't get me wrong. Ribs. Brisket. Chicken. Sausage. I'm an equal-opportunity eater, but their beans are amazing. Like, on a whole new level. But they're definitely not vegetarian. They have big chunks of applewood smoked bacon in them. Like, in case you're not getting enough meat with your order. But they are not to be missed, I promise you."

"Okay then, I'll be sure to get some."

"You won't be sorry," the woman said. Her face was placid but her nimble fingers sorted through a rack of beads, jumping from one bin to the next, restoring order like some kind of fairy magic. "So is there something you're looking for today?"

"I *was* looking for a piece of jewelry, but I think I'm in the wrong place."

"We have a lot of finished pieces here as well. In the case right here, if you want to take a look," the woman said. "Are you a beader?"

"Uh...no." Josie had never heard the term before, but she could figure out what it meant by her surroundings, that a beader meant *one who beads*, not a person with beady eyes. Or who was attracted to beads of moisture. Or something. "I'm not sure if I have the patience for it. But I can see how buying beads could be addictive."

The woman smiled. "That's how the habit starts. You get a few different colors, some different types. Suddenly you're spending your rent money on crystal seed beads, labradorite, and vintage glass cabochon—" At the blank look on Josie's face, she explained, "That means antique gewgaws."

While Josie examined the necklaces and pendants in the display case and considered buying one for her mother, a class let out from the back of the store. A stream of two dozen or more cackling women exited. Josie thought a cottage industry like this could actually do pretty well in the right conditions—and Austin was the right kind of eclectic mix for that.

"I hear Smiley's has a resident ghost, too," she told the woman.

"You know, I've been there a million times, but I have yet to make her acquaintance." The woman shrugged. "Maybe I'm just not lucky."

"Have you ever met the owner at Smiley's?"

"No, but I hear he's a loner. Keeps to himself. And gosh, doesn't that sound like every description of a murderer you've ever heard on the news?" The woman laughed.

Ah well, Josie would keep digging.

She selected a pendant she thought she might hang in her mother's room at the nursing home, and also an all-black, iridescent bracelet—a series of circles beaded onto circles with some kind of silver coin in the middle of one the foremost circle—for herself that looked like a Victorian mourning piece. She tried it on and thought it didn't clash too badly with her Joan Jett and The Runaways t-shirt.

"Nice choice. The coin in the center of your bracelet has a lot of history. Supposedly it belonged to a local woman who died for love. And while that sounds a little grim, it's actually a love charm. Or maybe, it means love can be a little harsh sometimes. I don't know. What do you think? It's open for interpretation. I got it at a flea market. I heard the story from the collector, so I wrote it down. In fact, I'm including a printed copy of the account in the bottom of your gift box if you want to read it sometime." She pulled out the corner of a piece of paper under the box.

Again with the ghost lore? This trip was headed down a rabbit hole. And fast.

"Huh. A love charm? No kidding," Josie said, sure the skepticism in her tone was ringing loud and clear. What the heck kind of coin was it? She peered at it more closely. Definitely not American currency. She could make out the letters R-O-M-A-N, but they were standard English letters. If it were a Roman coin, it certainly wouldn't be in English. Romani, maybe? And while the lettering around the outside of the silver shape had been worn enough to lessen the value on its own, the center was a beautiful silhouette of a woman riding horseback over the clouds. Whatever coin it was, it looked convincing enough to be a love charm.

And whatever the outcome of her current romantic situation with Drew was, she was going to have to make her own luck. Mostly by reigning in her tendency to get herself into trouble with her boneheaded moves.

"You made this bracelet?" The beadwork was nothing short of exquisite. Josie ran a finger along the hundreds of tiny beads woven into the spirals around her wrist. The woman must have had the patience of a clockmaker, the eyesight of a third grader, and the fingers of a surgeon.

"Yep. I did." She gave a cheerful smile, a pink flush coming into her cheeks at Josie's awestruck expression. "Anything else I can help you with?"

"Actually, I was looking for a ring. Maybe silver or something. Not beaded or anything. I mean, I love the beads—so sparkly—but not for this particular ring." She didn't want to insult the woman, but Drew wouldn't know what to do with a beaded engagement ring.

"Go to Hell."

"Excuse me?"

"Oops. Hell. It's the name of the boutique next door. Cool stuff in Hell."

The sign next door indeed said "Hell" in black painted letters on a placard covered in crystalline white rhinestones. She paused with her hand on the door, her new love charm bracelet dark and glinting from the streetlight overhead. *In for a penny, in for a pound?* She felt like she needed a more bracing battle cry before she entered Hell. *Curiouser and curiouser.* Well, that motto wasn't more macho, but at least it had an English devil-may-care flippancy.

Straightening her shoulders, she pushed through the door, and citrus incense and the olfactory sting of the latest Calvin Klein unisex cologne assaulted her nose. The fragrance said *youthful, trendy, and at least outwardly clean.* Appearances could be deceiving.

"Hey there. Let me know if I can help you find anything," a voice called out in a tone that was overly warm and friendly for a denizen of the underworld. As Josie's eyes adjusted, she located the source of the voice. A thin young man with dark hair in a t-shirt, black leather vest, and black jeans was bent over a display in the corner of the store. He had one of those heavy steel chains hanging out of his back pants pocket, securing his leather billfold wallet to his pants for all eternity. The emo manager of Hell.

Moody synthetic music that softly thrummed *oonst oonst oonst* drifted in through Hell's hidden speakers, and the store was chilly enough to have her wondering if the air conditioning was turned on even though it was late November. Black velvet drapery shut out the daylight and was pretty much how she pictured Hades—decor like a teen vampire movie on steroids. The whole setup reminded her of the living room of a web cam mathematics tutor of whom she'd recently made the acquaintance.

What did the curtains hide? Industrial walls, scuffs and scratches in the paint, flowery fun decals from a daycare of years gone by? *Pay no attention to the man behind the curtain.* She was mixing up her movie metaphors. She'd jumped from *Alice in Wonderland* to *The Wizard of Oz* when she was really in *Dazed and Confused*, searching for hidden motives, trying to be more transparent with her boyfriend in a world of lost love and mournful barbecue spirits.

Whatever. Keep moving. You're on a mission here. Find the ring. Toss it into Mordor.

Thick shag carpet underfoot made her journey to the right side of the store somewhat arduous as she ventured toward a display of feather boas. Some kind of costuming—red, pink like Georgia's Nails by Mattel, black, rainbow. But the feathers weren't boas, they were tails. She poked one with her finger so it turned on the rack. Spinning, spinning, flaunting its feathers. Each fluffy tail was attached to a heavy silver arrowhead—not a sharp one, but with a blunt point? How would a person wear a tail like that…?

What the actual heck?

She scanned the merchandise on the surrounding shelves only to confirm her realization that she wouldn't be finding a ring for Drew in *this* particular display. Toy after toy in lurid colors and outrageous shapes…and sizes.

Oh my gawd. I can't buy an engagement ring in a sex shop.

"Do you need any help?"

Josie almost jumped out of her skin when the denim-clad Millennial of Darkness appeared at her elbow. Apparently, shag carpet was good at muffling the slouched approach of fallen angels.

"I'm looking for a man's ring," she said and clarified in the same breath, "for him to wear. On his *finger*." Because she knew there were rings for other, more florid appendages. Her face felt like it might self-combust, her embarrassment fanning the flames. Skip the barbecue—she was flambéing herself.

His mouth twisted in a lazy half-smile. "Go through the door in the back of the store. You probably want to try the other side of the shop."

It seemed she had come through the rear entry of Hell.

CHAPTER 4

The other side of the building was pleasant and well-lit, with pale green carpet and shabby chic, feminine decor. Who knew parts of the underworld could be so charming? Clothing racks with funky feathered hats and pale, faceless mannequins lined the store, along with several jewelry cases arranged in angled ranks, like fish bones. What kind of baubles and ornaments would she find on the flip side of Hell? Was it any more or less worse to buy a man an engagement ring on this side of the store?

Yes, Josie was looking for a ring. A man's engagement ring for Drew. To get married. Her stomach gave a nervous flutter. Or maybe it was the half-slab of ribs. Or the last few days of copious amounts of meat consumption. Why did she confuse the two sensations? And why did confronting anything serious or emotional make her dyspeptic? This was a deep, philosophical third-degree, but one she didn't have time for right now. She had a bigger, more pressing question to think about.

Was now the right time to get engaged? Was there ever a correct moment to take the next step in a relationship? Adopt a dog. Buy a house. Have a kid or two. That was the normal route, right?

Not that she was normal by any stretch of the imagination.

She'd turned 29 years old in May, and Drew was a year and a half older. Friends since college, they'd been dating for only a short time. Recent events, however, had made it clear to her that she didn't want to waste any more time messing around without any reason or purpose—without making their relationship official and permanent. Maybe her sudden desire to get engaged had to do with a certain female doctor colleague who hadn't been able to keep her greedy little lips to herself. Maybe it had to do with Josie's repeated run-ins with death and incurable crazies that made her realize how short and precious life was. *Or something.*

Josie peered through the shiny glass countertop into the display cases. Because this was a small, non-chain kind of boutique, the rings were an unusual assortment of Celtic knots, dragons with gemstone eyes, and multi-piece bands woven through with black and opal. Nothing that even remotely made her think of her man-slash-BFF who'd put up with her foolhardy and sometimes self-destructive shenanigans for years now.

Toward the end of the second case, she found a few simpler rings, including a plain gold one. When she ducked down to look at the band from the side, through the front of the counter, she saw it had elvish scroll around it, like from *The Lord of the Rings.* She almost laughed out loud because she'd just been thinking it.

But this is definitely not the one ring to bind us.

At the very end of the case, just as she had stood up and turned to locate the door, another plain band caught her eye. Polished silver with a band of inky black running straight through stood out from the others because of its lovely simplicity.

"That's tungsten," the shop clerk behind the counter said. "Well, a tungsten alloy."

The young woman's high-contrast makeup riveted Josie. Too-dark hair parted in the center over a high forehead contrasted with her startling pale skin. A single diamond-studded piercing in her nose seemed conservative compared to what a lot of the other kids had been doing lately, based on Josie's recent college-campus adventure. The light blue color contacts and plumped up lips—which could have been clinically enhanced for all Josie knew—obscured her ethnicity. But then, did it really matter? All that was clear was who the girl wanted to be now, which was a friendly and helpful, albeit highly painted person. Artifice or facade versus substance—what was underneath mattered. And really, that was the important thing, wasn't it?

"It's what?"

"Tungsten. One of the hardest rare metals there is. I think the name is Swedish or Norwegian. Something Scandinavian. I used to know." The girl flipped her long brown hair over her shoulder. Josie gazed at her perfectly symmetrical painted-on eyebrows. "The military uses tungsten in missiles and bullets. And radiation shields. Stuff like that. It's 19 times denser than water. More like gold or uranium, and it has the highest melting point of all the elements."

"No kidding."

The girl pointed a dark purple fingernail at her own abundant cleavage, pale and miraculously untouched by the harsh Texas sun, which was clad in a deeply V-neck fuzzy black sweater. "Double major in Chem and Geology. Hook 'em, Horns." She flashed the Longhorn hand gesture. So this was what happened when Goth kids grew up. They became double majors in STEM. Awesome.

Josie nodded in appreciation. The girl knew her spiel. Whether it was true or not...well, who cared? "Basically, you're saying this ring is almost indestructible?"

"Yep. It should last a lifetime—more than a lifetime. And it's affordable, too."

"Sold."

"So tell me," Josie said as the girl rang up the ring—The Ring, as she was coming to think of it in capital letters, despite trying not to be so nerdy about it and her anxiety—"where should I go for the best barbecue around town?"

The girl's sculpted eyebrows rose. She had to have used a stencil to apply them so precisely. Maybe they were tattooed on. Josie had heard that was a thing. Never again would a walk of shame include smeared mascara and pale, bloodless lips. Eyebrows stayed in place even after vigorous scrubbing. Funeral home artists would need only to cover up the wounds and realign anything out of place. Her mind tripped over that.

If a façade is permanent, is it still just a façade?

"That's a controversial topic around this city. A lot of people have their favorites. Ruby's is great if you want some place to hang with your friends and have a few beers. Kinda trendy. Very tasty food, don't get me wrong. Their location at Lake Travis has some of the best views around and live music on the weekends. You can hear it even if you're in a boat on the water.

"If you're into organic and all that, you might like Off The Bone. It's not really authentic, but it's good. My friends and I hang there when we have non-meat-eaters with us. I mean, when they're with us and we're not making fun of them.

"There's The Mineral Lick, of course, but if you're going to go to all the trouble of driving out of town a little ways, you should go to Smiley's. It's totally authentic, from the building all the way down to the limestone it's sitting on. I mean, it's not the original building, but the sense of ambiance there is unbeatable." She took the price tag off and nestled the tungsten ring into a blue gift box with a white satin cushion. The box snapped shut with a muffled clap. Then she wrapped the whole thing in about twenty layers of tissue paper, oblivious to Josie's aborted protests.

The girl paused in thought, then said, "You'll see everyone eating at Smiley's. Not just the bubbas, but the bubba techs—computer nerds, but Texas style—old timers, kids, and regular people. It's a real cross-section of Austin and it's not even technically in Austin. It's north, in Leandro. But kind of Austin."

Barbecue as a common denominator? Well, other than for vegetarians and vegans, who would be a distinct absence in that slice of the population. Not to discount them in the slightest. In fact, her good friend Benjy had been vegan for a long period of time, which, incidentally, had coincided with his Pastafarian foray. That story was a long involved tale about parental defiance for another day.

"What happened to Smiley's first building?" Josie said as she took the shopping bag that the girl slid across the counter to her.

"It burned down." The girl shrugged her rounded shoulders. "One of the built-in dangers of running a smokehouse, I guess. If you cook with flames, I guess it's a given risk that you're going to have some big flare ups now and then. But Billy Blake—that's the owner—he rebuilt it in about 2007 just the same as it was before. Like *an exact replica* of the original building. He even picked the same wallpaper. I was just a kid, but I remember going to the grand opening with my parents. Or rather, the grand re-opening. And he still makes the best barbecue around in my opinion—not just mine, actually, according to a lot of people's opinions."

28

"What about the place being haunted?" Josie half-expected the girl to laugh her out of the store.

She gave a half-smile, her dark lips lifting just at the corners of her mouth. "Kind of local lore. Urban legend, you know."

Her flippant answer seemed to dismiss the possibility, but Josie sensed something more going on. Something in that funny half-smile made her delve a little more.

"You don't believe in ghosts?"

"I never said that." That same crooked smirk crossed the girl's face again. Nothing malevolent, just an impish thought behind the curtain that was trying to poke out. Something was making the girl want to laugh. An inside joke, maybe.

"What am I missing?" Josie frowned. "You believe in spirits and the undead presence who live among us?"

"Of course I do," the girl said. "I'm a ghost hunter."

CHAPTER 5

Josie blinked, calling to mind images of Ouija boards and Victorian séances, crystal balls and so-called mediums scamming little old ladies out of their life's savings in trying to talk to their dearly departed calico cats named Bernard and Muffin.

"You hunt ghosts? Seriously? Like Ghostbusters with ectoplasm, beeping machines, and the lights flashing? Crossing the streams, Egon, and everything?"

She didn't want to laugh at the girl, but she was pretty sure her disbelief-tinged-with-ridicule was coming across loud and clear. Josie had one of *those* faces. People said the eyes were the mirrors to the soul, but in her case, her face was a looking glass right into whatever ludicrous or skeptical thoughts she was entertaining at the moment. Super embarrassing. And, man, was she lousy at poker.

"Not exactly like that. But kind of." The girl crossed her arms, a defensive pose if Josie ever saw one. Looked like she had some ground to recover if she wanted Professor Venkman here to open up… "We have sensors, yeah. But we're not full-time hunters, obviously. We all have jobs and just hunt on the weekends when we can coordinate our schedules."

"And you have all the stuff?" Josie realized belatedly that her question could be taken in a number of ways.

The young woman's precision-crafted eyebrows crept up again. "You want to know more about the equipment?"

"Well, yeah." Josie's nosiness had gotten the better of her. Again. Not a big surprise there. Curiosity had almost killed the…snarky food critic…more than once in the past. Just because she was a non-believer in spirits walking the everyday world, for the most part, didn't mean she wasn't open to hearing more about it. Plus, she liked to hear what revved other people's engines, what made them tick. It helped with finding the key to the universe, so to speak, if she could just figure out the people around her to the smallest degree better.

"Okay, so like, there are about twenty people in the group. Well, nineteen because someone just left." She paused, dark fingernail scratching the corner of her matching lipsticked mouth. Puce—that was a color, right? Dark purple-brown, like dried blood. "He's born again, actually, and decided it was against his new religious beliefs as a Christian. But anyway, we usually go out in groups of three to four because of our schedules. It's honestly hard to get more people than that together at any given time, so we have a couple sets of equipment in a storage locker we can all access if something comes up."

"And the red phone rings and Janine the secretary rings the firehouse alarm?"

The girl brushed off Josie's sarcasm with an eye-roll and slow blink combo move. "Basically, you need an EMF detector for magnetic fields. Definitely a high def video cam. Some kind of thermometer for cold spots, though you can usually feel those just on your skin. You should have extra batteries, flashlights, first aid stuff—I mean, you're stumbling around in the dark, right? People are gonna get boo-boos. I think those are the basics."

"I get hurt just walking around my apartment at night." She had the bruises to prove it.

"I also like to add some baby powder to my kit to capture any footprints. If you sprinkle it around, the ghosts might step in it and leave their tracks."

"What kind of shoes do ghost generally wear?"

"Depends what century they're from."

"Have you ever gotten actual ghost footprints?"

"Yeah, a couple of times."

"Really?"

The girl shrugged. "The evidence is there. Sometimes you just have to let yourself believe it."

"'I want to believe.'"

The girl stared at her. "That's an X-Files quote, isn't it?" Her pursed mouth said she was starting to get somewhat ticked off at Josie's attitude.

Oops again.

It wasn't that she wanted to outright disparage the girl's hobby—her *beliefs*—but for Josie, *seeing* was believing. And she had never seen a ghost. Well, not really.

I mean, there was that one time out in the desert when I had that conversation with my father...but that wasn't a ghost, really. That was a hallucination. One that saved my life. But that was all in my head. Probably.

Josie brought her snark down a notch. "Have you ever seen the ghost at Smiley's?"

"No, but my cousin has. She was eating there a few weeks ago, and a woman appeared in a mirror right by the front door."

"A woman? Was it the wife of the owner?"

"Oh, you know about that? Yes, it was Mary Clare. My cousin said you could tell it was her because of her big hair and also the gold necklace around her neck that said her name."

Josie frowned. "Like one of those gangster girl necklaces?" She'd seen a few of them in Tucson when she was in high school. *Chola* necklaces, she thought, but didn't dare say out loud.

"Exactly. Except the script was smaller and classier. I think maybe with some diamond accents. Kind of 80's bling. My cousin thought the ghost was a picture on the wall, but then the sun hit it when someone opened the door and it turned out to be a mirror."

"So Mary Clare appeared to your cousin at the restaurant. Was she trying to warn her away? Was something wrong with the food that day? E.coli? Salmonella? Bad cole slaw?"

"No, nothing like that. In fact, the ghost was smiling, like she was welcoming people in."

A happy ghost? Was there such a thing? It seems contrary to popular belief.

Josie shook her head at herself. She needed to be convinced they existed first.

"Not only that," the girl said, "but their old house is haunted, too."

"What house—the one Mary Clare used to live in?"

"Yes. My cousin is a real estate agent. Cookie Casteñada. Her signs are all over town—bright yellow in the shape of a house. She's the second biggest selling agent in the whole city. She's been hired to list their former house in Bee Caves."

A little light went on in Josie's brain. Georgia, the woman from the Ruby's, had mentioned a big mansion-like house on the west side of town.

"How come it's going on the market after all these years?"

"I don't know. Maybe Billy Blake is getting ready to retire and he's finally downsizing. I mean, no one has lived there for years. He stays somewhere else. Maybe because it's haunted—and not by a settled spirit, but one that likes to break things and leave disgusting messes everywhere."

Gears were churning in Josie's head. She could almost hear the rust flaking off her mental cogs as they creaked into motion, groaning with effort.

"Would your cousin be willing to show us the house?"

"You want to see Billy Blake's haunted house? Like a tour? Or as a potential buyer?"

Josie cleared her throat, a little uncomfortable with admitting her...*undecided* status as to whether ghosts were part of reality. This girl would trust her more if she were a believer, whereas Josie would be more relieved if she'd been able to steadfastly deny their existence.

And here was where it got a little tricky. She didn't even know this girl's name yet. She'd known her for approximately thirty minutes, if that, and she was already asking for a favor.

Might as well just come right out with it.

"I was wondering if we—*you and I*—could go ghost hunting at the house."

The girl blinked. "Us—like you and me?"

"I'm doing this all backwards," Josie said, feeling her face get a little warm. Even self-professed antisocial grouches like her weren't immune to being embarrassed, after all—twice in one day, thanks to the adult toy shop.

She held out her hand. "I'm Josie Tucker. I'm a food blogger from Boston. I'm here doing a story on local barbecue, but as you can tell, I'm totally distracted by this story about Mary Clare and Billy Blake. I just want to find out more about what happened to her, and I think going to the house might help."

There. That was pretty much the truth. Josie felt self-congratulatory at the great strides she already seemed to be making. Not too much longer now and she'd be a fully self-realized grown up. Legit.

Instead of taking Josie's hand in greeting, the girl crossed her arms over her chest. After an extremely uncomfortable moment of silence, which could have been anywhere from thirty seconds to...oh, about five hours, she picked up the phone from behind the counter and held it between her cheek and her shoulder as she dialed.

Josie eyed the front door of the shop, thinking she might have to make a hasty retreat. If she took a circuitous route around the side of the shop, and maybe zig-zagged through some back alleys, the cops wouldn't be able to track her back to the hotel...

"Hey," the girl said into the phone, which made Josie think she might not be calling 9-1-1 for the police. "Yeah, this is Lizzie. Can you get me and my friend Josie in to see Billy Blake's house tonight? No? What about tomorrow night? No, it's not a big group of us. Just two girls. We won't track any dirt in, I swear. It'll be in exactly the same condition we find it when we leave. I swear on Grand-*mami*'s grave." She nodded. "Thursday night, it is. All right. Thanks."

The girl hung up and stuck her hand out to Josie and rattled off a bunch of Spanish. "First of all, *Lizabeta Del Valle Del Jabalí.* That's my name, but you can call me Lizzie. And second of all, it's not ghost hunting if you're looking for a specific ghost. It's ghost *investigation.*"

Good thing Josie had a private investigator's license. Not that it was worth anything in the spirit world.

CHAPTER 6

Josie returned to the hotel room around eight and found Drew lying face down on the bed. All the lights were on and he was fully dressed, but his one visible eye was closed. She eased off his shoes, and he gave a muffled groan as she kneaded the arches of his feet with her knuckles. He made another unintelligible sound that might've been an expression of gratitude. Or maybe he was dreaming about his mother's spaghetti. Josie could admit to having that dream more than once. The woman's cooking was the stuff of legends.

"Hey there, sleepyhead. Are you okay?" she asked near his ear as she sprawled next to him.

His dark lashes didn't even flutter as he muttered, "Vodka," which explained everything. Neither of them were big drinkers. Alcohol had gotten her into several idiotic predicaments in the past—one word: *burlesque*—and he was more of a beer fan. If they had been plying him with cocktails at the catered happy hour, he was pretty much done for the night.

She spied a pile of medical vendor brochures on the bedside table. No wonder he'd imbibed. This week's medical conference was focused on Geriatrics—which she imagined would have an ever-growing list of topics to discuss. Diabetes. Osteoporosis. Heart disease. *Yeesh.* A laundry list of reasons to die young and leave a beautiful corpse.

Okay, that *was a horrible sentiment.*

She'd *known* a young woman—a bride in Arizona—who'd done that very early death thing. And when death wasn't your choice, it was horrifying and wrong. She pursed her mouth in momentary apology to the woman's memory. Crap like that stuck with a person and colored her outlook on life, especially since she was lucky enough to be among the living.

She shook her head and thumbed through the stack of pamphlets before admitting her distinct lack of comprehension. New ways to test glucose, memory loss, balance. Or something. This medical conference was the first one Josie had ever gone to with Drew. He tried to attend at least one a year, sometimes in wonderfully warm and palm-tree filled places like San Diego. Texas was also nothing to spit at, considering the chilly weather back home in Boston this week.

Their friends Susan and Benjy were taking turns dog-sitting for Josie, so her phone had been bombed with texts from them, including photos of Bert refusing to walk down the icy front steps of her apartment building. The last photo in the sequence of messages had been of Benjy carrying Josie's enormous brown dog down the steps. Interesting. It meant Susan had gone with him, because she had taken the photo, which she'd then sent to Josie. Was romance finally afoot for those two?

Not holding my breath on that one.

Josie tried not to rustle too much as she took the ring she'd bought for Drew from its shopping bag and transferred it to the back pocket of her suitcase. Between the paper bag and the 58 layers of tissue paper, she was sure she was going to wake him up, vodka-induced coma or not. Ever the careful planner—*not*—she hadn't figured out how to pop The Question yet. A special dinner at a memorable restaurant? A sunset cruise on Lake Austin? She had no idea what to do. However, even *she* knew waking him from a boozy stupor to ask him if he wanted to get married probably wasn't the greatest idea.

Her stomach gave an unearthly howl, which might have been hunger, disgust, or anxiety—or a combo of the three. She squatted down in front of the room's mini-fridge and peered inside at the tower of takeout containers. Barbecue. Ribs. Brisket. Slaw. *Ugh.* She couldn't face another bite of meat at the moment. She needed to gird her loins for tomorrow's round of taste-testing. She wasn't in much of a people mood—was she ever?—but maybe the bar downstairs would have something green to eat like a little salad. Or a mojito, which had mint, and mint was green. Close enough to a vegetable.

One more glance told her Drew was out like a light, his face mashed against the decorative bolster pillow. He didn't even move when she pulled a blanket over him, so she grabbed her room key card and headed for the elevators.

"What can I get for you?" a twelve year-old boy with ear grommets and full sleeve tattoos asked her. After a double-take, she saw the strawberry blond soul patch and barely-there beard shadow on the bartender. It sucked to look so young sometimes—she could relate.

When you look underage, your opinions tend to be downgraded in relevance, even if hindsight proves your near infallibility. Not to toot my own horn too loudly.

She put down the parchment-paper menu. "Green beans, nachos, and an ice tea, please." Her order sounded mundane, but it was short-hand for French fried green beans with a chipotle aioli, black bean *carnitas* nachos with a lime-cilantro relish, and prickly pear iced tea—at the last minute, she'd decided to avoid the alcohol. Her late-night noshing was going to be pretty frickin' ritzy. Hopefully, her stomach wouldn't object. She was started to tiptoe around it as if it were a colicky baby who'd finally fallen asleep.

"You got it."

With a tattooed finger—she couldn't see what the tattoo was—he tapped her order into his handheld tablet and pulled a tall glass off the rack behind him for her tea. The bar ran along the back of the hotel's open atrium area, though her perch on a steel-legged stool still managed to feel secluded. Purple up-lights made the place feel kind of spaceshippy, as if a Ferengi from Star Trek might pull up a chair next to her and order something smoking with tentacles hanging out of it...or whatever. She made a note to start limiting her television consumption. Reruns were starting to color her view of the world. Something supernatural could occur and she might not even bat an eye.

"Have you checked out our world-famous bats and bat bridge?" he asked, setting down her drink. He had scars along the backs of his knuckles, as well as a Band-Aid over one. Maybe he worked in the kitchen as well as tended bar. Kitchen staff were always so macho about their scars.

"No, not yet. I didn't know if there was much to see this time of year."

"Yeah, it's the end of the season, I think, and it gets dark so early. But people have been telling me the little buggers are still around. You should give it a try if you have time. Are you here in town long?"

She noticed he didn't ask her if she was in town for the medical conference. In fact, no one had asked her, which wasn't a huge surprise. She didn't look *doctorly* in her worn jeans and tee, and she certainly didn't act it either. Even when Drew had a day off, he still managed to exude a certain authoritarian manner, an aura that said *I know what your cholesterol level is* and *You need to eat more fiber.*

"Just till the end of the week." The conference ran four days, Monday through Thursday. They were staying until Sunday morning, so they'd have a couple of days to relax and hit a few local sites together. Maybe they'd stroll down to the Congress Avenue Bridge if the weather was nice.

"Cool, cool. What have you seen so far?"

"Ruby's. The Mineral Lick. I'm headed up to Smiley's tomorrow."

"That's...a lot of meat. Welcome to Texas, I guess." He sounded a little *judgey.* Maybe he was one of those militant vegans the Internet was always talking about but she'd had yet to meet. Based on the tooled leather bracelet around his wrist, probably not anti-animal-consumption.

"Do you know anything about that restaurant?" Yeah, she was totally fishing for gossip as she had been all day, but she never knew when she would land something juicy, so it was worth it to keep casting her line. Plus, as far as she could tell, *everyone* in this town knew a little bit about everything. It wasn't too different from Tucson, the biggest small town she'd ever encountered in her life.

In fact, earlier in the day, she'd stacked the deck in her favor. Her breakfast waitress had mentioned the night bartender had once worked at Smiley's. Josie was fishing for gossip, but she knew where the fish might be biting, so to speak.

He wiped the bar down. She counted three strokes before he answered. "I started out there bussing tables and washing dishes when I was in high school. My mom lives about a mile from Smiley's, so I could ride my bike or skateboard there after school. Was really convenient for a first job."

Josie took a sip of her tea. She could sense an addendum coming—a *but*—and the best thing for her to do was to keep quiet and wait for it. She watched him, trying to tease out more of his story. He kept busy, though, and avoided eye contact. Then his attention was diverted elsewhere. A couple slid into seats at the end of the bar and he left to wait on them. After that, he brought Josie her dishes, tapped the counter once, and excused himself to fill some orders.

She was rarely wrong about sensing more to a story. But if that was the case, she wasn't going to hear it tonight. His tale needed a little more finessing.

CHAPTER 7

The prickly pear iced tea, as light as it sounded, packed a major caffeine punch. Maybe she should have gone with the mojito after all. She stayed up late seriously wired, working on notes for her blog post about Austin's barbecue scene and surfing the Internet. Then she looked for articles about Billy Blake and his wife Mary Clare.

While Drew mumbled about bone density and beta blockers in his sleep, Josie found some articles in the online archives of the local paper, *The Legislator*, dated almost five years after Mary Clare's disappearance.

MISSING PERSON REPORT FILED YEARS LATER

Mary Clare Blake (née Rogers), formerly of the Westview suburb of Dallas, hasn't been heard from since the morning of Sept. 28, 1995, when she spoke to her mother on the phone, according to police.

Her husband and owner of the popular restaurant Smiley's Smokehouse, Billy Blake, declined to report her disappearance. Family members have now reported her missing nearly three years later despite the fact that Blake insists she left the area of her own volition. Items found inside her home since her disappearance include her car keys and other personal items. Her 1994 Acura Integra still sits in the Blakes' five-car garage.

Multiple agencies have helped in the search for her, aided by volunteers, ATV's, horses, helicopters, and search dogs. No sign of the missing woman has been found.

Josie opened another tab on her browser and searched the Internet for Westview. She confirmed that Mary Clare's family lived in a ritzy suburb of Dallas—and still resided there, according to a more recent charity feature story. Her mother and three siblings still routinely made the society headlines. What a quaint and Southern tradition—publicizing the do-good intentions of the wealthy as they dressed up in their finery. Or maybe it wasn't relegated to the South. Though Josie had grown up in Arizona and Massachusetts, she hardly knew anything about the upper-crust of society.

But she knew someone who just might.

Maybe Josie's benefactor, Greta Williams, might know the Rogers family, though it was a serious long-shot. Greta traveled more in the New England blue blood circuit than anywhere else, but the woman seemed to have a finger in every pie. Greta's reach extended as far as San Francisco, so maybe she had some connections in Texas as well.

The clock on her computer screen said 12:36 a.m. While it wasn't too late to send Greta in Boston a text message—the older woman was either an insomniac or a vampire, Josie had yet to decide which—she didn't want to give Greta the impression that *she* was available at all hours of the night. The woman had boundary issues as it was, sending Josie across the country to do her legwork, getting her into sticky situations...Okay, to be fair, most of those tight spots were of Josie's own making. But she never would have had the funds or the initial kick in the seat of the pants to burrow in like a tick, seeking the truth.

She clicked on another article dated a few months later by an Austin investigative reporter named Skip Richmond.

WHERE IS MARY CLARE?

Speculation still swirls around the disappearance of Mary Clare Blake, wife of Smiley's owner, Billy Blake, and much of the suspicion falls on her husband. The taciturn yet well-respected restaurant owner has declined frequent requests for interviews.

According to sources within the Austin Police Department, multiple searches of the Blake mansion in the hills west of Austin did not turn up any signs of struggle or foul play. The only additional evidence of Mary Clare's absence is her missing purse.

A spokesperson from the APD has stated, "Mr. Blake has been questioned, and he will not face charges at this time."

Billy Blake maintains his statement that Mary Clare departed of her own free will. However, he has also stated his wife has not contacted him from her new location or advised him or anyone else of her well-being.

The news stories died down for a few years. No more public speculation surfaced after that, at least none that Josie could find in the online newspaper archives. Years later, a now-defunct Texas Hill Country magazine published a restaurant review of Smiley's. She did some hasty subtraction based on the dates. Was seven years the standard amount of time to let bygones be bygones?

Probably not, if she were to ask. Mary Clare's loved ones. Josie had lost her own father to an unexpected heart attack decades ago and the pain of loss still stung. Not as bad as an open wound, but what she imagined the pain would feel like from a missing arm.

Did they miss Mary Clare like a phantom limb?

"Hey," Drew's voice filtered into her subconscious. A large hand rubbed her back and swept her hair off her face. "Did you sleep the whole night on your laptop?"

Josie awoke to find herself slumped on the hotel room desk where countless other people had probably laid their city maps and rental car keys, half-full beverages cups and take-out containers, dirty feet and worse...and now, a small puddle of her drool made its home there as well.

Classy.

She wiped her chin and blinked sightlessly. "What time is it?" she croaked. Her voice sounded like she'd picked up a pack-a-day habit overnight.

"Ten after six."

"Why?"

Fortunately, Drew was fluent in early morning Josie-speak. *Why* meant, what was he doing up so early, and why was he waking her up to suffer with him?

"Coffee," he said.

She answered him by heaving herself off the desk and crawling into the bed he'd recently vacated. That part of the bed, deep under the blankets, was still warm. She nestled into the depression left by his body, breathing in his warm Drew scent.

When she woke up several hours later, she was alone, but a blanket was tucked around her chin. *Awwww.*

Her stomach was making some crazy lonely wolf noises, the *ooo-woohs* reverberating through her intestines, but the breakfast hour had long passed. She checked the clock again. If she got up and showered, she could waste just enough time until lunch. Smiley's was located about 45 minutes north of Austin in a small town called Leandro. So for now, a cup of room-brewed tea would do while she made use of the rainfall shower in the trendy black-slate tiled bathroom.

She'd slept soundly during the few last hours she'd been stretched out and horizontal in the plush bed, but she'd been visited by strange dreams. She'd been driving her Uncle Jack's 1957 T-bird down a desert road and had seen a hitchhiker. A ghostly woman in a white flowing gown with over-sprayed Kelly LeBrock hair circa *Weird Science* stood by the side of the road, trying to flag her down. Josie hadn't stopped the car—because who picked up hitchhikers these days?—but somehow, the woman appeared in the passenger seat next to her.

That was it, the full extent of the dream.

If Josie were a dream analysis kind of person, she might think the specter of Mary Clare Blake had attached itself to her and planned to ride shotgun during her stay in Austin. In light of the myriad bad decisions Josie had made throughout her life, maybe having another soul on board wasn't such a bad thing.

Depending on if Mary Clare were the vengeful spirit type or not.

CHAPTER 8

Smiley's didn't have a greeter at the front door of their low-ceilinged wood paneled dining room, no cheerful high-schooler hostess with flawless skin and dress-up yoga pants that failed to mask a perky backside and a raring metabolism. No laminated menus. No Hank Williams, Sr. or Willie Nelson as an audio backdrop to the clang of metal pans and the gruff curses emanating from the open fire pit in the kitchen.

Like Ruby's, Smiley's had a pickup counter along the back of the restaurant, but that was where the similarities ended. Where Ruby's could have been the flagship location of a budding franchise with its down-home kitsch and hand-painted signs, metal tables, and benches, Smiley's could have been Josie's uncle's garage back home in Arizona. It had a lived-in feel, if that made any sense for a restaurant. And she felt more at home here than in any other place in Austin.

Two of the walls had dark wood paneling. A third was covered with yellowed, peeling wallpaper that may have been bright and somewhat feminine when it was new. The fussy floral pattern reminded Josie of a Victorian house, from a time in which a family room might have been referred to as a "parlor," a place in which people sat upon a "Davenport." A cork bulletin board covered with hundreds of thumb-tacked business cards for locals hung from the wall—real estate agents, general contractors, plumbers, landscapers, and house sitters. The cards were in varying shades, from crisp white to downright sepia, thanks to the smoke that had probably filtered through Smiley's over the years, even since it had been rebuilt.

Josie wondered what the carcinogen intake level was here just breathing the air. She suspected it was akin to sucking on the exhaust pipe of an eighteen-wheeler.

"I thought this place burned down." She leaned her denim-clad elbow on the grimy counter and looked the guy behind it up and down. Her standard MO when she was sticking her nose where it didn't belong was to make nicey-nice with the natives until they accepted her as one of their own enough to blab all their secrets. Did her method work? Not very often. But she was thick-skulled enough to keep trying. Or was that the definition of insanity? She was lucky though. Most of the people she'd talked to so far were in the service industry—they were pretty much *required* to talk to her, so she didn't need to work her ethnically ambiguous, girl-next-door mojo on anyone yet.

"Yeah, that was a long time ago. 'Bout a decade, more or less. It got rebuilt. But now it's old again."

She guessed he was in his late forties, not taking into consideration any premature-by-smoke-inhalation aging. His flannel plaid outer shirt, Round Rock Fire Department t-shirt—what was it about firefighters and barbecue? They seemed to go hand in hand. Were they all pyros?—and stained John Deere cap would have made him right at home on the back of a tractor or a 125cc four-wheeler like they used to race up and down the dry wash beds in Arizona.

"The place was a total loss?"

He lifted his cap and re-fitted it over too-long hair curling over the tops of his ears. His disheveled locks weren't graying at all. She adjusted her age estimate downward a few years. He didn't look like the Just For Men type. Maybe it was soot. Dirty fingernails tipped the ends of his surprisingly nice-looking hands. If he'd had some busted knuckles and darker grease stains, he would have fit in better at a body shop.

"Pretty much." He sighed, his Texan drawl stretching out to full syrup mode as he realized she wasn't going to give him her order anytime soon. He adjusted from business to Southern chit-chat mode with the ease of a sleek nutria, an aquatic rodent sliding into lukewarm lake water. He eased his considerable bulk onto an elbow on the scarred countertop. "All the structure—wood frame—burned down, so that was a total re-do, but the original fire pit survived, even though they gutted it and scrubbed it out. I guess you can't burn down a stone fire pit, just in case you were planning on it."

"Nah," she said. "Not today."

She got a smile for that. The man had good teeth. No, she wasn't attracted to him, she had a boyfriend. This guy was just…magnetic, if she looked at him in an objective way.

"Smart move. Because I gotta tell ya, you can burn this place down, but it'll keep on going. It's a force of nature."

"I'm more of a food *aficionado* than a firebug. The only time I'm interested in smoke is if it's making the perfect pink smoke ring on my brisket."

He blinked. "You a chef?"

"I'm a fan of eating." She decided not to be coy since he seemed so down-home. "I'm a food critic and blogger."

"Huh."

She waited to see what that meant, since the conversation could go any number of directions from here. They were close enough to a technologically robust metropolis that a person like her making a living in the virtual blogosphere might be accepted instead of shunned, but she wasn't certain of her welcome, especially with old fashioned wallpaper like this.

"DJ," he said by way of introduction, sticking his big hand out. When he caught sight of how dirty it was, he quickly withdrew it and chuckled. "Whoa. I was restocking the wood. Mesquite. Hickory. Hardwood. Gotta keep the fires burning. Sorry about that."

"No problem. I'm Josie," she said, jabbing a thumb toward her sternum. She was straightforward with him, but to a point. If there had been any justice in the world, the paper P.I. license in her wallet would have spontaneously combusted at that moment. *Liar, liar, pants on fire.* Yes, she was a food blogger, but she was also a card-carrying P.I. with a big penchant for being nosy. Also, she hadn't exactly earned her P.I. license, and when she probably should have legitimately used it to identify herself—*like right now*—she purposefully chose to ignore it.

"I wasn't GM of this place back when the fire happened. Billy was doing it all by himself. I think the man just about lived here. I'm not kidding—he had a cot and a sleeping bag in the back office. Still does, actually. Truth is, I don't think he wanted to go home to that big ol' empty house by himself every night—you know that story, right?"

GM meant general manager, which was interesting. Essentially, this guy was Billy's right-hand man.

Josie wasn't sure which story about Smiley's, or Billy, he meant with such a stacked deck of cards to choose from. Mary Clare's disappearance and alleged murder. Her possible ghost sighting. Angry spirits at the Blake mansion. Josie went with a slight frown and tilted her head to encourage him to elaborate.

"His wife up and left him. Broke him up but good." He looked like he wanted to say more, and Josie had no idea which direction he would've headed conversation-wise. An anti-woman diatribe? The loss of a good woman leaving a man nothing but an empty shell?

"That must have been rough."

"They were college sweethearts, so yeah, about as rough as it could be. Guess that's why I'll be a bachelor until the day I die. If I need someone to cut my chest wide open and rip my heart out, all I need to do is keep rooting for the Cowboys. Hell, that happens on a yearly basis."

Loud guffaws filtered out from the back of the open kitchen. Josie enjoyed the trash talk as it flew fast and furiously for a few minutes—stuff about quarterbacks and Jimmy Someone that flew over her head for a while. She chocked it up to a native dialogue she didn't need to understand. Sadly, she was the same way about the Red Sox, and she lived within a stone's throw of Fenway Park.

"All right then, missy, what'll it be? We have—"

He was interrupted by a string of curse words the likes of which Josie hadn't heard since she'd taken her uncle's vintage Indian motorcycle for a midnight joyride.

A metal pan—a big rectangular one commercial kitchens use—skated across the kitchen's stone floor like a skateboard slipping out from under a kid's feet. It clattered to a noisy halt next to the fire pit. The swearing escalated in ferocity and volume from the back of the kitchen. Josie glanced around the restaurant, probably looking like a rabbit about to make a mad dash for the nearest exit. The other patrons had frozen, giving each other similar side-eye looks. One guy in a shirt and tie had a forkful of brisket lifted halfway to his mouth.

She was alarmed yet relieved to find the ruckus was an abnormal occurrence for Smiley's. Another muted clatter came from the back, this one accompanied by the distinct whack of a long mop or broom handle hitting the floor—someone had kicked the bucket at Smiley's. Literally.

She almost chuckled to herself, but the sound of the handle clattering to the floor resonated in her mind, taking on a life of its own, reverberating and replaying itself. Even though the mop and the bucket had stopped moving, that sound, the wooden clank of the handle hitting the red-orange stones of the floor echoed in her mind, making Smiley's kitchen fade from her vision, calling forth the sound of a shovel hitting hard dirt, bringing back the darkness of the Arizona desert, that night she'd been taken out to the desert by two very bad men intent on leaving her body there.

Black spots floated in front of her eyes and her view narrowed to near-pinpoint dots.

Oh crap. Don't pass out. Please don't pass out.

She ducked down on her side of the counter and squatted, releasing the muscles in her neck, dangling her head between her knees.

Breathe, you idiot.

She took a big, gasping inhalation. She smelled the dirt of the foot-worn rug under her feet and the laundry detergent she'd used on her jeans, felt the heat of the sweat forming on her upper lip and around her face.

Another breath. Not so hard for normal people.

The spots in her line of vision subsided. A rivulet of sweat ran down her waistband into the back of her pants where they gaped as she remained hunched over.

Just tying my shoe down here. Nothing to see.

As she came back to herself, she lifted her chin to see how far off she was from being able to stand. The blood rushed to her head, and she had to hang her head back down.

Three more breaths. That ought to do it. Three more and I'll be normal.

The hollow clanging of the wooden handle came back, and a wave of nausea washed over her. The stupid mop had sounded just like the tool that had almost taken her life.

She didn't think she could make it to the restroom, wherever it was, without losing her cookies.

Just let me get through this and I swear I will go talk to someone.

She had a therapist's card—Victor the counselor-slash-martial-arts-instructor's card—on her refrigerator at home. She pictured it in her mind. The magnet that held it to the fridge had a Ted DeGrazia painting on it of four blurry horses running—gold, black, tan, and white. The same painting had hung in her favorite Mexican restaurant in Tucson. She'd sat under the painting so often, she had nicknamed it *The Four Horsemen of the Taco-pocalypse.*

She raised herself up gingerly, feeling the ache of strain in her thighs. The front of her shirt stuck to her belly where she'd sweated through then pressed it against her own legs as she'd crouched. She gripped the front hem and flapped some cooler, smoke-scented air between the damp cotton Ziggy Stardust face on her t-shirt and her concave stomach, which made her shiver.

The countertop had a napkin dispenser from which she grabbed a few thin brown squares of paper and blotted the sweat from her face and under her nose.

Smiley's general manager who'd been talking with her was still looking the other way, distracted by the racket coming from the back of the kitchen. He hadn't noticed her disappearing trick or even her sudden return. A glance behind her showed all eyes were trained on the back of the kitchen, thank goodness.

The sub-human cursing and snarling coming into the kitchen had formed into less-inflammatory, more understandable words. "What in the hell do I pay my taxes for? Do those suit-wearing panty-waists only think I want my roads repaved? Their snot-nosed babies in this town's schools so they can spell better graffiti when they're vandalizing my restaurant? If Sheriff *Custard* wants to keep hauling me down to the station to harass me about things *which did not occur*, he can damn well stop those punks from interfering with my right to run my business, I can tell you that right here and right now. I am a God-fearing citizen trying to get along from day to day. I do not need to put up with this *shee-yit.*"

There was rustling, followed by a cardboard box that took flight halfway toward Josie, resulting in an explosion of plastic drink straws. One fell out of her hair onto the counter.

A big bear of a man emerged from the hallway at the back of the kitchen. Well over six feet tall, gray-haired and grizzled, with a face that hadn't seen a razor in a few days, he stormed into the kitchen, causing the cook staff to flee like backalley hobos under the beam of a cop's searchlight.

In fact, the only employee who hadn't budged—not so much as a flinch—was DJ, as he reclined with one large flannel-clad elbow on the counter across from Josie. Through sleepy eyelids, he observed his boss. Josie wasn't sure if his posture was belligerence or just his way of standing up to a challenge, whether it be physical or psychological, like the studied nonchalance in the face of a chest-beating silverback gorilla.

"S'up, Billy?" he said, his good ol' boy drawl back and thicker than ever.

Part 2: Smoke

You probably know that the proverb, "Where there's smoke, there's fire" means that where there are signs, clues, or *rumors*, there's usually a reason for it. It's a somewhat catty way of saying there's some truth to the gossip.

When you smoke meat—say, a brisket—there's a lovely pink ring that appears just below the outer crust of the cooked meat. This smoke ring, as it's called, is the result of a reaction between a protein in the meat called myoglobin with nitric oxide and carbon monoxide. It proves that the meat has been smoked well.

The fallacy is, however, is that you don't need smoke to cause the reaction. You can get the same pink ring reaction from using curing salts before you cook the meat in the oven. *With no smoke.*

Where there's a smoke ring, there's not always smoke. So what does gossip mean?

Not a darned thing.

—Josie Tucker, *Will Blog for Food*

CHAPTER 9

Billy Blake loomed large and seemed about eight feet tall, though Josie was aware her panic attack had skewed her perspective. He'd also looked like a bear for a few seconds.

She'd successfully wiped the sweat off her head and stuffed the napkin into the front pocket of her jeans as furtively as if she were shoplifting. A couple of deep breaths and her heart rate was back down from the stratosphere. Her nausea faded, and her vision peeled back to reveal the rest of the kitchen instead of just the narrow tube through which she'd been viewing the world.

She pressed her mental Reset button.

This time when she looked at Billy, she realized he was tall, but not inhumanly gigantic. He was upwards of six feet tall—still a beast compared to her five-two-and-three-quarters—and for a guy pushing 60, he looked solid. His blocky hands were reddish in color, the consequence of a fair-skinned person who labored in a kitchen. Extra weight padded his midsection and barrel chest. His chin and neck were also pink, grizzled with white scruff, and on the jowly side of heavy. His eyebrows were doing that older man thing, growing out in unruly wisps, and his forehead looked as if his creator had pressed a thumb against the ruddy flesh above either eye and mashed his brow downward. A perpetual scowl of distrust cast two pale green, almost yellow, eyes in shadow.

"What's going on, Billy?" DJ said again. Not really a question, but still questioning, if that made any sense at all. He spoke during a lapse in what had been a non-stop stream of cussing and countrified epithets about come-to-Jesus-meetings and tanning people's hides, peppered with f-bombs and a plethora of *shee-yits.*

"Some damned fool spray-painted obscene nonsense all over the side of the smokehouse."

"Is that right?" DJ straightened up, alert and sharp-eyed. "What, like gang tags?"

"Go see for yourself," the bigger man said and stalked off toward a door on the other side of the kitchen. The back office, she guessed, as he slammed the door.

Most of the people in the restaurant had gone back to their lunches when the show was over. The drama had died down, and they were back to their ribs and beans and Dr. Peppers, probably on work schedules with timecards that had to be punched back in.

Josie wasn't on a schedule or agenda for the day. Her time was her own. So when DJ headed for the back hallway that led out of the kitchen, she skirted the counter and followed him. Behind her, about a quarter of the patrons got up and filed out the front door, anxious to get a glimpse at what had made the big man so hopping mad.

Pure instinct had her heading through the kitchen rather than backtracking out the front door of Smiley's. She'd worked in her mother's restaurant before things had gone south with her mother's mind. Josie still felt more comfortable on the other side of the counter. Maybe presumptuous on her part, but DJ didn't seem to mind as he held the back door open when they headed outside and around the side of the building.

This part of the structure, at least, was brick, and it didn't look original to Josie. Common sense had prevailed, at least for this wall. Based on all the limestone homes and office complexes Josie had seen up and down the major roads, like the Mo-Pac Expressway and I-35, stone seemed plentiful here. There was no reason *not to rebuild* with brick, especially a smokehouse and barbecue place. Especially one that had already burned down once.

A crowd of about a dozen people, mostly plaid-wearing old-timers, had gathered at the side of Smiley's.

"Darn kids," was the first thing Josie heard.

Her line of sight turned from the good ol' boy spectators to the wall as she stepped from behind DJ, who was a bit of a wall himself, though not as formidable as his rampaging boss.

Scrawled across the wall in dripped-dry black painted letters were the words, "GO TO HELL U MUDERER WIFE BEATER LIER."

"Not much of a speller, were they? Could benefit from some punctuation, too," DJ said in his sleepy, taciturn fashion that Josie was coming to learn was anything but either of those things. It was no wonder Billy trusted him to run the place. There was more to Smiley's GM than met the eye.

Josie was silent, staring at the words, trying to glean any clues as to the identity of the writer. The use of the letter "U" in place of the word "you" could have meant that the person was used to typing online or on a phone in text messages where people did that all that time. The writer had also left out a letter in the word "murderer." Maybe that showed they were used to autocorrect for spelling errors.

She found the misspelling of the word "liar" more puzzling. Did the writer honestly not know how to spell the word, or was it a deliberate mistake so that they would appear uneducated or juvenile?

She took out her phone and stepped back a few feet to get the whole span of the graffiti in her camera's viewfinder before snapping a couple of pictures. "Are you going to call the police?"

DJ sighed and ran a hand across his scruffy chin. "The sheriff? You probably heard Billy's feelings on the man a few minutes ago. He and Billy are not what you call *friendly*, but I guess I'd better call this one in just in case we have any more problems later. Can't be too cautious with vandals. Could be nothing or it might turn out to be something. You never know."

"So you've had other incidents like this before?" Josie followed him as he headed back inside, holding the door for her once more. Very chivalrous. She didn't know if it was a Texas thing or just unique to him, but no one really did that for her ever. Not that Drew wasn't gentlemanly. More like Josie didn't give off the vibe that she needed to be coddled. Taken care of…well, yes, at times, thanks to her natural bull-headedness and propensity for getting into trouble.

I'm way over-thinking this, but that's pretty much my signature move.

She made her way around the counter back to the customer side. He was already lounging on his big elbow, looking like he'd never left, only this time he had the restaurant's phone in his meaty hand. He dialed as he answered her question.

"A few over the years. Nothing recently. More like Billy's in-laws taking out a full-page ad in the local paper accusing him of hiding details that may have led to the whereabouts of their daughter."

"Wow. That's a lot more passive aggressive than sending a lawyer or a detective after him."

DJ shrugged. "Oh, they did that, too, believe you me. They covered all the bases money could buy. A big money reward for information. Appearances on the local news morning shows. They pulled out all the stops."

The other end of the phone line picked up and he cut off their conversation to report the vandalism. "Bernie, that you? Yeah, it's me. We've got some spray paint all over the side of Smiley's right where we had those eggs that one time. Y'all want to add this to your file? Yeah, you can send Louie, but don't expect me to hold his hand and wipe his nose for him. He's got a couple more hours of daylight if he wants to take photos today. All right. Yeah, I'll be at the game. See you on Saturday."

He hung up the phone and, by way of explanation, told her, "City basketball league on Saturday. We're the Spurs. We're playing the Rockets. Bernie plays center because he's tallest, but he can't move for the life of him."

"Is your friend a cop?"

"Oh, yeah. He'll take care of the report without involving the sheriff. It's better that way. As you can tell, the sheriff don't like Billy much. "

It sounded like the local sheriff had it out for Billy Blake. Maybe he'd already made up his mind about the BBQ man's guilt. Josie imagined not being able to solve a decade's old murder would stick in a person's craw, especially when the suspect was living and working daily in the community. She wondered if the sheriff was a fan of Smiley's food. That would make it worse, not being able to go to a favorite place to eat because of an *irritation* like that.

CHAPTER 10

Josie dawdled in Smiley's over a platter of brisket and beans—she couldn't skip the beans after all the fuss people had made over them. They were impressive, as it turned out—spicy and sweet in just the right proportions of both. Full of flavor—probably a mountain of brown sugar, without a doubt—and chunks of smoked bacon.

She snapped a few photos of the food and the restaurant for her blog, capturing DJ behind the counter mid-laugh and gabbing to a regular customer. A full slab of ribs on the fire pit. A closeup of the sepia wallpaper. The smoke-tainted business cards lining the community bulletin board. A few tables with people hunched over their lunch plates. The row of unsmiling old-timers with flat stares, who glared at her as if she were an alien.

Maybe she'd just imagined that part, feeling like a perpetual outsider.

She lingered over her lunch at a table toward the side of the main room, away from the other people eating, but within sight of the door. From her vantage point, she could still see most of the restaurant in a broad sweep of the room, including the large picture mirror at the front.

Lizzie, the geology-Goth girl, had said the mirror was haunted, but Josie didn't know if the item was supposed to be the ghost's home or if she had free range over the whole place. She would have to ask Lizzie what the going theories were. So far, she hadn't seen a lick of anything supernatural, other than the crisp of smoked bacon bits in the sweet-smoky beans at Smiley's. How in the world did he get the bacon to stay crunchy in it?

She was still eating when a man from the local sheriff's office showed up. He roared up in his shiny government-issued black-and-white car and threw open the front door, hands on his skinny hips, feet braced wide apart.

A crusty older patron had sniped at him, "We take our hats off when we're indoors, *son*," which caused him to flush bright red and slouch. He swiped off his wide-brimmed deputy hat as he approached the counter. He was so wiry, she could see the wallpaper between the legs of his uniform pants as he walked.

"Some of us weren't raised in a barn."

"Wait 'til I tell his mama. I see her at VFW later this week. She'll give him a what-for."

"I ought to write a letter to the editor about them kids these days."

For his part, DJ treated the officer from the sheriff's office as if he were brain damaged, speaking in slow, over-pronounced syllables. He went so far as to grab him by the epaulet on his uniform shoulder to lead him out to the side of the restaurant where the spray paint stood out in stark relief on the light brown brick in the fading sunlight. Josie tagged along to watch the interaction.

"Write this down in your little notebook, Deputy Louie," DJ told him. "You remember to bring something to write with? I'll wait while you check your pockets."

The officer didn't seem much younger than DJ, but was clearly beneath him in pecking order. His face turned bright scarlet, from his neck all the way up through the tips of his somewhat pointy ears. His ginger buzzcut did little to hide the flush on his scalp. His pursed lips, white with anger, indicated to Josie that he was, in fact, not mentally deficient in any way and that his treatment was the result of a contentious history between them.

"I got it, DJ." He fished in his pocket for a writing utensil, bobbled his cell phone, and ended up dropping the pen on the ground. Probably due to agitation. He was just as tall as DJ—everything in Texas did seem bigger to Josie in her limited experience so far—but probably half the bigger man's body weight. Maybe a buck sixty-five soaking wet, as Josie's Uncle Jack might say.

"Do you now, you sumbitch?" DJ's temped flared. His pinkish face had gone a little florid over the collar of his plaid shirt. His back had straightened up as much as his virtual hackles, like a junkyard dog defending his lot.

"That's *Officer*, even to you, DJ." As skinny as he was, the deputy didn't back down or lose his temper—Josie was impressed—though his ears had gone a deeper shade of red. He had a shaving nick on his neck right above his khaki uniform collar that looked fresh and painful. Josie didn't know it was possible for someone to look both middle-aged and untried at the same time. He was like the smallest kid in her high school class, all grown up but still exactly the same. His skin had wear and tear, sun damage, and creases at his forehead and eyes, but his expression said he still didn't know what he was doing or how he'd gotten there.

"I used to babysit *Officer* Sumbitch here," DJ told Josie. "I was in high school and this punk was in diapers. I used to wipe his butt and feed him in a high chair while his mama was at work. Now he thinks he's better than all of us. Thinks he can get to be a super cop by arresting innocent men for murder."

"I didn't arrest Billy. I took him in for questioning," the deputy said. "We all know the sheriff wanted him brought in. I didn't have anything to do with that decision, so you can stop taking it out on me already. I was just doing my job."

DJ poked a broad finger at the deputy's narrow chest. "Well, sometimes the damn job is wrong."

Josie paid her lunch tab, completely forgetting until after the fact that she had a business credit card for her expenses. Drew was trying to help her get organized, but after a lifetime of paying cash—what little she had, when she had it—she was pretty terrible at acting like a grownup with paperwork, taxes, and receipts. She also had one of those black credit cards in the very back of her wallet courtesy of Greta Williams. Josie had only recently learned that the card didn't have a credit limit. Like, she thought maybe she could buy a jet plane with it, if the circumstances called for a James Bond type of getaway.

So far, she hadn't used it for anything that exciting. Apparently, Greta thought she might be incurring more medical expenses based on her past behavior.

Pah. That's not happening again.

DJ rang her ticket up, one eye on the door, probably watching for the deputy still. "You enjoy your lunch? And the show, too?"

She laughed. "Never a dull moment around here, I'm guessing."

He shook his head, more rueful than amused. "Billy's not always like that. He does have a notoriously short fuse, but for the past decade he's had it under control for the most part. It's just when this idiotic business periodically comes up, he loses his mind."

She got the feeling DJ was just shooting the breeze with her, not trying to sway her blog post in any way. Smiley's had enough local and tourist business to keep afloat for the next thousand years, if she had to make a rough estimate. If the building was still standing, it would be them and the cockroaches surviving the next comet impact. A few snarky words on a little-known blog weren't going to make or break them.

"But you don't believe any of it?"

How else could DJ work for a man so closely? Be *his right-hand man* for so many years? But he surprised her.

"That, I don't know. All I know is the guy I see every day when I come to work. Never shorted me a paycheck. In fact, gave me raises when I didn't ask for them. Took care of my advance when my car broke down. Never treated me or any of his employees with anything but fairness."

"So this isn't the work of a disgruntled employee, someone that he fired?"

"Didn't say that either. If you're a pain in the ass and deserve to be fired, Billy will hunt and destroy you faster than a duck on a tick. Same goes if you steal from him or lie to him. People get what they deserve, but I've never seen a man more fair or had a better boss than him. He'd give you the shirt off his back if you needed it, but the minute you turn on him, you're out. Don't let the door hit you where the good Lord split you, if you know what I'm saying."

Josie laughed and thanked him, though she didn't miss the undercurrent of seriousness in everything he said. He wasn't joking around when it came to Billy Blake and the loyalty he gave to and demanded from others, cute country aphorisms or not.

CHAPTER 11

On the faded blacktop outside Smiley's, Josie found Deputy Louie leaning against the hood of her rented car, legs crossed, arms folded against his narrow chest. Her heart thumped in her chest for a minute— her gut-reaction to anyone in a badge, a leftover from her misspent youth trying to avoid the Pima County Juvenile Detention Center. She'd had a lot of close calls in those days thanks to a massive chip on her shoulder and the misfortune of being the new kid at her high school mid-year.

Did the Sheriff's Office issue parking tickets? I thought that was a Police Department thing? Maybe there's only the Sheriff in tiny Leandro. Why on earth would I be getting a ticket? This frickin' lot doesn't even have any painted lines.

"Can I help you?" She lobbed this generic conversation opener at the deputy, hoping she didn't sound as defensive as she felt. She tried to school the frown off her face but knew she was only partly successful. She probably had on what her friends called her "dragon lady scowl," which kind of sounded racist because of her being part-Asian, but she wore it with pride.

"Hi there," he said, all friendly-like. The smile on his face seemed sincere enough, though not flattering on his lean face. He looked like a wild dog hoping for scraps, upper lip lifted in submission. Josie's dog, Bert, wasn't a submission-smiler, but his Golden Retriever buddy down the street from her apartment was.

She didn't say anything, just raised her eyebrows.

"I see you're friendly with ol' DJ in there."

She didn't bother to enlighten him that she'd only met the man a couple hours ago, though she felt they had bonded a little hanging out at the counter before his boss's crazy outburst.

"I was wondering if you could assist me with something."

Her face must have taken a turn for the skeptical because he held up his hands placatingly.

"Whoa, whoa, whoa. I'm not going to ask you for nothing too bad. Anyhow, I'm off duty now."

Like that made her feel better. She'd *seen* the TV shows.

He straightened up, digging a hand into his back pocket. "You see, the thing is, my mama really likes Billy's brisket and cornbread. I'm about to go visit her house to fix the kitchen sink which has a leak under the cabinet. But that's neither here nor there. The point I'm getting to is, I'd really like to take her some lunch, but the thing is, I'm blacklisted from ordering food in the restaurant. Just because of doing my job."

"Because you arrested Billy."

"I did not *arrest* him," he said, sticking his hands on his hips, bony elbows jutting out. "I was required *by my job* to escort him to the station for questioning. My personal inclinations in the matter are not relevant. Neither are my past affiliations with the Blake family and Ms. Mary Clare, may she rest in peace."

Josie blinked, a slightly unethical scheme hatching in her brain. "You know she's dead for sure?"

She expected Louie to backpedal or deny having implied it.

"Well, duh," he said. "Everybody knows that."

Josie must have looked surprised. Darned transparent face and all.

He said, "I told you I'm off duty. I'm allowed to say what I want. And it's just plain as the nose on my face that the woman has passed on. She hasn't called her family. Her mother near about worried herself to death over the years. And as much as she and Billy supposedly were at each other's throats, I know those two loved each other up until the very end. I've known them since before I was born and it's always been the case. Volatile as firecrackers in a butane factory, but devoted to each other as much as Elvis and Priscilla. As much as Lyndon B. and Lady Bird. As much as…"

"I *get it*. I understand," Josie said, sticking her hand out, fingers wiggling. "Give me the money."

He gave her a crisp twenty from his beat-up leather wallet. "Brisket platter with cornbread and slaw. Extra side of beans. Mama loves those, too."

So did most of Austin, apparently.

"Nothing for you?" Maybe he'd soured on Smiley's barbecue himself. Though, personally, being banned from a restaurant would probably make Josie crave it more, as perverse as her nature was.

"Nah." He got a hangdog look on his face, his shoulders slumping. The posture looked more natural on him than his hands-on-hips Superman stance at the front of the restaurant when he'd first burst in. His true half-glass-empty nature showed through.

"Now wait a minute," she said. "Don't tell me you're denying yourself because you feel like you don't deserve it."

His eyes flicked to the right—her left—and up, a basic tell. He'd handed her money with his right hand from his wallet, which had been in his right back pocket. Looked like he was right-handed, so it would follow that shifting his eyes up and to the right meant he was fibbing.

She stood there, rolling her own eyes until he caved. His resolve melted like a cone of cotton candy in a rainstorm.

"Fine. I betrayed Billy. It's true. I feel like I don't deserve to partake of his multiple-award-winning barbecue anymore. Even though he practically raised me—well, on certain days of the week, along with his mother. Not until I make it up to him somehow." The deputy picked at his fingernails for second. "Which is never."

"Why never?"

"Because he did it. And there's not a damn thing I can do to change that fact."

She shook her head. "What if I could help you feel better about it…in a small way. I mean, no promises, but I can try."

"Just what are you talking about? Are you digging up that old business again?"

"It seems like it was never buried to begin with."

He shrugged. "Fair enough."

"So if I get your mama's lunch, you need to do something for me."

Yeah. So maybe she was taking advantage of what she thought might be a simple guy just to get more information out of him, but she couldn't let the opportunity pass her by. Then again, maybe he knew things…and he wouldn't mind chatting with an outsider who had no stake in the game.

His eyes narrowed. "And just what would that be?"

Or maybe not.

"Just answer a few questions."

"About Billy?"

"Yep. And his wife. And the restaurant."

He kicked his boot at a weed growing through the cracked pavement. "You're not going to record me, are you? Are you a reporter?"

"Nope. Not a reporter. This is purely off-record just to satisfy my own curiosity. I want to see if I can figure this out."

"Even though hundreds of people have already looked into it? Even though tons of people were out whacking the bushes looking for her remains and not a single one of them found anything?"

Well, when he put it like that…

"Yep."

"And what makes you think you're so special, missy?"

She gave him a pass on his condescension, even though the instinct to kick him in the shins was nearly overpowering. He'd asked a fair question. What made her different from anyone else who'd gone before her?

Her innate curiosity? Any number of people had that. She could walk out her front door at home and count five people who knew her dog's walk schedule and that Josie had a weakness for Girl Scout cookies.

Her track record on solving mysteries? Not so much. The last one had unraveled on its own right in front of her eyes. She was still having trouble living that one down, at least in her own mind.

Her unerring common sense and gut reactions? *Meh.* She'd used to think she was a good judge of people, but she knew her ability to survive hits to the head and stabs in the back was pure luck.

"Not a darned thing."

CHAPTER 12

Luckily, DJ wasn't at the counter when Josie went back inside Smiley's to buy lunch for the deputy's mother, so she didn't have to explain herself. She stuck to the deputy's order to the letter. It had briefly crossed her mind to be a Good Samaritan and throw in an extra side of the famous beans for the officer, but she decided against it. Who was she to interfere with the dynamics of the feud? Well, besides being an insufferable busybody who normally would do *exactly* that...But in this case, the deputy seemed to be doing a self-imposed penance. It would have been wrong of her to be an interloper when she only had a tip of the facts iceberg in sight.

They'd bargained for her to accompany him to his mother's house with the food in exchange for her being able to ask him a few questions. She slid into the passenger side of his department SUV, staring at the millions of buttons and gadgets on his dash. A stand between them had a laptop mounted to it, and she wondered how that wasn't a cause of distracted driving.

He waited for her to buckle up, the partitioned takeout container balanced on her knees, before he pulled out onto the highway. "You've got 15 minutes there and another 15 on the way back. Now what exactly is it you want to ask me?" He glanced at the food, then at her face—his priorities in line—before focusing back on the road. She had to use her time wisely, so she figured she'd cut to the chase.

"If everyone thinks Billy killed Mary Clare, why do they still go to his restaurant?" She'd thought Texans would be less forgiving than to eat at the establishment of a wife killer, no matter how good his food was.

"That's the thing. There's no proof that he did it." Narrow shoulders bobbled in a shrug under his polyester uniform. She could see the glint of silver in his closely shorn hair—he was older than he looked.

"Even though you said everyone knows he's guilty."

"Well, yeah. Unless he's tried and convicted in a court of law, he's a contributing member of this community. Until that day, we'll all eat there. I mean, everyone but me."

"Her body was never found, was it?"

"No, ma'am. But she never contacted her family, her best friends, or anyone else to speak of after that day in 1995. In my book, that's as good as dead. Even if she was aiming to flee across the Mexican border and start over, I think she would have contacted someone eventually. People are creatures of habit. It'd take a special kind of heartlessness to be able to cut off all ties like that."

And the food at Smiley's was *that good*.

Josie watched the landscape speed by outside her window. Gnarled live oak trees dotted the landscape, their twisted branches clawing against the gray afternoon sky. It was flatter out here than in the rolling limestone covered hills in the city. She'd never sat in the front of a police vehicle before. The backseat once or twice when she was younger, yes, but never up front riding shotgun.

She eyed the deputy's actual shotgun, mounted inside the vehicle next to his seat. Riding up front was a whole new perspective on life—not feeling like a criminal. The trip was kind of...fun since her heart wasn't pounding with dread.

"What places did they search for her?"

"The house and, of course, the restaurant. Lake Austin, Lady Bird Lake, also Barton Creek—thanks to a dead-end tip on the hotline. We got so many false leads thanks to that thing. People were calling in the kiddie ball pit at Highland Mall, for the love of God. 'Course, that mall's closed now. They turned it into the community college, but that's neither here nor there. The point is, we searched a lot of places, but it was hit or miss, you know? There were a lot of eyes out there looking—hundreds of volunteers putting in man hours. I kept expecting some jogger or some old geezer out walking his dog to call it in. Even the Boy Scouts were out in troops, but no one found anything. Neither hide nor hair."

An image passed through Josie's mind of Mary Clare's hairsprayed coif, her bloodless face with unseeing eyes open, lying in the Texas dirt. She took an unsteady breath. She didn't know if Mary Clare's restless

70

spirit had unfinished business here, but it certainly was making her feel unsettled.

"Needle in a haystack," she said, trying to keep the quaver out of her voice. A crackle in the police radio helped disguise her weakness, for which she counted herself grateful. Her professionalism hung by a tenuous thread here as it did in most situations.

"That's right."

He clicked his turn signal and took them west. She needed to ramp up her line of questioning because they were almost at his mother's, though she still had the return trip to Smiley's to ask him more.

"Okay, so let's assume Mary Clare is dead." It seemed heartless, but Josie was trying to look at the situation theoretically. If she stopped and thought about it too much, she'd freeze in her tracks, like a lot of the other situations in her life.

"Right. This is the path we went down. I mean, we hoped she was alive, but nothing turned up either way. But in a case with a woman in possible danger, we always talk to the husband first. Sad to say, but there's a lot of menfolk out there beatin' up on their women."

Bringing in Billy for questioning was what had revoked Deputy Louie's barbecue privileges. Even his life had changed that day.

"But you guys didn't bring him in for years after she went missing."

"That's because Billy kept telling us she was still alive. He kept insisting that she'd just up and left him and that we should let him wallow in his misery and quit harassing him."

"And you believed him?"

The deputy pursed his mouth for a minute before answering. "Listen. It's possible mistakes were made. But the thing is, Billy Blake is a respected member of the Leandro community. He and his wife, for all intents and purposes, were both well-liked, were faithful to each other, and from what everyone could tell, in love, even though he's a grumpy bastard and has always been one. We didn't have any reason not to believe him."

Josie did a little math in her head—not her strong suit, but she did her best. Mary Clare had gone missing in 1995. Billy Blake had been taken in for questioning about three years later.

"Just how old were you when you had to go get Billy and bring him in to the Sheriff's office?"

Deputy Louie jutted out his lean lower jaw, a sign of frustrated resignation, perhaps. "Nineteen. Fresh out of training. Not my happiest day, I tell you what."

"Stay right here. I'm going to drop this off with Mama," the deputy told Josie as he reached through her window to take the Smiley's container from her. "And don't touch anything."

Well, that's putting a lot of trust where it hasn't been merited.

She eyed the siren box and its "yelp" and "wail" settings. She would have given in to temptation to play with the buttons and flip switches, but he'd warned her that his mother would be napping. She worked the early morning shift in the local grocery store bakery decorating cakes, and Josie respected that. Her own mother had gotten up before the sun many times to prep for her restaurant. The woman deserved her naps.

He re-emerged from the modest single-story house just a little while later, empty-handed.

"Thanks for that," he said, sliding back behind the steering wheel. "She'll be pleased to wake up to the smell of Smiley's in her kitchen. Lord knows I would be."

If the woman's house had been more lavish and if she'd been taking her rest on a velvet fainting couch, Josie would have been inclined to think he was trying to buy himself into his mom's favor. Maybe get a bigger inheritance. The right meal could make Josie have a change of heart about almost anyone. But the house was modest, the yard tiny but tidy. Had Josie been the type of person who was in touch with her feelings with words at the ready for expressing those emotions, she would have told the deputy he was a good son. Instead, she remained silent and stared out the windshield straight ahead of them.

They'd pulled back onto the road before Josie asked her next question.

"How long after Mary Clare went missing did Smiley's burn down?"

"She disappeared in fall of '95. Smiley's didn't burn down until 2007."

"Huh. More than a decade later. Twelve years."

Any evidence that might have been destroyed by the fire would have been sitting around for anyone to discover for a dozen years. If the fire at Smiley's had been arson, it didn't strike Josie as having been an urgent attempt to destroy evidence, to put it mildly.

"There was an arson investigation, as you can imagine," the deputy said. "For insurance purposes. They didn't find any accelerants or points of origin of the fire other than the fire pit. I think the official finding was that it was ember or spark that caused the whole place to go up. Purely accidental."

"Who investigated the fire?"

"Funny you should ask that. There were two separate investigations. One was conducted by the Leandro Fire Department. They have something like three investigators on payroll that searched for the cause and origin of the fire. There was some question about spoliation."

Josie felt her forehead crinkle. Her confusion probably made her look like a Shar-Pei.

"Well, when a crew of firefighters goes to a scene, they can sometimes ruin potential evidence while they're putting out the fire. Not on purpose, of course, just in the rush to get the flames out."

"But that wouldn't destroy evidence of, say, an accelerant, right?"

"Nah, I don't think so. The chemicals would still be there."

Josie frowned. "And there was a second investigation?"

"Yes, Mary Clare's parents hired an independent expert from California—some fire bigwig who's written a bunch of books and teaches forensics classes somewhere. They brought him in not two weeks later. He comes poking around, stirring things up, stepping on toes over at the Leandro FD. But his report came back as it being one hundred percent accidental. No question about it."

"Wow, I'll bet they were disappointed. Probably not what they were hoping after going to all that trouble and expense."

He shrugged. "I'm sure they spent a pretty penny on him, but I guess he told them to drop it because there was nothing there. Mary Clare's family—her mama in particular—kind of let it go after that."

"I imagine it's a pain in the neck to insure a smokehouse against accidental fire."

"Like living on the Gulf and trying to get homeowner's insurance to protect against hurricanes," he agreed. "You got to be richer than God."

"Or get crappy coverage."

Which was an interesting thought. Which case was Billy Blake? Rich or poorly insured?

"What about Mary Clare's assets? I heard her family was fairly wealthy. They're up in Dallas, right?"

He hedged a bit as he turned the vehicle back onto the main highway, spinning the steering wheel with the heel of his hand. "I've heard they're well-to-do. You know, some people are flashy-rich and others just are. I think they are the latter. To be honest, that's only what I've seen on the news. I haven't had any personal interaction with them. I'll tell you what, though...if Billy killed her for money, he sure wasn't greedy about it. Other than their big ol' house that's just sitting there empty, he's living the exact same life he was always living. Wears the same shirts until they get holes. Drives the same old truck until...well, he still is driving it."

"How long do you have to wait after a person goes missing before you can get them legally declared dead?"

"That's generally seven years," he said. "If you don't have any evidence the person is actually not alive, all you have to do is wait it out seven years. Say, you've seen your neighbor get swept away by flood waters, but they've never been found. You last saw them in a situation of 'great peril,' so it would be more likely a judge would declare them dead before the seven years timespan was up."

Josie drummed her fingers on the door's arm rest. More mental math, which was probably making smoke come out of her ears. She was really only good at calculating cooking conversions—teaspoons to tablespoons, ounces to cups.

"So, seven years after Mary Clare's disappearance would have been around fall of 2005. Billy could have gotten her declared dead by then, collected any life insurance money or other funds tied up in her name— anything that wasn't already jointly owned, and fixed up the restaurant legitimately. He wouldn't necessarily had to have waited until 2007 to burn the place down if it was all about money."

She knew there could've been other unseen factors at work. A mistress. Blackmail. A gambling debt. Addiction. Any number of things could have created a huge need for cash on Billy's part that would have been hidden from an outsider like her all these years later.

"Of course, all this is off the record," the deputy said, turning back into the lot at Smiley's. He drew up alongside her rental car. "Lots of gossip about Billy and Mary Clare. Nothing ever came of it. And you have to know, every one of those old-timers in there." He stabbed a long, bony finger in the direction of the restaurant. "Every soccer mom, software programmer, or what have you, who comes to eat here has his or her own theory about what happened to Mary Clare. And not one of those theories has held water. *Not one.*"

He gave her a pointed look, which she understood to mean he thought she didn't have a chance in hell of unraveling the mystery.

She turned back after opening the door on her side. "I appreciate you taking the time to talk with me."

He knuckled his forehead, tipping an imaginary hat. "It was a good trade-off."

"And I think you're being too hard on yourself." She nodded toward the restaurant.

Because even she could admit, those were some darned good beans.

CHAPTER 13

"What'd you do today?" Drew asked as he dunked a French fry into a splatter of mayo on his plate, trying to hide the fact that he preferred the ecru goo over ketchup on his fries. As if she didn't know by now. As if she would kick him to the curb for this minor though disgusting character flaw.

"Chased down some crazy and fascinating barbecue leads," she said, not exactly fibbing, sipping her microbrew ginger ale through a straw — spicy, bubbly, and delightful, if overly trendy. "What about you?"

They were sitting outside, tucked away in the back patio of a cute little beer bar in the warehouse district, enjoying what had turned out to be a mild night. If this was late fall in Austin, she was almost ready to give up her primo apartment with its grandfathered-in low rent. Cold was cold. Enjoying patio weather in November was priceless.

Drew was drinking some kind of stout with chocolatey overtones — she shivered just thinking about it. *Ew*, not her thing either, like the mayo. But she liked to watch him — *her man* — drink it.

"New directions in monitoring diabetes."

She nodded, trying to keep an interested expression on her face — it wasn't too difficult. Though she wasn't as fascinated by his topic as he was, she was engaged *by him*. He gestured with his hands while he talked, like all the people in his large Italian family. Whenever she pictured his mom, Andrea was standing in her little kitchen gesticulating at her kids with a spatula. Maybe that was part of Josie's instant love for him and his family — they were always cooking, and the love of food was at the heart of her existence, her essence. Along with family and friends, of course. She wasn't a complete hedonist.

As the daylight faded around them and the fairy lights intertwined through the tree branches overhead sparkled on, she listened to the deep thrum of Drew's voice and thought, *This would have been a perfect evening to ask him if he wanted to get married.* Of course, she'd left the ring in the hotel room, and she had no idea if she had ketchup on her chin. So perfect was a relative notion.

"Hey," he said, breaking off from his somewhat one-sided medical speech. "There's something I've been meaning to ask you. I was waiting for the right time, but now seems about as good as any."

She blinked at him, a swallow of ginger ale caught on her tongue in limbo before she squeezed it down her throat. He couldn't possibly be asking her The Question. He was so much more prepared than this. He'd do something big, make a grand gesture. Violins came to mind. Him on bended knee. A ring in a fancy box. Basically the opposite of anything she would come up with. So, no, there was no way he could be pre-empting her popping the question.

Do a couple of inhale-exhales and he won't notice my freakout.

Just as she got her breathing back to normal, he said, "You haven't been sleeping much lately, have you?"

Her lack of REM was not a topic she wanted to discuss. In fact, she'd been actively avoiding it because then she'd have to admit her nightmares had been ramping up, never mind the little panic episode she'd had in Smiley's this afternoon.

So she did what any other woman of the world would do.

"It's fine," she said. "I'm fine."

The thing was, lying was not second nature to Josie. She couldn't even school her face to follow through with the B.S. coming out of her mouth.

As soon as she reiterated her state of fine-ness to Drew, he laughed. He paused to take a swig of his stout, but burst out laughing again at what must have been a sour look on her face. "Tell me another good one," he said.

Laugh it up, fuzzball.

"A man walks into a bar," she said.

"That must have hurt."

She took a sip of ginger ale and contemplated spitting it at him. The bubbles stung going down her throat.

"Why did the chicken cross the road?"

"To get away from the person who was asking her why she's not sleeping at night." He added, "*Chicken.*" Just in case she wasn't following him.

"Why doesn't a rooster wear pants?"

"Because his pecker is on his—Hey, are you calling me a peckerhead?"

She gave up, having burned through the three lousy jokes in her repertoire.

They sat in silence for a few more rounds of sipping their drinks, with him giving her that half-smile accompanied by an occasional shake of his dark head. After he flagged the server down for another beer, she threw in the white flag.

"I'll go see someone when we get home," she said at last, having been worn down by his blasted, indomitable good nature.

He nodded his head, not adding an *I told you so* or anything at all, for that matter. He knew when to back off, especially after a victory like that. Smart man.

And more than a match for her thick-skulled pig-headedness.

CHAPTER 14

Josie was due for a good night's sleep, but her sub-consciousness wasn't about to pay that debt. She spent the night tossing and turning until she moved to the second queen bed in the room, afraid that her nocturnal Pilates would wake up Drew.

Her new location wasn't much better. In fact, it had the added drawback of being cold and lonely. Eventually, she got out her cell phone, aiming the light away from Drew, and started watching videos of a street vigilante who trawls the seedy L.A. streets at night rescuing stray dogs. Though she would deny it by daylight, a tear or two may have leaked from the corners of her sleep-deprived eyes.

Just after 10:00 a.m., she woke up to an empty but pitch black room. Drew must have drawn the funky, geometric blackout drapes and hung the Do Not Disturb placard on the hotel room door handle, thoughtful guy that he was. She peeled her face off her phone and used her shirt to rub off the greasy impression of her cheek and half her mouth from the touch screen.

It took three futile presses of the power button on her phone to realize its battery had died. Scrubbing a hand over her face, she sat on the second hotel bed and waited for her brain to come back online. Somewhere deep inside her skull, a puny fluorescent light box was flashing sporadically, powered by a weak backup generator, the last outpost in deep, dark, pitch-black space.

Tink, tink, tink...

After a few minutes, she gave up on being fully functional and dragged herself out of bed to her suitcase. She swiped her hand inside the front of it, then the back and sides, searching for her phone charger. She managed to unfold almost every article of clothing left in her bag and brush her knuckles against the box with the ring she'd bought for Drew, reminding her she'd yet to come up with a plan to ask him.

When she failed to locate her charging cord in her suitcase, she opened Drew's to borrow his. He might have taken it with him for the day, but it was worth a look—she didn't want to invade his privacy, but he'd be more upset with her if she walked around without a phone.

When she tipped back the lid and saw all the neatly folded piles of socks and t-shirts, she sat back on her heels, knocked for a loop by the beautiful order. A glance back at the disarray of her bag compared to his, laid out a dilemma in front of her as plain as day.

What is he doing with me?

Here was a handsome guy who had all his ducks in a row, as his mother would say. *All his crap together*, as she herself would say. He was solid, loyal, smart... Yeah, she could go on about his good qualities, his generosity, his thoughtfulness, and how he turned her on like nobody's business. She could even list his annoyances and foibles with a certain bemused affection.

Like insisting on giving directions using "north," "south," "east," and "west" as if she carried a compass with her. Or falling asleep the second his head hit the pillow while she stared at the bedroom ceiling. Or the way he'd somehow mesmerized her dog into loving him more than the mutt loved her.

Here she was, wanting to grab Drew and hold on to him forever because he was clearly the best thing in her life, but...she was mess. A non-sleeping, possibly PTSD-having, food critic fraud who couldn't eat most of the time. An over-thinking busybody with a made-up career blogging about food and philosophy, who had a bad habit of getting herself into stupid situations. And yet another bad habit of pushing people away when they got too close.

A puff of air escaped her mouth and blew back her hair from her eyes.

Am I dragging him down for my own selfish reasons?

She closed his neat, organized suitcase, the little window into his world. Her search for a phone charger didn't feel important just now. And some thoughts were better left unthought for the moment. Especially first thing in the morning, and especially on an empty stomach.

Downstairs in the hotel's atrium restaurant that swept upward into several cavernous stories of the glass hotel lobby, Josie opened her laptop at her table and pushed aside a salmon salad that failed to hold her interest. She spent some time answering comments on her blog, blocking a few lewd trolls and spammers, and checking her ad revenue. Before coming to Texas, she'd set up and scheduled a blog post to go live later this afternoon, so she was covered for a while. After she got back to Boston, she'd have time to go through her photos and write up her trip later.

Her income-rustling work taken care of for the time being, she went back to a couple articles about Mary Clare she'd bookmarked for reading.

In the late 1980's, Mary Clare had competed but not placed in a Dallas Fort-Worth area beauty pageant. Josie found a group photo of all the contestants of that pageant that particular season, but couldn't determine which puffy-headed, toothy grin was Mary Clare's in the huge mass of skin and swimsuits. The women—or teens, actually—in the front row of the photo were 1980's-thin, stomachs sucked in further to make their ribs jut out.

The website that hosted the article was pro-pageant and made no beans about it. In flowery terms, it extolled the virtues of pageants, listing the high demands they expected from participants in terms of talent, time, and qualifications. It also enumerated the vast sums of scholarship money it doled out to winners.

Okay, fine. They're not just beauty contests, they're scholarship pageants. In which you have to display your abs. While wearing high heels.

During one of her more-sick-than-well episodes with her stomach, Josie had become more acquainted with reality TV than she'd ever publicly admit. She'd watched a few shows about children and beauty contests with the same avid and equal amounts of horror she'd devoted to *Ghost Seekers* and *Aliens Built the Egyptian Pyramids*. She wasn't proud of it, but it made her feel slightly more patriotic, more American. At least she knew what people were talking about a little more now.

She was wary about beauty…pageants, but at the same time, she knew they were a long-revered tradition in many of the Southern states, most assuredly including Texas. As far as she could tell from her Internet searches, Mary Clare had a short-lived history with them. Just one and done.

What she needed to track down was someone who'd done more research on the woman. Why backtrack through all the scraps and breadcrumbs when someone might have done all the legwork?

She scrolled back through some of the other articles about Mary Clare that she'd saved until she found the follow-up one about Billy being taken in for questioning written by a reporter named Skip Richmond.

A few more clicks determined that he still occasionally contributed to the local paper. She dug in her back pocket for her cell phone but came up empty. Not only was her phone still up in the room, but it was dead because she'd never found a charger.

Darn it.

That was a drag. She was going to have to go use the room phone.

Well, well, well, how quickly the technophobe becomes the addict.

"I take it that's a no-go on the salad?" the bartender with the young face said. He had come to clear her dishes and stood over her with one ginger eyebrow cocked.

She shrugged. "No offense to the salmon. I'm just not into it. It's all the meat I've been eating this week. I've had more animal-based protein this week than in the last year. I think it's making me more aggressive, too."

In fact, now that she was thinking about it, Baby-Faced Bartender here was the one who'd shut down the minute she'd mentioned Smiley's earlier. She reached out with a hand on his wrist as he was picking up her plate. His pretentious black finger nail polish was mostly chipped off.

"Not done after all?" he asked. His blond soul-patch jutted out from his chin when he grinned.

"Tell me," she said. "How come you don't like Smiley's?"

Speaking of smiles, his immediately faded. He pulled his wrist away, but she tightened her fingers just a little. Her strongest rendition of being a bad cop—a pinch on the wrist.

He glanced at the bar where another bartender was handling the light afternoon clientele. Then he pulled out the chair next to her and flopped down, legs apart, hands with various silver rings dangling between them. His knuckles were all banged up.

"Look," he said. "It's not that I don't like him. It's just...it was my first job. I thought it was totally lame. I mean, who has good memories of their first job? Seriously."

She'd give him that. Her first job was in her mother's restaurant wiping down tables and filling sauce bottles. Although...she'd kind of liked it. But she would have been inclined to believe him had his eyes not gone up and to his right—and he was wearing a watch on his left wrist. There was that ridiculously easy tell to spot again. She wanted to shake her head in disbelief.

If people only knew how common the eye giveaway is.

She wondered, for a second, if she could train herself to avoid the tell herself, but what was the use? She couldn't even keep a straight face when she was telling a joke, never mind a lie.

"Why'd you leave Smiley's?"

He shrugged and ran a hand through his hair, his dark fingernails showing through the blond strands. He had one of those trendy undercut buzzes with the floppy part on top that seemed to require him to play with it often.

"I didn't really like bussing tables like a low-life scrub, so I found a better job. I don't mean this job here—I left Billy's a couple years ago." He was quick to add that part, as if she were going to call up his past workplaces for verification. If she were more detail-oriented, she would've gotten right on that task. She had a feeling there was more to his story than he was willing to impart, but instead of doing the tedious legwork, she was hoping he'd make it easy on her and just spill the beans.

"I'm working on my sculptures now. I work with steel." He dug in his back pocket and handed her a card that said *My Band Is Better Than Yours works of art in steel.*

"That's uh...an unusual name for an art exhibit."

He shrugged. "It's supposed to be ironic."

So ironic, she didn't get it.

He pointed to his hands. "I really mess up my hands sometimes working with metal. I need to be more careful, but I get so caught up in my work in progress that I forget to watch what I'm doing until it's too late."

Though it was a turn-off to be served by someone with open sores, at least they were acquired in the name of art. She could get behind that.

"So you were moving onto bigger and better things, pretty much. Did something specific happen to make you quit Smiley's?"

"Nah, yeah," he said.

Whatever that meant. And there went the hand through the hair again. He was going to be sporting a bald patch by the end of their conversation. She waited for him to settle on one answer.

"I mean, Billy was cool and all." His eyes went up to the right.

Pants on fire.

"Yeah?" she asked. "I hear he has kind of a reputation." She was careful not to say more.

"People always talk about his crazy temper, but I never saw anything like that." He didn't elaborate, but his gaze was straight forward—no twitching and no playing with his hair. Whatever beef he had with Billy hadn't involved the man's epic outbursts.

"So he was pretty good to work for?"

"Yeah, I mean, it was just the job that sucked." His eyes were back to their shifty dance. Something had happened between him and Billy, but she wasn't able to pry it out of him.

"You know what? You're totally right," she said, closing her laptop. "First jobs are good for what they are, but we always have to move on, you know?"

He was back to smiling, which was good. She didn't want to be forced to go elsewhere for breakfast.

CHAPTER 15

Upstairs in the room, Josie found her phone charger under a bed, hidden half under the bed covers that had slid to the floor when she'd gotten up. She plugged the cord in and opened her laptop to search for a phone number for *The Legislator*. She picked up the room phone and dialed out, making a mental note to tidy up the explosion of tees and jeans coming out of her suitcase. Not for her sake, but to be less annoying to Drew, or so she aimed to be. She squinted...how'd her hairbrush end up under the chair? That explained why finger-combing her unruly mop of dark hair had been her only choice after her shower.

By some miracle, her call wound through the tortuous newspaper switchboard and reached Skip Richmond's desk line. She figured she'd leave a message and hope against hope that he'd call *her*, some unknown out-of-towner digging up old news.

Yeah right. Might as well start playing the lottery.

"Y'ello," he said, his voice a twangy croak like a knife being dragged across a coat hanger—some kind of homespun instrument that would have been at home fronting a jug band.

She paused in shock, long enough that he repeated his greeting, the second time sounding like he'd been getting more than his fair share of robocalls, telemarketers, and angry readers today.

"Mr. Richmond," she said, hoping he wouldn't flip her the digital dial tone. "I'm interested in an article you wrote many years ago." She paused to figure out the best way to proceed. Leaving a message on his voicemail would have been a lot easier.

"Lady, I've been at this desk for three decades. I have underwear older than most of the people who work here. You're going to have to be more specific than that."

She could hear him shuffle papers and move things around on his end of the phone, clearly interested in doing anything at all other than talk to her. A slurp and a thunk suggested he was a late-afternoon coffee drinker.

"It's about Mary Clare Blake."

First silence, then a stream of creative cursing warbled through the line. Something about the son of God and crackers. Very derivative New Testament. She was impressed.

"You people from *Exposé Tonight* and all those other trash rags, your so-called investigative reporting, need to leave me in peace. That poor woman's been gone now for nearly 22 years and you keep dragging her story out like a rotted corpse on display. For what? To sell ads. To get higher ratings. Whatever happened to common human decency? Just like that little JonBenét girl in Colorado. We all know her family did it, for the love of God. Why don't you find some other dead horse to beat? Because not even the blowflies will touch this one."

His voice grew faint at the end of his diatribe, like he was on a crash course to slamming down the receiver. She had to figure out what to say. And quick.

"Mr. Richmond, I'm not a reporter," she yelled. She froze and squinted, as if that would make her hear better, waiting to see if her words had had any effect.

Well, pretty much not a reporter. Blogging doesn't count, does it? Semi-philosophical food-obsessed ramblings.

"And I'm not a detective."

Another little white lie. The P.I. license in her pocket made her face burn with the fib, but *in her heart*, she knew she wasn't a P.I. because the thought of that was ridiculous. She was a nosy bumbler at best. A half-Thai female Columbo. The last time she'd been on an official case, she'd been next to useless and then paraded out like a hero on local TV. She was still trying to live that one down. The thought of it embarrassed her so much, she had to shove it to the back of her mind whenever it resurfaced or her face turned bright red. Which was often, thanks to her friends.

"I swear I'm not in this for profit or glory. I don't want to make a buck or write a story. I just want to know what happened to that poor woman and maybe help bring a modicum of peace to her family."

The silence bloomed over the line, and she couldn't tell if he'd hung up while she'd been fast-talking. She sighed. Talking to him could have cleared so much up. Now she'd have to muddle through this riddle the old fashioned way...by speculation and gossip. Certainly not as effective, but with her knack for ferreting out the truth, or at least pushing people until they eventually gave it up, she might have a small chance in finding out what happened to the missing woman.

Okay, a small snowball's chance in a Tucson summer.

At last, he said, "Well then, who are you? And what do you know about Mary Clare?"

Josie's heart thumped. "I'm just a person who has a knack for figuring things out. I heard the story over lunch the other day and it stuck with me. It's like a pricker in the ankle band of my sock and it won't stop bothering me."

"Well, what is it you want to know about her?"

"I want to know whatever you know."

Skip, as he'd asked Josie to call him, was in his sixties, kind of an aging hippie. He was thin, slightly built and looked desiccated, skeletal, and dried out, like the spines of a cactus. He was a mostly brownish-gray person—hair, skin, and clothing alike. Yet he also had a timeless look as if he could have been sitting there in a toga, a set of Wild West Davy Crockett skins, or tie-dye and a fringed vest and looked equally at home in any state.

She met him while he was on his third cup of java in a coffeehouse-slash-café that specialized in what they called "bespoke donuts." In fact, there was a brochure in papyrus font on recycled elephant dung paper in a hemp basket that explained the philosophy of made-to-order fried dough. Josie put the brochure back and discreetly wiped her hand on her jeans. It seemed their napkins were made of the same pachydermal by-product, which they proudly proclaimed. She set aside the napkins and made a note not to order anything with powdered sugar. As grossed out as she was by wiping her mouth on it, the threat of a little animal poo contamination didn't stop her from putting in an order for a half-dozen. Who knew—maybe it would help mend her grumpy gut or whatever was wrong with her.

Josie shook Skip's dry, weathered hand across the metal bistro table.

"I can't believe you're interested in Mary Clare, after all these years. I mean, I get all kinds of calls from crackpots and weirdos. This case was as big as the UT sniper, Charles Whitman case. Or the case of David Villarreal, 'The Rainbow Killer,' who slashed and hammered men to death. Or the one about Joe Ball, the 'Butcher of Elmendorf' over in Bexar County. That guy kept an alligator pit. People were coming out of the woodwork trying to get into the limelight with their false leads and so-called tips. Others were calling up just trying to get details out of us. What is people's fascination with the misery of others? Or, even worse, murder fetish types who like to tour the homes of dead people."

Josie swallowed hard, discomfort making her mouth dry. Her appointment with Lizzie the Goth ghost hunter later that night was making her feel a tad ghoulish under his scrutiny.

Skip anchored his longish gray hair behind his ear and heaved a large shoulder bag onto his lap. "You sound really sincere. And after I hung up, I checked out your blog and background. No lawsuits. No arrest record, at least as an adult. Good education. Married once, no kids—"

Her eyes bugged out as he recited her background in bullet points. *And what the* hell? *That quickie mistake marriage had been annulled.* Technically it didn't exist, at least in the eyes of the Pope or whoever. She was working hard to forget it herself.

"—Looks like you've had your fair share of hospital stays."

"How do you know all this? That information isn't public record." Anxiety zinged down her spine. Her stomach went numb for once, which was disconcerting after months of mostly pain. She had enemies and a half-hearted Internet stalker who sent her blurry pictures of his anatomy every few months, almost on a quarterly schedule. Her entire life was available to those people? Elephant dung in her donuts was the least of her worries now.

"Relax," he said. "I have my ways, methods of finding things out that are not available to mere mortals." His thin, colorless lips curled up in a sardonic smile. He had so many wrinkles in his face, she was concerned about his hydration level.

His vague reassurance that he had skills beyond the average Googler didn't make her feel better. A guy wearing—she looked under the table to confirm her suspicion—sandals in November shouldn't be so adept in this stuff, should he? She studied his face. Maybe his bloodshot gray eyes were hiding more intelligence than she'd given him credit. And duh, he was a legitimate journalist, unlike her.

"Moreover, your secrets are safe with me. I keep my findings strictly confidential. That is, unless I'm legally bound to inform law enforcement. I'm not a priest, after all." He dropped an overstuffed accordion folder case on the table between them, jostling his mug. The drops of coffee that splashed on the front flap weren't the first to adorn it.

"Here's everything I have. And I have to warn you, these are not duplicates. All these papers are the real thing, the last of their kind. This is my original file, so anything you want to copy, we have to find a copy machine."

She could already tell the file was his original collection by the various impressionist shades of caffeine that painted it. She bet if she scraped DNA samples off the coffee splashes, she could track a path from Indonesia all the way back to Juan Valdez.

"Go ahead. Dig in," he said with a nod toward the file as he drained his cup. He craned his neck to look at the café's counter. "The line's down and I need a refill."

CHAPTER 16

As creeped out as Josie had been by the amount of details Skip had dug up about her, she was enthralled by how much information he had about Mary Clare as she rifled through the pockets of the accordion file. She figured she'd paid the price by sacrificing her privacy.

His info on the supposedly dead woman was pay-dirt. Bank statements. Cancelled checks. Grocery store receipts. Her junior high school report cards. Two thank you notes addressed to her from charities—the Horton House and her college alumni fund. Three articles from the society column of a Texas Hill Country magazine. A paid-in-full billing statement from a dentist that mentioned an edentulous space and prosthesis, whatever that was. A cassette tape marked "voicemail outgoing message."

She'd have to ask him about the tape. How in the world did people play tapes anymore? The last tape player she'd seen was in the Green Giant, her '75 Lincoln Continental currently undergoing reconstruction at a celebrity chop shop.

I'm being unfair. John Dwyer is a legitimate mechanical engineer, even if he was the star of a reality TV show.

Whatever, she mentally warred with herself. Without her car, she felt edgy and more bitter than usual. Not that she drove it very often—it was a two-ton security blanket that reminded her of her family in Arizona who'd given it to her. In any case, she didn't have a car or a cassette tape player handy.

One pocket of the file contained a stack of dog-eared pages, a typed transcript of a conversation that had taken place in June 1996, approximately nine months after the disappearance. Josie looked closer. The speakers' names, marked in brackets, were Skip Richmond and someone named Bunny Rogers. Josie set aside the rest of the file to read the interaction. She skimmed through the requisite greetings and verbal permission for him to tape the conversation.

[SKIP RICHMOND] Can you please tell me about the last interaction you had with your daughter Mary Clare?

[BUNNY ROGERS] Yes. It was a telephone call. She called me the morning of September 28. We had a normal conversation, just chit-chatting about this and that. We talked in the morning several times a week, but I've since checked on my day planner, in case you're wondering how I know the date. Also, I've been asked many, many times this same question by the police.

[SKIP RICHMOND] Of course. I'm sorry if it's annoying. I just want to get it in my records.

[BUNNY ROGERS] To tell you the truth, I don't mind at all if it helps someone figure out what happened to my Mary Clare. One little fact, one little tidbit of information—if there's anything I know that will help one person figure this out, I'm willing to keep repeating myself till my last breath.

[SKIP RICHMOND] I'll do my best, ma'am. I've had a lot of successes in the past, but I don't want to get your hopes up too much. I've just had a lot of experience in these types of things.

[BUNNY ROGERS] Yes, well, I think other people have reached dead end after dead end and some have just plain given up. So I'm open to exploring other options now.

[SKIP RICHMOND] What kind of other options?

[BUNNY ROGERS] My sister brought me a psychic. My son, Brian, has some friends in the Army Corps of Engineers who want to do something with radar or sonar to look for underground heat signatures. I don't understand the specifics. They seem to think she's being held alive underground somewhere, like that bus full of kidnapped children.

[SKIP RICHMOND] Chowchilla?

[BUNNY ROGERS] Yes, that's the one I mean. They were buried alive by some maniac.

[SKIP RICHMOND] Do you think Mary Clare is being held somewhere and that she's alive?

[BUNNY ROGERS] Well, she could be. I mean, I hope to God she's alive and coming home. But we haven't received a ransom note or had any proof of her being alive. In the beginning, I couldn't think of anything else but her being out there somewhere. That someone had taken her. But now, I just don't know. If she's alive, how could she be healthy and well after all these months? If she's been alive this whole time… I just don't know what to pray for anymore.

[SKIP RICHMOND] I'm so sorry. Do you need some tissues?

[BUNNY ROGERS] I have some, thank you. I come well-prepared. This is what my life is now, such as it is. Truly, no one can ever fathom what I have been through. To lose my best friend like this. It's just completely turned my life upside down. I can never go back to the way it was.

[SKIP RICHMOND] I understand. I'm very sorry for you. Going back to that telephone call, the last time you spoke with your daughter, how did she seem?

[BUNNY ROGERS] The same as always. I didn't sense anything unusual. I honestly thought I would be talking to her again a few hours later. We talked one or two times a day. Especially when she moved to Austin with Billy Blake.

[SKIP RICHMOND] So you were very close.

[BUNNY ROGERS] We were like sisters.

[SKIP RICHMOND] Uh-huh. And how many other children do you have? You mentioned a son earlier?

[BUNNY ROGERS] I have three boys and Mary Clare. So, as you can imagine, she was my heart and soul. I just don't know what I'm going to do without her. She'll never have my grandchildren. She'll never be by my side as I get older and need her help. It's just unfathomable sometimes. I have the boys, of course, but they go off and leave you. A daughter always stays.

[SKIP RICHMOND] Do you know of anyone who would want to harm her?

[BUNNY ROGERS] Not any of her brothers, if that's what you're implying.

[SKIP RICHMOND] No, of course not. But did she have any rivals at school, things of that nature?

[BUNNY ROGERS] Absolutely not. Everyone loved her.

[SKIP RICHMOND] But she competed in beauty pageants. Surely she had rivals?

[BUNNY ROGERS] She competed in pageants until she was a freshman in high school. And she was a very good, a very strong competitor. However, when she reached her sweet sixteen, we mutually agreed that she should concentrate on other things in her life, like her studies and charity projects. She was very active with the community and wanted to join the Junior League when she got old enough. But in terms of rivalries with other contestants, some of those girls had grown up with her on the beauty circuit. They were all very supportive of each other. I don't know a single one of them who would have wished any harm come to her.

[SKIP RICHMOND] Uh-huh.

[BUNNY ROGERS] I don't like what your tone is implying, Mr. Richmond.

[SKIP RICHMOND] I'm sorry. I didn't mean to imply anything.

[BUNNY ROGERS] You think I'm just another air-headed woman who bullied her air-headed daughter into doing fluff competitions where the girls are evil snakes and not serious about anything in their lives. Well, you're very mistaken.

[SKIP RICHMOND] I can see I touched a nerve here. I certainly didn't mean to give impression that I think anything of that nature.

[BUNNY ROGERS] I'm sure you didn't.

[SKIP RICHMOND] I apologize. I absolutely did not. But just a few more questions, if you don't mind. To help your daughter.

[BUNNY ROGERS] All right.

[SKIP RICHMOND] Did she have a good relationship with her father? With Mr. Rogers?

[BUNNY ROGERS] Pardon me?

[SKIP RICHMOND] Were Mary Clare and her father particularly close? I mean, in an entirely appropriate fashion.

[BUNNY ROGERS] That's enough. I think we're done here.

The interview ended there, with a thinly veiled accusation of molestation of Mary Clare by her father. Not very subtle, Skip. Though Josie wouldn't guarantee she wouldn't have done the same thing.

CHAPTER 17

An insulated beverage cup—hopefully not made from elephant poo—thunked down on the table in front of Josie next to her forgotten box of donuts. She was about to tell Skip she didn't drink coffee when he told her it was tea.

"Wow. Your research is flawless," she told him, taking the lid off the cup and reaching for the bottle of honey on the table next to them. She'd never been able to stomach coffee, though it might have been helpful to her socially. People were always getting together for coffee, meeting in cafés.

Coffee can be such an ice-breaker when you're trying to coax the truth out of bad guys. If they like coffee. Scratch that. Liquor probably works better.

"Aha, a tea drinker. I was right! That's what I like to call a 'wild-ass guess,'" he said, his raspy voice cracking as he crowed in triumph. He gestured to the files, nearly splashing his own coffee over the edge of his cup. "So what'd you think of all that?"

"I was just reading your chat with Mommy Dearest."

"Oh yeah. Wasn't she a piece of work? Don't let the cute, fluffy name fool you. She's a force to be reckoned with. I think those diminutive female names are a Southern thing. They're all Dixieland generals underneath their strings of pearls." He took a massive gulp of his steaming hot coffee, and she wondered if his mouth was coated with scar tissue from previous burns. He didn't even flinch. The inside of his mouth probably looked like the Elephant Man, thick-hided and malformed. If that was the case, he deserved to enjoy his piping-hot coffee. He'd darn well earned his superpower.

"What's Bunny's story? Any skeletons in her closet?"

"Oh, plenty. If you go back one generation, you find an aunt like that poor Rosemary Kennedy girl, institutionalized and lobotomized by the very family that was supposed to have loved her best."

"Holy geeze."

Josie had heard the story of the poor Kennedy girl, older sister to JFK and RFK, Eunice, and the others. She'd suffered a traumatic birth and had been developmentally delayed—but happy—her entire life. When she grew older, she became rebellious and more subject to fits of violence outside the norm of her family, hence the failed experimental lobotomy. By that standard, Josie would have been a vegetable in a padded room by age 24 as well.

"Yeah, it was Bunny's mother's older sister. Barbaric and tragic. She ended up dying of natural causes in a home outside of Houston. Why is it that these poor people always live long, long lives after they've been turned into mental third graders?"

Josie shuddered. "Do you know what the aunt's diagnosis was that caused her family to do this to her?"

"I did read one account in some letters once, but it was just some weird general terms like 'hysteria' and other bull. Honestly, it could have been anything from schizophrenia to PMS back then and the treatment would have been the same. Dark ages of medicine, pretty much. In fact, Bunny went to nursing school. She dropped out to get married, but I think one of the reasons she chose it was her aunt."

"Brrr. Nurse Ratched."

"No kidding. It's time for your sponge bath now, mister." He made a mock motion of snapping on gloves.

"Was Bunny hiding other things when you talked with her?"

"Well, duh, of course she was. Everyone does. But about her daughter, I don't think she knows where she is or what happened to her. That part was genuine."

"Which is why you went after the father angle at the end there?"

"I may have hit that hammer a little too hard on that nail. But I was trying new directions, trying to be thorough."

"In that case, did you find anything about the brothers?"

"In terms of molestation? Nothing ever came up. They seem like normal, prep-school frat boys. All married with kids at the time. Two lawyers and one some kind of local politician. All still in the Dallas area with their families, but from what I could find out, they only get together on the holidays. As for Bunny's husband, he died in December of 1999 of some type of cancer. His obit didn't specify what kind, which probably means testicular or prostate. Something unspeakable for a man. Maybe even breast cancer," he speculated out loud.

"So, can you take me through the day that Mary Clare went missing? I imagine there was a timeline created along with establishing her husband's alibi and things like that?"

"Sure, sure." He pulled a spiral notebook out of the back of the file and flipped it open before perching some tortoiseshell drugstore granny reader glasses on the end of his nose. "Since Mary Clare's last known interaction was with her mother at about 9:30 the morning of her disappearance, the events of the day before were more important to nail down. During the afternoon, she attended a planning committee meeting in honor of Ann Richards, who was about to step down as governor. It was down on 6th Street in their private dining room. Multiple witnesses interacted with her there until about 4:30 in the afternoon."

"Do you know if she was acting normal that day? Not agitated or upset in any way?"

He flipped through his notes. "There was one thing. A woman named Yvonne Lugnar, who also knew Mary Clare from the pageant circuit when they were younger, incidentally, said that Mary Clare knocked over a drink at the meeting and swore a blue streak, shocking her. None of the other attendees that I tracked down mentioned anything out of the ordinary. One other saw the drink mishap but didn't hear any cursing. Yvonne seemed to be hoping to get her name in the paper, however. As I recall, she spelled her name for me three times."

Josie nodded. Though she couldn't relate to fame hounds, she knew they existed. Several of them sent her weekly emails through her website's contact form suggesting stories for her to cover, which she didn't do as a rule, or asked her to write their biographies, which also wasn't her thing.

"At about quarter to nine that night, call records from their home phone showed someone called Smiley's restaurant and spoke to someone there for about ten minutes. Billy confirmed that his wife did call the restaurant to see when he was coming home. He often worked late into the night, ten to twelve hour days at Smiley's, so he wouldn't see her when he returned home. He says that was the case for that night as well. He got home late, saw her briefly in the morning before he returned to the restaurant, and that was the last time anyone saw her."

Never good when the last person to see her alive was the spouse. At least, not good for him. Never mind the fact that about forty percent of all murdered women are killed by their partners. Not good for him either.

"And his alibi checks out?"

"Yep. The guy was and still is a workhorse. Constantly at his restaurant, with a good forty-minute drive between the house and the restaurant when there's no traffic." He snorted at that last part.

"And what about this tape?" She tapped the voicemail cassette with her finger.

"Just a standard outgoing message for an old voicemail machine. Not very exciting in terms of evidence. Just a little clip of her voice saying to leave a message at the beep." He hemmed and hawed and pursed his lips as if mulling over the state of his soul's eternal salvation. "In fact...you can have that, if you want."

She blinked, wondering if she was supposed to want it.

"I mean, it's something to hear Mary Clare's actual voice. Just to put a bit of life into the person you're reading about and looking at in pictures." Still, he looked doubtful—tortured, in fact—about whether he really wanted to turn it over to her when she didn't really think it was as valuable an artifact as his struggle seemed to merit. She wasn't positive she wanted to take it. Taking his crummy old tape was akin to having a distant relative bequeath her a collection of troll dolls.

"Are you sure you want me to have it?" She knew she didn't sound very grateful to have been selected for this honor, but he was making a gesture of camaraderie, of a partnership of sorts. She should accept it with gratitude.

"Yes," he said at last with a touch more conviction, sliding it across the table to her. "I want you to have a little piece of her."

She took the plastic little relic of the past and turned it over in her hand. She wished she had more time with the rest of his file, but at least the tape was something.

"Speaking of little pieces, how in the heck did you get all these receipts?" She fanned out the papers, sorting through them, an odd assortment of the minutiae of Mary Clare's life, even some early glimpses into it. She had gone to a private school for girls, apparently, and had earned all As except for a C in Etiquette. Sounded like torture to Josie, too. All of a sudden, she felt a kinship with the missing woman. The file was more thorough than all of the scraps of Josie's childhood lumped together in the shoebox at the bottom of her closet.

"That was almost twenty years ago. I was really into dumpster diving and stealing people's trash just to get a story. The things I turned over in the name of research back then...Believe me, those days are over. Climbing in and out of garbage bins and lugging junk around. I got aches and pains in places I didn't even know existed. Like the Lost Pines of arthritis."

Josie hadn't stooped to sifting through trash yet. She hoped she would never voluntarily dig through people's curbside Heftys.

Never say never. As soon as you say it, "never" turns out to be tomorrow.

CHAPTER 18

"What about Mary Clare's friends? Did you manage to track any of them down?"

"Let's see. I already told you about that wily one, Yvonne, from the pageant circuit. But I don't think they were truly friends. More like frenemies. It's hard to take any of those ladies at face value. They're always trained to put their best face forward, to show the best version of themselves even if it's not the real version. I did find a couple of girls she knew from private school, but most of those friendships dropped off when she graduated and turned eighteen."

Josie hadn't kept any of her friends from high school either, but she'd only known most of them for a half-year. She didn't think it was normal for a person to completely cut herself off from all her previous friendships unless there was some kind of abrupt rift.

"Was she well-liked in school or more of a loner?"

"From what I can tell based on class photos and yearbooks, she was one of the popular kids everyone likes to hate. Outgoing, even. Debate team. Dance. Newspaper editor, though I couldn't find anything actually written by her. Always smiling in the photos. So, yeah, it doesn't sit well that she didn't keep in contact with her school friends. Makes you wonder if they were all secretly stabbing each other in the back, all the time smiling on the outside."

"Too bad Facebook and Snapchat weren't around back then. Or hateful text messages. Those would be really helpful right about now. We could probably dig up some dirt if we had something like that."

Skip snorted. "Kids these days. Not very subtle or sneaky, especially when they think they are."

Josie shuddered to think what her life would have been like if any of those things had been readily available while she was a kid and the dumb things she'd done that could have been recorded for all of posterity to see. When she'd graduated high school in 2004, she hadn't even had her own cell phone, or anyone who might have wanted to call her on one.

"What about Mary Clare's college friends? Any of those around?"

"Other than Billy Blake, none pop up on the radar."

"Do you think that's weird?"

Skip swirled his coffee mug around once before taking a gulp. "You know, I thought about that. But she and Billy met right after she started college classes. Some couples, when they meet the love of their lives, tend to shut out the rest of world. They start staying home instead of going out. They rent a movie, get take out, and start living like their friends don't exist. That could have been the case for these two."

A powerful and exclusionary relationship? Josie was willing to give that theory some merit, though it wasn't the case in her own personal life. She and Drew had Benjy and Susan…but not much else beyond them in terms of social life. That was Josie's fault, however. She was pretty much asocial. Possibly antisocial. She'd probably be happy living off a dirt road fifty acres away from her nearest neighbor as long as she had a solid Internet connection.

Or perhaps a controlled and isolated existence. Had Mary Clare been subjected to an abusive relationship with a controlling husband?

"Tell me what you know about Billy," Josie said.

Skip nodded, as if he approved of her train of thought. "Of course, he was always the main suspect. The spouse always is, but he had such a rock-solid alibi for the entire 72-hour period around the time she went missing that other than a murder-for-hire scenario, nothing ever stuck. No theories ever held water. He was at the restaurant during the time she last spoke to her mother. And she was missing by the time he got home, almost ten hours later."

"What was the first sign that she was missing?"

"She had an appointment to get her hair done the next day, but she missed it and also didn't pick up a butcher order she'd requested for that evening. Apparently Billy ended up getting it. Since he had a relationship with the meat market for the restaurant, they always got their home order from the same guy at a discount. Not like they needed a coupon at their income bracket, but isn't it always the way it works?

"Eventually, Mary Clare's mother forced him into filing a missing person's report. But since it was so much later, details were fuzzy in people's minds and nothing was investigated in that essential first 48 hours after she went missing."

"So you don't think Billy's notoriously bad temper came into play?"

Skip rubbed his narrow chin, eliciting a noise like fine-grit sandpaper. "You know, for as much as we've all learned about his fiery temperament, I've never once heard about him raising his voice to his wife. Or any woman, for that matter. In fact, most of his tantrums have been directed at inanimate objects. He's punched the wall at Smiley's two or three times, also kicked a hole in his office door there. Threw a garbage can around. Yelled at a busboy or two. But never at a female—God bless the chauvinism of a Southern gentleman in this case—and never at a customer, as far as I've heard."

Pies and bread, too, had met their demise at the hands of Billy Blake, if Josie remembered what Georgia from Ruby's had told her correctly. Depending on the quality of the bakery, that was a major crime in her book. A guy so out of control of his rage that he could ruin perfectly beautiful pies was a danger to anything defenseless and lovely. Probably.

She didn't like to think about people—*anyone*—getting hit or abused by other people. She hoped it wasn't this situation in Mary Clare's case. Josie had complete, body-racking empathy for situations where a big man beat a smaller, more vulnerable person.

And maybe a flashback or two.

CHAPTER 19

After a couple hours chatting with Skip, Josie decided she wanted his file—*needed* it with the fiery heat of a thousand suns. If only she could snatch it out of his dry, withered grasp and bolt down Lavaca Street, trailing Mary Clare's report cards all the way back to the hotel. Josie felt as itchy fingered as a nine year old girl in a drug store in front of a lip gloss display. It was the brass carousel ring she wanted to grab—no, it was the prize that yanking the ring would get her. It was the open back door of an armored truck, money bags fat with bills just within reach.

If she was going to find out what happened to Mary Clare, it wasn't going to be through communing with the dead woman's spirit. If any scrap of evidence existed that pointed to her whereabouts, Josie had a feeling it was in Skip's file. *Something* had to be there.

She eyed Skip as he clutched it to his sweater-covered chest, the criss-cross java stains on the folder neatly lining up with the argyle pattern on his pullover.

No, she wasn't going to steal it. Taking it from him without his permission when he was a fellow subversive would be utterly dishonorable. Even she couldn't stomach the thought. But how could she convince him to give it—*lend it*—to her? Use some kind of flirtatious voodoo on him?

He set his folder in his lap and took a swig from his coffee cup, slurping loudly as if he were a customer at a noodle cart on a Hong Kong street corner. She cringed.

Yeah, no.

Also, even if she hadn't given Drew his ring yet—hadn't presented him with the physical token of her commitment to him—she still intended to honor their bond no matter what. That included role playing in the course of an investigation for the sake of the job.

Job? Non-paying past-time. Perilous hobby. Exercise in stupidity. Whatever. She wasn't going to start out their official relationship pretending to flirt with someone just to get some information.

But that file, though...

"Want a treat?" Skip asked her.

"Huh?"

"Cookie or a muffin, maybe? You're not gluten-free, are you? They have them here, but I call them 'vampire muffins.'" He looked at her expectantly, but she didn't know how to respond. "When you bite into them, they crumble into dust. Like when you stab a vampire and it turns to ash. Right? Because the gluten holds everything together. Makes it yummy."

"Oh, right."

He stood. "So that's a no on the muffin?"

"Ah, no, thanks. I'm good." She'd lost her taste for food just then, especially when he stood and left the folder on the table.

"Keep an eye on that, would you?"

Left alone with Skip's pride and joy, the spark of Josie's moral dilemma flared to a roaring inferno. What if she replaced some of the pages with...something...and tucked a few important ones into the front of her jacket? She wasn't wearing her denim jacket at the moment, but she could probably slip it on with the pages tucked inside.

Skip turned his back turned toward her as he navigated the line in search of his not-vampiric snack. She placed her hand on the top of the folder, half-expecting lightning to strike her. She flipped it open and paused, then turned the first page. The papers lay nearly two inches thick. Studying them would take her weeks, more time than she had left in the rest of her Texas stay.

And what did she expect to learn that Skip had not uncovered in decades of the feeding, nurturing, and care of the file? She was being ridiculous to think she might glean some mind-shattering conclusion he had neglected to come up with after all this time.

He'd said she could copy some of the pages. But she didn't have the time to rifle through them, traveling well-trod ground, inserting coins into a library copy machine like a grad student research assistant when she could be finding answers in avenues as of yet unexplored.

She glanced again at Skip's back as he reached the counter and placed his order, pointing through the glass at his choice.

Stealing, scamming, cajoling, and flirting were out. What if she took photos of some of the papers with her phone? She patted her pockets, but to her dismay, she didn't have her phone with her, remembering belatedly that she'd left it plugged into the charger in the hotel room. Drew would kill her if he found out she'd gone out—driving around in a strange city without her phone's GPS and a way to call for help if she got into trouble. She didn't intend to, but it certainly would have been helpful in taking a few snapshots of Skip's papers.

She stroked her hand over the papers, sliding a few more over so she could skim the ones underneath. No way was she going to be able to speed-read fast enough to get through them.

"I know you said you didn't want anything, but you have got to see this monstrosity," Skip said. "I bought you one just for the heck of it. You don't have to try it, but I wanted you to have one. Take it home. Varnish it. Make a doorstop out of it. I don't care…Behold."

With a heavy thunk, a white plate came down on top of the file, nearly catching her hand as she drew it away, but also effectively pinning the file to the table at the same time. A muffin about six inches in diameter across and about the same shade of gray as Skip's hair sat in the center of the plate in a paper baking cup. Across the top of the muffin, chia and sunflower seeds jutted out like gravel in a concrete aggregate mix. Josie was sure it would scrape off the roof of her mouth if she tried to bite into it.

"Undead, am I right?" he asked, nodding his head, eyebrows bobbing.

"So, Skip," Josie said, as they were gathering up their things to depart, "I know how much Mary Clare's file means to you. Will you lend it to me for 24 hours?"

She barreled ahead before his inevitable and probably emphatic *no*, but she had to at least try her worst and last-ditch attempt to get it—

honesty. Like math and taxes, it was not her strong suit. She would have preferred to go with a strength, but her last resort was all she had at the moment.

"I'll take good care of it. I'm not going to say 'you can trust me' because people who say that are usually the least trustworthy ones out there. But I know what you've put into this file, this investigation. I know it's near and dear to your heart."

She patted her pockets until she located her wallet, which she flipped open. "I'll give you my driver's license as collateral until I return the file."

"That's ridiculous," he said.

"Wait—before you say no—I'll give you…"

She flipped past her P.I. license. That thing wasn't worth the paper it was printed on in her mind. What about her I.D. card for a self-insured blogger with outrageous premiums and co-pays? He probably didn't want that.

She reached the last flap of her wallet where a black card lurked. Her limitless credit card from Greta Williams. Josie's friends had been impressed by it—jaws dropping, actually—but Josie wasn't as wowed by it as they were. She had forgotten it was in her wallet. As she started to pull it out, Skip stopped her.

"I meant, it's crazy to think I'd ask you to drive around without I.D. Have you ever met member of the Texas law enforcement? Those dudes do not mess around. They're all 'ma'am' and 'sir,' but they mean business. Next thing you know, you're being frisked and tossed into the tank with a guy with a Confederate flag tattooed on his butt. Not that it's happened to me."

As a matter of fact, she had just met the local law yesterday, but she wasn't sure where Skip was going with his hesitation, so she didn't bring it up. He seemed to be mulling over her question and she wasn't inclined to interrupt him.

"Just one day," she reiterated. She nodded, as solemn-faced as she could manage.

"I know what room you're staying in at your hotel. In fact, I know your home address. I'm not worried I won't be able to track you down. I trust you." He took the coffin-ready muffin off the table and shoved the file in her direction. "You can take it. What's one day going to hurt after years of it sitting in my desk drawer? And you know what? I'm not afraid of you absconding with it. To be honest, I'm just worried I'll get my hopes up that you'll find Mary Clare."

CHAPTER 20

"Hey, where are you?" Drew's voicemail said. "Did you forget your phone again? Sorry to leave a message like this. A bunch of us are taking off early from the conference and going to this movie theater place where you can order a burger and a beer while you're watching a movie. I don't even know what's playing, but it sounds awesome. If you get this message and want to meet us, it's called The Alamo Drafthouse. Otherwise, I'll see you later tonight. Sorry about this...I'll make it up to you."

Ugh, this is going to be tricky.

Back in the hotel room with Skip's file spread out across the comforter, Josie sat on the edge of the bed pinching the bridge of her nose. If Drew got back after ten, she wouldn't be in the room, but if he got back before ten and was still awake by the time she had to meet Lizzie downstairs, she'd still have to explain what she was doing.

Is this what being in a committed relationship is all about? Guilt and subterfuge?

She didn't think so, but she didn't really have anyone to ask. All the same, she was reluctant to tell him about her plans for the evening. First, she was slightly embarrassed about going on a wild ghost chase. Second, she'd have to admit that she'd once again stuck her nose into someone's— Mary Clare's, Billy's, all of the town of Leandro's—business where it didn't belong. And how many times had he admonished her about her inability to keep herself out of harm's way? This wasn't the best plan to stick to that agenda, even she could see that.

Drew had helped her on the last investigation—the field trip to Bader College. He'd said he understood it was a part of her to be...well, nosy, and he was learning to accept it. However, that was less than three months ago. He probably didn't expect her to jump back into the investigation fray so quickly.

Maybe.

She had a second message on her phone from her police friend in San Francisco, Maxwell Lopez. After a suggestive greeting that was in true form to his somewhat pervy flirtatious nature, he said he'd read on her blog that she was in Texas and reminding her that his cousin, Juan Pablo, owned a restaurant in San Antonio called El Chino if she was in the area. She and Drew had a couple extra days after his conference was finished. Maybe they could drive south, see the Riverwalk, and try the restaurant while they were in Texas. She'd heard it was nice, that you could ride in a boat up the river and see the sights that way.

In the meantime, she had 24 hours—less time now—to get through Skip's file. As she stared at the mass of paper spread across the bed, she realized she didn't even have time to think of a better way to approach the sheer number of details other than to wade directly into—and through—them. Time to buckle down and do some hardcore speed reading.

And there was no time like the present.

Two hours later, her head was pounding and her stomach growling. She picked up the phone to order something to eat—maybe another round of those fried green beans off the bar menu downstairs. She continued avoiding the meat leftovers in the mini-fridge. The Ghost of Barbecue Past and Present were menacing her. She certainly didn't want to invoke BBQ Future if it meant worshipping the porcelain god at 3:00 in the morning, huddled on the bathroom floor.

Been there. Done that. Ruined the t-shirt.

"What else can we tempt you with this evening?" the room service guy, Gary, asked after she requested her beans.

She scanned the in-room menu and picked a small label root beer, and then asked, "Do you have any brownies?"

The guy scoffed and gave an abbreviated snort, which she appreciated. His snarky banter made her feel right at home. "Would you prefer the Mexican chocolate with a little bit of a hot pepper kick, or the double-dark molten lava brownie?"

She picked the volcano thingy. Duh. It probably had more of a kick than a double shot of espresso, though. She was going to need it if she wanted to get through her Mary Clare cram-slash-study session this evening. Sugar and chocolate might propel her through ghost hunting all the way until morning, but until then, she had some more grocery store receipts to peruse. So far...her research had been fruitless. All she knew was that someone had been partial to limes and tequila.

Throw in some chips and salsa, and you've got a party.

But she intended to keep going until her time was up. She didn't want to fail Skip. Or Mary Clare. There had to be something...

"One more question," she said. "Do you know where I can borrow a cassette tape player?"

As it turned out, he did. Or rather, Manny, the receiving man down in the facilities and maintenance part of the hotel owned one. Apparently, he liked to record movies and then listen to the just the audio tracks while he was logging deliveries. Even better, he was on vacation for the week, so Josie was able to borrow his ancient Sony boombox.

"Good lord. How old is this thing?" Josie asked when Gary delivered it on the rolling cart with her dinner.

"Older than you, so be super careful with it, if you don't mind me saying. If anything happens to that, I'll not only be out of a job, I may also have to enter the witness protection program. Manny is kind of...intense."

"Is he going to dust it for prints when he gets back?" Josie was joking, but Gary's expression said he considered it a possibility.

"Just go easy on it. And call my direct extension when you're done with it. I don't want it to go missing. Someone would take one look at that thing and pitch it in the dumpster."

"Or sell it online," Josie said. "This old beauty is rare. A true antique."

"Kind of irreplaceable. Kind of like me, so let's make sure nothing happens to either of us." He gave her a pointed look and opened the lids of her dinner with a flourish.

She only needed it to listen to the message on the tape—and it wasn't an issue of burning curiosity, but she felt obligated to give it a whirl since Skip had treasured it so highly.

So when Gary left after one last admonishment, Josie popped the cassette tape into the player and pressed the Play button as she took a sip of root beer.

"Hi, you've reached Mary Clare and Billy's. We can't answer right now. Please leave a message after the beep. We'll return your call shortly."

The woman's voice was medium-range, not too high, not too low, and a little smoky—not Kathleen Turner. More like Katharine Hepburn, but slightly Texan. Very pleasant, actually.

Josie set down her bottle and waited for more, but after the greeting, there was nothing. Not even a beep. But the tone was on the machine itself, wasn't it? Josie tried to remember when her parents had had a voicemail machine.

She sighed and forked her hands through her already messy hair, massaging her scalp, and paced the edges of the mattress where the papers were scattered. She shuffled through the stack, reading paper after paper.

What do I know about Mary Clare based on these papers from various periods of her life?

Upper class. Overbearing mother. Full dental work. Cultured. Classy. A reader, but not good about returning her books to the library on time. The Austin Public Library had sent her a notice just a short while before she'd gone missing. What books did she like to read?

Josie skimmed the form letter to the bottom where it had been personalized with the list of Mary Clare's overdue books. John Grisham, Patricia Cornwell, Sue Grafton. The girl liked a good mystery. At the bottom of the list were three books on container gardening and *The Bartender's Black Book*. Maybe Smiley's had been intending to beef up their bar offerings. After all, nothing had a bigger profit margin than alcohol. She set the letter down and sorted through more, one after another.

Unfortunately, no invoices for psychiatric care. No red flags. No receipts for large amounts of pseudoephedrine or whatever else they used to cook drugs from home. Everything seemed fairly normal. Even a life insurance premium was for a modest quarter million. Probably not enough to rebuild the restaurant after the fire. Nothing stuck out.

She racked her brains. In this heap of details, this mountain of paper, what didn't fit?

"Kiss me, daddy. Like you used to do. That mean way I used to like," a woman said. Josie stared at the wall where it sounded like the occupants of the room next door had returned. The woman's voice was so faint and slurred, she could barely make out the words. "What do you want from me? I don't even know what you want from me."

A man's voice, less inebriated, said, "Hush now. I don't want anything."

Waitaminute.

Josie lunged for the tape player and knocked her root beer bottle over, splashing the boombox. The voices were on the recording, way at the end of the tape. She'd left the tape playing while she'd been sorting through the file.

Frantic, she grabbed a t-shirt off the top of her laundry pile and sopped up the spilled soda, trying to keep the sticky puddle from ruining the tape player.

"I don't know what I'm supposed to do. I don't know who I am," Mary Clare said.

"No, don't hit me. Settle down now."

"I don't know what I'm supposed to be."

"You're you, honey. You don't need to be anything."

"But I do. I can't be nothing."

"You're the woman I married, sweetheart."

"I'm not her. She's nothing." There was a pause. "What are you doing?"

"I'm just recording this a little, so you can hear yourself tomorrow."

"Why would I want to do that? I already know what I sound like."

"No, honey, so you know how bad you get. So maybe you'll get some help."

"I don't need any help. I'm fine. You're all I need. Just kiss me."

Josie waited through some ambient noises. Some shifting and light shuffling, but not much else. Maybe they had stopped talking to make love. Maybe, as drunk as she was, she had passed out. She hoped Billy would come back to the tape recorder and explain what he'd wanted to capture, what he witnessed, what he wanted to prove to his wife.

But the tape ended there.

Part 3: Flame

Fire is the rapid oxidation of a material like wood, paper, charcoal briquettes, a marshmallow, or the family home in the chemical process or reaction of combustion. The flame is what we see during the ignition point of the reaction.

Little bit dry, right? Forgive the pun.

Let's think of it the way the Ancient Greeks did.

Thank you, Prometheus, for stealing the flames from Mount Olympus to give us the means of searing our ribeye steaks, powering our combustion engines, putting that lovely golden crackle on our creme brûlées, and covering our tracks when the evidence must be destroyed.

—Josie Tucker, *Will Blog for Food*

CHAPTER 21

As Josie sat stock-still and shocked with her sticky t-shirt clutched in her hand, root beer dripped off the night table and onto the hotel carpet. Drops hit a soggy, apricot-sized stain on the carpet with a *pit pit pit* sound like carbonated, sucrose-filled Chinese water torture.

"Oh crap."

She dove for the brown bottle, which had wobbled and gone over again while she'd been trying to clean off the tape player. Another small pool had collected under the tape player again. She sent up a frantic prayer to the god of small electronics that she hadn't destroyed it, like a WALL-E robot deity in the sky. Samsung-*ishna*. Then she cringed, hoping her religious bastardization wouldn't get her struck by a bolt of lightning through her hotel window. Not that she was superstitious. Much.

"Please don't be broken. Please don't be ruined."

With frantic dabs, she cleaned up the table, floor, and Manny's sacred boombox. Her stomach plunged in trepidation. Could she have broken it? She didn't want to think about it. Not poor Gary. Not now. Not yet.

When she'd soaked all the soda up, she retrieved a damp cloth from the bathroom and cleaned up the rest of the syrup. When she lifted the tape player, however, more root beer dripped out from the bottom.

"No, no, no."

Heart pounding, she pressed the Play button, but nothing happened. Then she remembered the tape had played to the end, so she pressed Rewind. *Nothing.* Maybe rewinding didn't work on this player, although Gary hadn't mentioned that. Surely Manny had kept it in perfect working order since he loved it so much.

Pressing Eject successfully popped the tape out, but that didn't require anything electrical—the button just pushed open the tape door. She slid out the cassette. Maybe if she played the other side.

That's how these stupid things work, right? A side and B side.

It had been so long since she'd used a boombox—high school, maybe?—she started to question herself, thanks to her panic. But she pulled herself together, inserted the tape, flipped over, shut the door, and pressed Play again.

Nothing.

Her stomach twisted in a knot. She and Gary were dead meat.

"Okay, let's think this through."

While she was freaking out, she retreated into the bathroom to rinse out her soda-soaked t-shirt while she tried to figure out how to salvage this screw up. She had about fifteen minutes until Lizzie was coming to pick her up. Fifteen minutes to repair this situation and to save a life.

The water came on cold, which was good for stains, wasn't it? Her spoiled t-shirt was a Def Leppard one, so she didn't feel so bad. Their song about pouring some sugar on someone popped into her head and a half-hysterical giggle escaped from her throat. But how could she laugh at a time like this when Gary's life was on the line?

Never mind that she was stunned by what she'd heard on the tape.

Was Mary Clare an addict? An alcoholic? Maybe. Emotionally troubled? Definitely, which *might* have been coupled with some kind of substance use. The slurred voice was in sharp contrast to the calm, smoky tone of the greeting at the beginning of the tape. Was there a deeply troubled woman behind the façade of the socialite and former beauty queen?

Josie *had* to listen to the tape again, just to confirm she wasn't making things up in her mind. Had she really heard all that?

She hung up her shirt to dry on the towel bar in the shower and returned to the other room to retrieve the tape off the bedside table. Maybe the boombox just needed to dry out, like how she'd dropped her phone in the sink one day and needed to let it sit overnight in a bowl of uncooked rice...Unfortunately, she didn't have that kind of time. She had ten minutes—nine to be exact now.

With a growl of frustration, she yanked open the drawer of the desk and caught the hotel pen that rolled toward her over the monogrammed notepad. Just what she needed, a manual rewind button. Old-school style. She gently wedged the end of the pen into one of the cassette tape holes and unwound the tape—after she figured out which way to turn it—going slowly so she didn't create any gaps or folds in the fragile strip. She'd be even worse off if she damaged Skip's tape.

Carefully, she again lifted the tape player and went over it with the damp towel, catching any drops that came from its plastic seams and screw holes. When she opened the battery compartment, she was relieved to find it dry and free of root beer. She slid the tape back into the slot, pressed the door shut, crossed her fingers, and pressed Play.

She almost cried with relief when the gears inside the player started whirling, winding the tape ahead. *Whew. Not broken.* She'd freaked herself out over a flaky old appliance—the boombox had been fine. However, her jumpy nerves were messing with her. She'd rewound the tape to a blank spot before the voices came back on, but rather than risk screwing things up again with more button pressing, she let it play through the silence until the voices came back.

Mary Clare, slurred and pleading. Billy placating and...*tender.*

The recording showed a true devotion between the pair, and possibly an unhealthy co-dependency as well. Josie was no counselor, but the heightened emotion in Billy's and Mary Clare's voices made even her cold, shriveled heart hurt just a bit.

Her phone rang just as she finished listening all the way through the second time. She let the tape run as she fumbled for her phone.

Lizzie, sounding a bit breathless, said, "I'm running about forty-five minutes late. I'm so sorry, but I'm still coming. I was babysitting my nieces and my sister didn't get home until just now. I'm going to swing by the storage unit and pick up some equipment, but I'll meet you downstairs at 10:45. I'm super stoked about this. So don't worry. I'm on my way."

Glancing at the clock on the night table, Josie discovered it was past ten now. Time had flown while she'd been panicking. Where the heck was Drew? She bit her lip. At this rate, she was going to have to leave him a message explaining where she was. *Not good.*

Face to face would have been so much better, but what were her options now? Could she scribble some cryptic message on the hotel insignia notepad and hope he didn't get ticked off at her? *Ugh.*

"No worries," she told Lizzie, making sure her voice was strong and upbeat because, for Pete's sake, she was an adult and could figure this out. "Don't even park. I'll be waiting for you at the curb."

In the end, Josie only half faced up to her fear about telling Drew where she was going and texted him. She had wrestled with the idea of calling him, but convinced herself it was okay to message him because he was still at the movie theater. So maybe she was a big chicken and texting him was giving herself a convenient out. And so what if he was with a bunch of medical professionals who were probably all used to getting inconvenient phone calls and random butt-buzzing muted alerts in their pockets? She didn't want to annoy him if he was relaxing and having a good time.

Josie: Hey I need to go out so I might not be here when u get back

After a couple minutes of silence in which she tapped her foot and drummed her fingers on the desk, he texted back.

Drew: Whats up

Josie: Meeting a new friend to follow up on something I found out

She waited in low-key agony after that, not sure if he was cursing or if he'd stopped looking at his phone to order more beer, or what. She paced the short length of the room and then sat on the edge of the bed again.

Drew: Who died

Josie: Um

In the next pause, she knew for sure he was muttering to himself under his breath.

Drew: Ur serious

Josie: Yeah I am tbh

To be honest. And *she was* being honest. Mostly. She was *trying* to be, at least. It just didn't come naturally to her. In time, it would probably come with practice. The trick was to keep practicing facing the truth. And she would, if it weren't so darned hard.

Another long, drawn-out pause made her wish she hadn't eaten anything earlier. She was having heart palpitations, though the brownie probably had less to do with the discomfort in her chest and stomach than her anxiety. But she was right to tell him, she knew. Even though it was hard for her to be open and communicative. She would much rather just go and do, not stop and talk about it.

Drew: Im sighing rn

Josie: I know I'm sorry

Drew: It's ok just b careful and now I might need another beer

Josie: Just don't drive

Drew: Ur telling me to b careful now

Josie: Now Im sighing

Drew: Don't worry I'll get a cab or something

She wanted to say she was sorry again, but she didn't think it would make the situation better. What was she doing here? Aggravating him with her constant need to meddle in other people's business and sticking her neck out, getting into potential sticky situations. He'd said he understood this was a part of her...but she wasn't sure if he really accepted it. She needed to talk with him about it, or at least stop moving away from him when she wanted to tie them tighter together.

She wanted this trip to end with an engagement, but she seemed to be making the wrong choices for that to happen. She just didn't have time to stop and fix it right now. But she would.

Just soon as she got back from tromping through Billy Blake's haunted house with Lizzie.

CHAPTER 22

"Okay, so here's the deal," Lizzie said, making room for Josie in the passenger seat next to her. "Billy's house isn't on the market yet because it's not ready. I mean, he pretty much just decided to do this, spur of the moment, and hired my cousin because he didn't know where to start. It was a total coup for her—the notoriety and the potential six percent fee, even if she has to split it with the buyer's agent. A lot of other agents were kind of pissed off they didn't get hired for this, but it's going to be a lot of work—no joke.

"The house still has a lot of personal effects in it, and it needs fresh paint and new carpet and to be staged. You know, made all pretty for the website photos and the open house days. All the personal effects put away. All the counter surfaces cleaned off. Cozy seating areas set up. Beds all made with too many pillows. And since this house is so pricy, my cousin is getting a professional home stager to come and do it up right."

Josie's young ghostbuster friend had thrown a shoulder bag and some other miscellaneous papers into the backseat of her older model Pathfinder. The SUV was maybe a 2006 from when they'd gotten big again, Josie guessed. Her great uncle's car obsession had left its mark on her during her high school years and now she'd couldn't *not* pay attention to them. As she used the *oh crap* bar to hoist herself up, she realized it kind of kept him close in her thoughts even though he was physically far away. She looked into the seat behind them. Lizzie had the thing packed full of junk.

What the heck is all this junk?

Black plastic garbage bags. Bright orange construction buckets filled with tools and...paper towels. A mop. Some Pine-Sol. Were they ghost hunting or house cleaning? Would they be encountering ectoplasm goo?

Did she need a smock? She hadn't been told to wear any type of protective clothing.

She glanced at her cohort for the evening. Other than the glint of the diamond stud in Lizzie's nose, she wore all dark colors. If Josie had to give her look a name, it was Neo Goth Burglar Ghost Hunter. Josie didn't know if the dark colors were for sneaking around in the dark or just Lizzie's personal fashion sense. So far, she had seen her only in black and purple, but Josie hoped she knew what she was doing, that it was more of a uniform than a style. Misgivings zinged through her stomach.

"Is it good or bad that their things are still in the house?" she asked.

She knew what home staging was—she'd watched some home improvement TV shows like *Hovel To Home* and *Apartment Bling* when she'd been hanging out on her couch dealing with her testy stomach. Okay, so she'd been addicted to some of them. However, she didn't know if a cluttered house was better for ghosts. As far as she was concerned, seeing some of Billy's natural habitat and his belongings, and possibly some of Mary Clare's, too, was a good thing. More of a mess meant more potential clues. Somewhere, something had to tell the story of what had happened to the woman.

"Neither empty nor populated for paranormal investigations. I've heard stories of empty homes being chock-a-block full of restless spirits, as well as spirits following items to the auction house. In our case with Billy Blake's house, it just means that the owner's possessions are still inside and so if we get caught in there, we're kind of on the wrong side of the law, if you know what I mean."

Josie muddled this over for about three seconds. "So you're saying it's not breaking and entering necessarily? But definitely trespassing, and if anything ends up missing or broken, it's our necks on the block?"

Crap. She wondered how fast she could track down a lawyer if she needed one. Of all the stupid situations she'd gotten herself into in her life, this was one she'd never been forced to test. Yet. Maybe Greta Williams, whom she hadn't called yet to see what she knew about Bunny Rogers, also knew a good lawyer.

Who am I kidding? Greta probably owns her own fleet of lawyers. Keeps 'em in her closet in racks right next to her Kate Spade shoes. Or in her garage in the bay next to her Bentley.

Josie conjured up the image of a cluster of men and women in dark suits with briefcases sitting in a clump in Greta's multi-car garage out in the suburbs of Massachusetts.

Lizzie broke into her thoughts, saying, "Yeah, and also my cousin will deny any knowledge of us being there if we do. She is a career woman with her whole future in real estate ahead of her, and she will leave our asses out in the cold, if it comes right down to it. Are you okay with that?" She cast her a side-eyed glance through her mascara as she drove westward out of town, the moon shining down on the road in front of them.

Josie watched the light reflect off Lake Austin and the big, swooping semi-circle bridge over it. Penny-something Bridge. Pennybacker? Pennybaker? Lizzie had called it the 360 Bridge, and it had taken Josie a minute or two before she realized that the bridge, despite being a semi-circular swoop rising above the water, was not 360 degrees, but that *the road* was Highway 360. Seemed like a little bit of a letdown. Though it was pretty, she'd been hoping for a big bubble of a bridge.

"We'll be careful," Josie said, though she wasn't a hundred percent sure if she was capable of exercising caution. Her skepticism extended to almost every other aspect of her life. But how often did she say things she didn't mean, only to find out that she *did* mean them after all?

She'd proven her rhino-in-a-china-shop tendencies many times in the past—not so much physical as social. Her blunders were renowned, the tales of which were often retold by her small group of friends. But who was to say this time would be like the others?

Okay, that sounded like a lame argument even in her own mind. She shored up her confidence, *screwed her courage to the sticking place*, as Lady Macbeth put it, though Josie's was attached more by chewing gum and Elmer's glue than strength of will. Yes, this evening, *she was* going to make a supreme effort not to wind up in jail. Or the hospital.

In less than an hour, they reached the neighborhood the Blake house was in. Thanks to the late hour, they didn't find much traffic on the roads. By the time they reached the far west suburb where Billy's house was, all traffic had dwindled to just the occasional Range Rover or Lincoln SUV.

Josie peered through the windshield, leaning forward in her seat, her curiosity ramping up. Lizzie knew where they were going, but she was using her phone's GPS nonetheless. Out here in the twisting turns and hidden hills by the lake and the gnarled, thick trees, they needed all the help they could get.

"Is this it?" Josie asked, looking out the window at the nothingness of scrub brush and silhouettes, then back at the bright screen of Lizzie's phone with her real-time map app.

"Should be right here—oh, there it is." Lizzie steered them around the last blind corner.

"Holy crap."

The spit dried up in Josie's mouth. She had to wait for it to come back before she could ask, "What…price range did your cousin say this house is?"

Rising up behind the last sloped turn of the smooth, paved drive, the house's two-story multicolored peach and cream stone stood out against the velvety blue night sky thanks to dramatic landscape lights. Part Italianate and part modern with geometric picture windows—Josie didn't know how to describe it. It wasn't symmetrical, but it seemed totally balanced, the wings of the house rising together in a fulcrum of a round…thing—rotunda?—in the center. She was no architecture expert. All she could say with certainty was that it was gorgeous and took her breath away. However, the full impact of breaking and entering a mansion hadn't sunk in until that very moment.

"I dunno. Maybe about seven million," Lizzie said. "It's like eleven thousand square feet, my cousin said. I think there's a tennis court and a zero horizon pool out back."

Josie gulped. Well, that explained it. Grandeur wasn't cheap. Would her prison sentence be more for breaking into a place like this? She was in awe, and not enough to stop the quaking that arced through her stomach. She couldn't imagine living here. Not that she would know what to do with all of this space other than get all of her friends to live with her and maybe adopt about 23 dogs. And a pygmy goat or two. How could two people, just Billy and Mary Clare, have lived in a place like this by themselves?

Lizzie steered up the circular drive, past a multi-tiered fountain, and parked close to the front door, which in and of itself was intimidating. Eight feet tall, double doors with the windows to either side, glass from top down to about waist-high, covered with ornate wrought iron work with stars in the middle. Very Texan, very majestic. *Bubba Royale*, she wanted to call it. *Pardner Palatial* or *Regal Rancherio*. Her spike of misgiving was making her slap-happy.

"We're going through the front?" Josie had expected something more...covert, more dark of night, more ninja. Yeah, she was a little disappointed. And also, they were sitting ducks for any rent-a-cop the ritzy neighborhood might have prowling these exclusive, twisty streets.

"Yeah." Lizzie pointed a dark fingernail at the wooden front door. "It has a lockbox and my cousin gave me the combo."

Sure enough, when Josie peered through her window, she saw the right side of the majestic double door had a mundane-looking, beige plastic realtor's box hanging from the handle. She didn't feel it warranted mentioning to Lizzie, but all Josie needed was a super flat little piece of metal and she could get them into the lockbox in just a couple minutes thanks to a tutorial from her friend of many shady talents, Tiffany, she'd just met a couple months ago.

They climbed out of the SUV, and Lizzie popped the trunk hatch open. Josie met her around the back and watched her dig through the bags, selecting and discarding item after item, tossing them into a shoulder bag. Minutes went by, and Josie's self-doubt escalated.

"Uh...I didn't bring anything." She'd barely remembered to pocket her cell phone before hopping in Lizzie's SUV. Girl Scout, she was not. She'd been a more likely candidate for juvenile offender of the week. Sadly, that didn't make her any more prepared for this potential felony trespassing.

"I got you covered." Lizzie unzipped her tote bag to show Josie a variety of gadgets. "EMF detector. That's for electromagnetic fields. EVP recorder for Electronic Voice Phenomena. It records in multiple digital formats, but we all think WAV format is better that MP3. It's crisper and picks up more things from other planes. Extra batteries. Flashlight.

Thermometer for cold spots. And a red light so we have better night vision."

"Aha," Josie said, although there was very little comprehension in her exclamation. She hoped she at least sounded less skeptical than before. Maybe even supportive of Lizzie's efforts. After all, without her, Josie wouldn't be about to trespass onto her number one suspect's property.

Standing outside the very ritzy mansion, nay, castle—her mental Lady Macbeth reference earlier had been more apt than she'd known—in the dark with a person of unknown good judgment whom she'd just met for the first time briefly this same week, Josie questioned her own sanity yet again. How many times could one reasonably doubt oneself in the space of an hour?

Why am I here if I don't believe in ghosts?

Because I want to see if Mary Clare is up in his attic like Norman Bates's mummified mother, sitting in her rocking chair, swaddled in a flag of Texas and preserved with AquaNet.

She put her hands on her hips and paced a few steps, the top of her head tingling the way it always did when she was about to do something stupid.

There's still time to back out. Or at least say I'll wait in the car.

But that was ridiculous. She wasn't in this weird position because of luck or happenstance. She had chosen the various forks in the road that had led her to this single situation, this unique point in time. Josie was the one who'd ask Lizzie to come on this wild ghost chase in the first place. In for a penny, as her Aunt Ruth always said.

Josie cracked her knuckles and shook out her wrists, jangling the black beaded bracelet she'd bought the other day. Her finger brushed the coin embedded in the center. No time to have second thoughts now, except maybe she could just...

"Awww yeah, look who remembered the combo on the first try, girl. We're in like flint," Lizzie said, swinging the door open.

Josie took a deep breath and jogged up the steps, the bottoms of her Converse low-tops slapping the stones. She stepped over the threshold, trailing Lizzie into the house.

"You mean, *in like Flynn*—whoa, check out those stairs. Robin Hood definitely could've had a sword fight on those."

Inside the massive foyer, a staircase spiraled upward, following along the exterior wall and then disappearing up into the darkness. The stairs swirled around, emphasizing the grandeur and sweep of the rounded...turret? Dome? Once again, she was stumped for the right word. Big, huge, impressive rounded roof thingy that went up really high.

Though the foyer was blanketed in darkness, she could still see a lot of detail in the wrought iron railing on the staircase, the rustic dark-wood window frames, and the contrast of what looked like a fluffy white area rug in the center of the dark stone floor in the entryway. She made a note to avoid stepping on the carpet. As plush as it looked—good enough to drag in front of a TV and collapse into a Netflix stupor—every bit of dust on her Chucks would be sucked into its fibers. She'd probably leave a trail of dirt across it, like that messy Pig Pen kid from Charlie Brown.

Speaking of TV, Josie had watched her fair share of black and white movies and reruns, so she was familiar with the old saying. Errol Flynn, the swashbuckling actor who had played Robin Hood, had been slick, or "in," with both the ladies *and* gentlemen during the Golden Age of Hollywood. She was no Remington Steele, but she knew some fairly useless trivia.

"In like *flint*, dummy," Lizzie said. "Flint is sharp and makes fires. It's a hard, crystalline form of mineral quartz. It was used for early tools because you could split it into sharp layers, like knife blades. Like, so you could cut *into* things. But if you strike it against something like steel, it makes a spark. It actually got replaced by a man-made substance. So when campers are making campfires, that's not really flint they're using anymore."

Their voices echoed in the entryway, seeming to spiral upward into the darkness much like the stairs. Josie lowered her voice to a whisper.

"But the saying is 'in like Flynn.'"

"No way." Lizzie pointed to her chest with a dark purple nail. "Geology major, remember? *Flint*. Why would it be 'in like a flin?' That makes no sense. What's a 'flin–?' Like, a fin on a fish?"

"It doesn't have anything to do with rocks and minerals. Flynn was—"

Somewhere deep inside the house, glass shattered.

CHAPTER 23

"I thought you said no one was supposed to be here," Josie hissed, acutely aware that they themselves were also not supposed to be in the house. Dual urges battled inside her—one to sprint out the front door, the other to find the closest light switch and slap it on. Though they hadn't been here for long, the dark was getting on her nerves. *Big time.*

"Shhhh," Lizzie said, batting the air in Josie's general direction. For being a semi-seasoned ghost hunter, Lizzie looked unnerved. Her eyes had gone wide enough that Josie could see the whites of them in the shadowy darkness where they still stood.

"Okay," Josie said and Lizzie hushed her again, frozen and listening for more sounds. At least, that's what Josie figured, but Lizzie had gripped her arm and her nails were poking into the meaty part of Josie's left biceps—*ow*—so she didn't ask.

Josie waited. She assumed Lizzie would want to dig out some of her ghost detection equipment. For her own part, she assumed a broken window or whatever had gotten damaged meant there were other *living* bodies in the house. And people doing things in the dark were rarely up to any good. Including them.

Lizzie stood frozen and didn't seem inclined to start gathering data in any way.

"Aren't you going to investigate? Don't you want to get out your...gadget...thingy?" Josie whispered. She made a vague hand gesture approximating the size of the handheld device she'd seen earlier in Lizzie's bag.

"I've never encountered an actual spirit before." Lizzie's voice was more of a squeak.

"What? Never? But you said—"

Lizzie shook her head.

"What was all that talk about the powder? You said you've captured footprints in baby powder." To demonstrate, Josie shuffled her foot on the gorgeous floor. Dark slate? Man, it was pretty. "Was all that footprint talk a fib?"

"Noooo," Lizzie said—whispered—in that tone of voice Josie always used when she herself was fibbing. "I mean, *theoretically*, I have captured footprints in baby powder."

"What do you mean 'theoretically?' How would that work on a non-actual level?"

"Well, you know, we have practicums."

Josie blinked. "What...never mind." She took Lizzie's bag from her shoulder and dug around in it. She pulled out the little handheld thing with all the buttons and lights, then tossed it back in. Digging around some more, she found the red flashlight. She handed the bag back to Lizzie. Far be it from her to let the girl blow her first chance at experiencing the real thing. Not that Josie believed there was a ghost in the house. She just didn't want Lizzie to be disappointed in herself later. Josie believed in fostering the youth and encouraging their budding interests. At least for the kids who weren't total idiots.

I can be a sarcastic jerk at times, but geeze, I'm not completely heartless.

With the weird, cavernous setup of the house, it was hard to tell where the sound of breaking glass had come from. Echoes sent the smallest noises up into the domed ceiling and back down again. It seemed unlikely that someone would have broken an upstairs window...unless it was a really big bat. Not a cute little cartoon bat like she'd seen all over tourist t-shirts downtown, but a big-ass Dracula sized. Josie shook her head to clear the creepy thoughts making her heart pound.

Yes, she was having panic attacks these days, so she might as well control the dumber, conscious thoughts she *knew* could scare her. None of the tourist brochures had mentioned the downside to bats. Surely they would have mentioned bloodsucking vampires had they been spotted as well.

"Downstairs it is," she muttered. She clicked on the flashlight, bathing their path in a blood-red light, and gestured for Lizzie to follow.

They followed an offshoot of the curved wall that led to the back of the house, which opened up to a massive sitting room and an open kitchen and bar area. Slouchy brown leather couches. Wood everywhere, including the walls. Antlers. Texas stars. Cow hides. Antique rifles mounted over the stone fireplaces, of which there were two, fully stocked with chopped wood. A massive stuffed owl glared at them from a sideboard. The room was a decorating style Josie would categorize as Early-Modern Bubba with a Taxidermist Influence. The red beam of the flashlight painting the room made it all that much more ghoulish.

Josie stepped into the room, Lizzie so close on her heels she could feel the girl's breath on the back of her hair, which was as comforting as it was encroaching on her personal space. At least no one could sneak up behind her with a knife or a shovel or…an expected bout of PTSD. In fact, Josie hadn't even had a quake of her nerves with Lizzie around.

Hmm. Maybe I could hire the kid full-time. Would probably be cheaper than therapy. Though more of a stop-gap Band-Aid than a permanent cure.

She walked the room's perimeter, checking first for broken windows, but she didn't find any. A collection of three chunky crystal liquor decanters lined a table by a winged-back chair, but none of them were broken. In fact, they looked so heavy that if any of them hit the floor, they'd probably gouge the wood rather than shatter.

Using the hem of her t-shirt so she wouldn't leave any trace of herself, she lifted the stopper off one of the bottles and sniffed. She wrinkled her nose. Bourbon. *Gross*, but not vinegar yet or whatever happened when booze turned bad. She flicked her light across the top of the nearest side table, did a double-take, and shined the light over it again. No dust. In the adjacent kitchen, the refrigerator hummed.

Someone was staying here. The house showed all the signs of upkeep and habitation. If Billy Blake was living at his restaurant, who was living here at the house?

"Over there," Lizzie said, prodding Josie's shoulder blade and pointing in the direction of the kitchen. "I see a doorway on the other side."

Josie massaged her shoulder where Lizzie's nails had poked her. Sure enough, when she squinted, she could make out just the very vaguest shape of a door opposite the fridge. How Lizzie could see anything in this darkened part of the house was beyond Josie. Maybe she'd learned how to in one of her *practicums. How to Sharpen Your Night Vision for Burglaries 101* and *Eating Carrots for The Serious Nighttime Hobbyist.*

In the meantime, Lizzie had regained her composure and dug the ghost-detecting machines out of her bag. In one hand, she held her thermometer. In the other, she wielded the one with the lights and...antenna? Were ghosts broadcasting on a specific frequency? Or maybe they were beaming messages directly into people's minds.

What's the frequency, Lizzie?

As they scooted through the kitchen across the slick marble floor, Josie stopped them long enough to peek into the stainless steel fridge, again using the hem of her shirt to open the door. If she kept up this B&E gig for real, she was going to have to invest in a pair of burglar gloves. Or maybe a pack of disposables. She wasn't sure which of those options would look more suspicious if found later in her possession.

The light from inside the stainless steel side-by-side nearly blinded her. As she yanked her head back squinting, she bumped into Lizzie, who also stepped back. In front of them, shelf after gleaming shelf stood empty except for just a few sparse items. The beauty of the unfilled refrigerator left her seriously jonesing to fill it with kitchen staples and basic ingredients. A squirt tube of minced garlic. A beef roast aging in the back corner. Numerous jars of pesto and pickles that no one but her would ever eat... Okay, maybe that was just her vision.

But great Julia Child in heaven, what would it be like to come home to an appliance—a whole kitchen—like this every day?

"You want a yogurt?" Lizzie asked, looking over her shoulder. "It's organic. And locally sourced."

She looked at the rest of the fridge's contents. Greek yogurt, hummus, mozzarella cheese sticks, natural peanut butter, and a screw top bottle of fruity red sangria. *What the heck?*

"I hate hummus," Lizzie said with a shudder. "It's disgusting. If you want me to eat garbanzo beans, just say it to my face. Don't try to trick me. I don't need that kind of two-faced, toxic relationship in my life."

Josie frowned over her shoulder. "Don't eat store-bought hummus. Make it yourself. It's totally different, like night and day. And I thought we were being quiet."

"Any ghost that's here already knows we're here now. We're not exactly subtle infiltrators." Ninjas, they were not. A squadron of senior citizen cloggers was closer to the truth.

"It's not the ghosts I'm worried about."

In her experience, people could be *the worst*. Like, murdering, violent monsters. So until she met a ghost, she was willing to give them the benefit of the doubt.

Josie shut the fridge and had to wait a few seconds for her eyes to readjust to the near-dark, bathed in blood, thanks to the stupid ghost light. She passed through the kitchen and reached for the handle on the door Lizzie had pointed out.

"No broken glass in here. It's a pantry," she said.

And an empty one at that. Too bad. It was more spacious than her closet at home—almost bigger than her entire bedroom back in Boston. She took a few seconds to indulge in an almost pornographic foodie fantasy about the white wood shelves of the storage area being fully stocked with dry goods, gourmet pickles, and a 50-gallon tub of spicy brown mustard. Heck, why not? The pantry had room for more than one trip to the food warehouse store. She could even get a gallon of sun-dried tomatoes to go with it. Or 20 pounds of dried apricots. With a storage space like this, nothing could stop her...except an empty wallet and someone else pointing out her idiocy.

She backed out of the pantry and edged farther down the hallway in the semi-dark with Lizzie close behind her. The next door led to the garage, the first two bays of which were empty, other than a puddle of oil stains in the one closest to the door. The third bay, however, was occupied by what Josie realized was a car.

A dark green older model Acura—Mary Clare's car.

CHAPTER 24

Yes, they were in a hurry. They didn't have all night to jump on the beds and try out every bowl of porridge. True, she didn't know who had broken the glass—or if there was a homicidal maniac roaming the house with them—but here was Mary Clare's car. *Right in front of her.*

The car was a sporty, two-door 1994 Acura Integra in that dark metallic green that had been so popular, with a spoiler—the same vehicle that Josie remembered reading about in the article online.

She peeked in the driver's side window, shining her creepy red light inside. She listed off the features she could see—automatic transmission, leather seats. In the nineties, this would have been a nice, classy car to drive, and 1994 had been a major redesign in terms of looks. Very trendy and sleek. Other than a thin layer of dust, it looked to be in like-new condition.

She checked each of the windows and none were broken, so this wasn't the source of the shattering glass sound. And otherwise, the garage was empty. No person-sized shadows lurking in the corners. She swept her flashlight around just to make sure.

And holy crap, what is that?

When she shined the flashlight on the wall ahead of the car, the beam of bloody red light caught a massive portrait of the dead woman and what looked to be a homemade memorial. Pink and white silk flowers tied together with broad, silk white ribbon, arranged in a large heart shape surrounded the painting, framing Mary Clare's face and frozen Mona Lisa half-smile. *Super creepy.*

Lizzie also issued a sharp intake of air as she caught sight of the display. "What the—?"

"It's just the funeral flowers," Josie said, trying to reassure herself as well. "It's the portrait and stand from the ceremony. Someone hung it on the wall. Nothing to worry about. No big deal."

Yeah, like it was totally normal to display that stuff on the wall in your garage. The silk flowers had kept well, though. Not a surprise—it was cold and quiet as a tomb in here.

Lizzie rubbed her arms, clearly wigged out by it. Josie was, too, but she kept it to herself.

On one hand, the wall memorial was unnerving as heck. On the other, mourning his wife was bittersweet and natural. This memorial brought to Josie's mind the patient and loving Billy she had heard on the cassette tape. Making this wall hanging might have been his personal way of facing her death. Maybe he wasn't a natural-born artist, but his crafting ability was beyond reproach.

She moved in for a closer look and peered at the flowers, noting each bunch had been attached into the drywall with what looked to be staples from a high-powered staple gun.

The sound that would have made...that decisive and final *chunk chunk chunk* of the staples sinking into the wall, pinning the silk there permanently. Okay, that gave her the chills.

"Did you know the heart shape is really not representative of the two sides of a human heart like a lot of people think?" Lizzie said. "It's actually from ancient times and was drawn to imitate the leaf of the silphium plant, which was also used for brothel signs."

"What?...How do you know all this stuff?" *And yet, still not know who Errol Flynn was.*

"I like to read," she said.

But what in the world was she reading?

"Fair enough," Josie said. She made up her mind not to mock Lizzie again about the Flynn thing. At least, not out loud. The kid was a reader, and that made her a rare breed these days, although she was kind of stubborn.

Turning back to the car, Josie lifted up the driver's side door handle using the hem of her t-shirt. She'd been hoping for an easy way in, but it was locked.

"What are you doing? Don't touch that. What if it has an alarm?"

If the car had truly been sitting here in this garage since Mary Clare vanished all those years ago, even if it did have an alarm system, chances were good that the battery was long dead. In any case, she took the risk of yanking on the handle and was lucky that no alarm went off. Not lucky enough to have found the car unlocked, though. She edged around the hood of the car and tried the passenger side, which was also locked, unfortunately. She would've liked to check out the glove box.

Most people who spent any amount of time in their cars treated them like a home away from home—receipts, fast food wrappers, coins, lost business cards. Anything under the seats or on the floors could hold a clue to where the woman had vanished. A long, unexpected colored hair, even. Animal fur. Seed pods of a faraway plant. Something that investigators before her might have missed.

Peering into the small, triangular backseat window, she tried to remember if the glass on this model rolled down or if it was just cosmetic. From what she could see, the backseat looked empty, though there could have been something on the floor, which was hidden in shadow. She attempted to angle her light downward, but it didn't reach the darkest recesses. She'd have to go back to the other side to shine it across, but that still would give her only a partial view of the interior.

If she hurried, maybe she could unlock a door. Sweeping her light around, she spied a workbench and toolbox along the far side of the garage. All she needed was a screwdriver and she could get in that car. She'd be in like—she side-eyed Lizzie—*Flynn*.

"Stop that. What are you doing? You're going to bring the cops here."

Josie rummaged around in the toolbox and found just what she needed: a nice Craftsman flathead screwdriver. No, she wasn't going to hot-wire Mary Clare's car. Not that she remembered how. She merely wanted to search the inside of it. Thanks to her Uncle Jack, she knew how. All she had to do was pry back the rubber strip around one of the windows and create a gap for her hand, slip her arm inside, and pop the lock. Luckily, the Acura's door locks were up near the top of the door because her arms were short—proportionally short, not extra short. She was only five-two and three quarters.

And sensitive about it, thank you very much.

"Just give me five minutes." Fingertips just inches from the car, she paused. "Hey, do you happen to have gloves in your kit?"

"Holy smokes, you got inside that car in under four minutes. My God, I'm glad you use your powers for good and not evil." Lizzie had timed her using her phone's stopwatch, which up-lit her face with a ghostly pallor. She'd tossed one of her gadgets back into her bag in favor of her smartphone so she could use the clock app. "How'd you learn how to do that?"

"My uncle works with cars," Josie said, handing her the screwdriver and snapping the too-big latex gloves from Lizzie tighter while she slid into the passenger seat. When Lizzie slid her a suspicious look, she added, "He has a legitimate garage, not a chop shop."

Okay, so it was a slight *exaggeration.*

After retiring from McDonnell Douglas, the airplane manufacturer, her Uncle Jack had begun collecting antique cars on his property in Tucson. He loved autos from all historical eras, but only worked on modern cars when he owed people favors—which wasn't often, but important when it happened. He had on occasion helped a friend out who had locked keys in a car in the middle of the night in South Tucson. Or had Josie open a locked car that had been towed to his lot for repayment of one debt or another. Off the books. Not a lot of questions asked, only the necessary ones, like *how fast do you need this back?*

Maybe that was where Josie had acquired her slippery, relativistic view of the law.

She checked the glove box first, but found only the car manual and Mary Clare's printed proof of insurance that expired at the end of 1995. No DNA-filled gum wrappers, no used pregnancy tests, no scary heroin needles. No candlestick, rope, or knife. Yeah, maybe it was a bit too much to hope for a smoking gun after all these years.

A sweep of her flashlight between the seats yielded nothing, so she slid out beside the car and crouched down to look under the seats. Again, nothing. She leaned across the driver's seat to open the hatchback, almost popping the hood with the button on the dash before she remembered the trunk release was down on the floor with the gas cap lever. She'd detailed her uncle's loaner Acura of a similar make many times, so she was intimately and depressingly familiar with the layout. Getting Arizona dust out of A/C ducts was no joke. And if she'd been particularly mouthy with her aunt or uncle that week, he'd hand her a bag of Q-Tips and cotton balls and tell her to get the job done using them.

Totally deserved it, every time.

As she worked her way around to the back of the car, she noted that Lizzie had gotten her ghost detection equipment working and was walking around the garage now, waving the gadget with the lights and buttons in front of her as she walked, reminding Josie of a red-shirted Star Trek extra. Hopefully not one of the disposable ones.

"Any signs of life?" Josie asked and shook her head at her choice of words. Signs of *afterlife* would have been more fitting.

"Nothing yet, but I'm patient. The key to being a good ghost hunter is to be good at waiting for something to happen, some spirit to decide to expose itself."

You'll be waitin' a long time, Josie thought as she bent forward into the open hatchback, trying to hurry, yet be thorough. This was probably her last chance to find something in the car. She ran her gloved fingers under the edge of the trunk board and lifted it up. The spare tire in the trunk well looked clean and intact. No dust on it, even. In fact, it looked as if the car had been detailed.

But being anal retentive about the state of a car wasn't a proof of guilt, she reminded herself, though she wanted to declare otherwise. Taking care of her car could have been a way of honoring his wife's memory. Just because it was squeaky, show-room clean didn't mean it *had been* covered with incriminating DNA evidence. It didn't mean that Billy Blake had murdered his wife and transported her body out to the Texas wilderness using her own car. Though, now Josie was picturing that very thing in her mind and shivered as she let the board back down and closed the trunk with a *thunk*. "Well, that was a bust."

Dang it. She'd really hoped to find something incriminating. Or just find anything at all. Instead, she'd come up with a big, fat zero.

"Let's go back in the house. There's nothing here. And it's creepy," Lizzie said.

"Truth."

They'd wasted precious minutes in her fruitless search of the car when they still hadn't found the cause of the broken glass. The house was big enough that the intruder—or spirit, Josie was willing to allow, just this once and only because she felt bad for breaking into the car—might have left already without revealing itself.

One could only hope.

Josie didn't particularly want to encounter anything vengeful, mercenary, or violent, whether corporeal or otherworldly. She preferred not to get injured. She was willing to admit that maybe she'd been unconsciously traveling in the opposite direction of the shattering glass in self-preservation.

However, as they rounded the corner into the kitchen, they came face to face with a breathtakingly horrible, bikini-clad apparition.

CHAPTER 25

Four-inch cork wedge high heels. Heroin-chic legs, minus the chic part. Denim cut-off short-shorts that failed to hide a distinctly male crotch. Abs of an anorexic teenage girl. Hot pink string bikini top. Turkey-waddle neck. Stained, wispy gray beard. All topped by a sunken, toothless face.

The three of them shrieked, and Josie's hearing was blocked out for a few seconds until she swallowed hard to open her ears back up. When the screaming stopped, the bikini man—whom she now recognized from her near collision with him earlier downtown—bent over with a hand to his heaving chest, and Josie hoped to God she wouldn't have to perform CPR on that mouth.

"What are you ladies doing here?" he demanded.

Okay, not a ghost. And hello, did you just assume my gender?

"No, you first. What are *you* doing here?" Lizzie asked, clearly territorial on behalf of her realtor cousin.

"Don't make me pull one of those antique guns off the wall, because I'm a pacifist. I don't like to hurt people, but if you corner me, I'll go honey badger on your butts. And I'll have you know, I'm a legal renter. I have a month-to-month lease in writing."

Though he lisped horribly because of his lack of teeth, Josie realized he was lucid and not too badly spoken. He didn't have any fresh track marks on his arms, so if he was using, it was in some other way. At this very moment, he was as sane as either one of them.

"Seriously? You're paying to live here?" Josie asked. What kind of income did he have to afford it and how could she get in on a gig like this?

"No. I'm being *paid* to live here. This is my humble abode."

"That's impossible. Who would pay you to do that?" Lizzie asked, her shock and awe clear as the starkly drawn eyebrows on her face.

"Look, I'll show you my rental contract. It's in my suitcase. I just need to clean this up first." He gestured to the double sink where he'd been rinsing a blood-covered towel. "Don't get too close," he said, and visions of hepatitis tests flooded through Josie's mind. Hep C was no laughing matter. But then he added, "Red wine stains horribly. I lost a chiffon prom dress to merlot just last week. Just about broke my heart. I cried for days. Love your bracelet, by the way. Kind of weird with the gloves, though. It's so you. Kind of dark and broody, but classy, in a way."

In a way? Come on. What wasn't classy about her? She quickly snapped off her gloves and smoothed back her messy hair.

He finished wringing out the towel and led them outside through the patio doors. His Daisy Dukes were giving him a serious wedgie, and Josie averted her eyes too late to avoid seeing his emaciated cheeks. Under the covered pergola on the patio, he'd set up a lounge chair with a sleeping bag next to a suitcase on rollers. A large splash of red wine marred the cream-colored cement decking next to the chair.

"Watch out. I'm going to need to get the garden hose before that stains. I think I got all the glass, but you never know. Little slivers can get right into your skin and next thing you know, you got sepsis. I had that once. And hypothermia. Lost two toes—makes my platforms fit better, so there's a flip side to everything. But that was before I came to Austin. I was living in Oklahoma, but it's just too damn cold up there."

And definitely more conservative than Austin, Josie speculated. Especially for a cross-dresser. Or trans-person, not that she wanted to assume anything.

"My name's Marion," he said, not pausing in his mopping up of the spilled wine. "Like John Wayne, you know? His real name before Hollywood got ahold of him was Marion. But not John Wayne Gacy. What a way to ruin a name. That guy was a creep. I hate clowns."

Clowns? What about serial murderers?

"What are y'all doing here anyway?" He straightened up and jutted out a hip bone, propping a hand on it. Pink nail polish, Josie noted. A more subtle shade than her friend, Barbecue Barbie, had been wearing. A shade Josie herself wouldn't have minded wearing if she ever were to paint her nails.

"We're looking for ghosts. Seen any around?" she asked.

Might as well be honest with him. When she'd asked Lizzie to come out to Billy's house, she had no idea she'd find an actual living resident. She was caught off guard by the whole situation and with her emotional drawbridge down, she'd been accidentally forthright.

He didn't seem the least bit phased by their nighttime adventuring in the house, like there was some underground cultural with which he was familiar that didn't adhere to strict daylight hours or boundaries like locked doors. Nocturnal trespassers. Denizens of the night, like street kids or vampires.

"Ghosts. Spirits. Specters. Phantoms. You should hear all the noises in the house at night," he said, making her more aware of words with the letter S than she'd ever been before.

He reached across the lounger for his suitcase and set aside a vintage rhinestone tiara and a pair of acrylic platform stripper heels before pulling out a packet of dog-eared papers.

"They don't bother me much. I only use the washroom and the fridge, so I'm not inside much. I sleep out here on the chair. Mostly because I can't stand to be in closed spaces. That's what you get when your mother locks you in a closet at night so she can go out hooking. Oops—was that too much sharing? I was in group therapy once in a place I stayed at. I got used to telling everyone what I was feeling, and now I just can't stop. Anyway, all the details are right there in the agreement." He pointed to the line with his cotton candy colored nail as Josie skimmed through the contract.

Lizzie, reading over Josie's shoulder, shrieked in her ear, making her head ring and her ear close up. Again. She swallowed hard as if she were on an airplane and managed to get a little hearing back.

"Good God, girl, you got a set of pipes on you. If there are any ghosts around tonight, you certainly woke them up now." Marion's mouth hung open, giving Josie a good view of the pits in the front of it where his teeth used to be. His gums weren't all that healthy looking either. That explained all the soft foods in the fridge. Hummus was probably his friend.

"Jessica Rubiak!" Lizzie said, pointing to the top of the contract, disgust and outrage turbo-charging the volume of her voice up to level eleven. "The number one real estate agent in the city. And my cousin's rival. She's letting *him* squat here so she can sabotage the sale." She shot Marion the evil eye.

"I resent that, missy," he said, his voice even raspier with protest. "I'm no squatter." He pronounced it *th'kwatter*. "I'm a paid renter. It's a job. Not only is this is my place of employ, it just so happened to be also where I hang my tiara at night."

"How is this legal?" Josie asked, more to herself than them as she scanned the contract. She knew Billy Blake had hired Cookie Casteñada to sell his home, but who had hired her rival, Jessica Rubiak? Had someone purposely pit the two saleswoman gladiators against each other to sabotage the sale? This lease packet had to have more clues.

She kept flipping through the pages, pausing at the important headings in all caps.

DAMAGE TO PREMISES...

RIGHT OF INSPECTION...

HOLDOVER...

BINDING EFFECT...

Blah, blah, blah.

NOISE... PETS... BICYCLES...

Speaking of bikes, Marion had leaned his against the pergola wall. Had he ridden all the way out here in his cork wedges from downtown where she'd first run into him? Had he weathered that crazy, thunderous storm out here huddled in his sleeping bag? And was it still better than living in Oklahoma?

Probably.

She read the last page, expecting to see Billy Blake's name on the line for the landlord. Maybe someone had acted on his behalf or forged his signature. DJ worked as his right-hand man at the restaurant. Maybe Billy had someone like that here at the house. He was a busy man and relatively wealthy. It would make sense if he had an assistant or even a lawyer take care of all of these details.

But it wasn't Billy's name on the last page of the lease. Instead, Josie saw another name.

Bunny Rogers.

Mary Clare's mother had hired Marion to squat at the house. Did she want him here to discourage buyers? Josie didn't think it was out of the goodness of the woman's heart. After reading that transcript of her conversation with Skip, it was hard for Josie to picture her as kind and generous.

"But why?" Josie said again, frowning at the lease form.

Unless uptight Bunny Rogers was acting illegally as a landlord—highly unlikely based on what Josie knew about her character so far—that meant she was probably part-owner of this house. Had Mary Clare left her portion of the estate to her mother instead of her husband? Josie knew Texas was a communal property state thanks to some research from a previous case, which meant if spouses died or divorced, their property was divided evenly. But if Mary Clare had a will in which she left all of her belongings to her mother, Bunny Rogers would be joint owner of Billy's home.

Or maybe Bunny Rogers's name had been on the mortgage from the very beginning. A behemoth house like that required some serious financing behind it, possibly more than what Mary Clare was entitled to on her own. Billy Blake was a simple restaurateur, not a Vegas high roller. They would've needed a fat bank account behind a massive house like this. Looking up who had signed the note on the house would be easy—Josie could probably even access the public record of it from her phone, if she could actually get a signal in these limestone hills.

Marion scratched his beard. *Skrich skrich skrich.* "I don't know why she hired me to stay here, honey. Sometimes your job in life is just to enjoy each day as it's handed to you. All I can say is I'm living in the lap of luxury for the foreseeable future, and I'm loving it."

"Oooh, my cousin is going to be so cheesed off. I need to call her," Lizzie said, but Josie noticed she didn't immediately reach for her phone.

Maybe *prima who denies all knowledge* of their midnight foray hadn't earned Lizzie's full respect and support after all. Or maybe Lizzie wasn't fully convinced Marion wasn't a ghost, though her ghost measuring device hung limply at her side for now.

Marion had stretched out on his chaise lounge, showing the scuffed bottoms of his sky-high heels, and crossed his smooth shaven showgirl flamingo-like legs with the spider webs of veins and bruises running up and down them. Josie would kill for a little length in the legs, some extra extension of the tibia and fibula. The guy had been gifted in that department. He raised his arms and cradled the back of his head with his hands, tufts of gray underarm hair jutting out by his string bikini top, and she had no idea where to begin assuming his gender even if she'd been forced to decide.

Lizzie squeaked in dismay and turned her face slightly to the side so she wasn't looking directly at Marion's fluffy pits. Nevertheless, Josie's young friend collected herself enough to ask, "But what about those ghosts you mentioned hearing—can you see them, too?"

Marion sat up. "You can see them, too? Oh my lord, I thought I was the only one. Can hardly sleep at night with the racket. It's like living on the streets. One eye always open."

"What? Where?"

Lizzie's device with the buttons and lights was back up at eye level. They all stared at it, but none of the indicators flashed. She whacked it with the palm of her hand and a row of them blinked on briefly, then turned dark.

"I've seen one of those before," Marion exclaimed.

"You have?" Josie couldn't imagine where he would have seen anything remotely like it. Was he a former mechanic? Maybe he'd worked in a lab at the university and had experience with...she didn't know what...seismic instruments? She found herself, along with Lizzie, leaning closer to him as he lowered his voice.

"CIA listening device, right? Real retro, too. Nowadays they're so small, they can get into your bloodstream with nanobots. First it was the fluoride mind control. That's why I stopped brushing my teeth." He paused to point at his gaping, toothless maw. "Now it's microscopic technology invented by a 14 year old doctoral candidate at Johns Hopkins

University. They inject it into you when you get the flu shot. That's why I never get it. I'm off the grid, girls. You should think about it. It's the only way to survive."

"Survive what?" Lizzie asked.

"What about the ghosts?" Josie interrupted. She didn't want to delve too far into Marion's conspiracy theories or his psyche. They didn't have all night, *literally*. It had already been late when they'd arrived here.

"All around us, every day. They won't shut up with their *woo-woo-woos*. They're here right now. Don't you see them? Buzzing around like big mosquitos in bedsheets. Holes cut out for their eyes. They think they're so clever when they look like amateur hour." His face brightened up. "But I've seen JFK and Marilyn. They like to dance in the kitchen to old Benny Goodman tunes."

CHAPTER 26

After Marion left for his Thursday night Bunco game—"bunch of reformed hippies in the neighborhood invite me over every week...not really my thing, but they make a kickin' sangria"—and told them to lock up on their way out, Josie was about ready to throw in the towel for the night. Lying her way into seeing Billy Blake's house had not only been unethical, but disappointingly fruitless.

She'd wondered for a minute if the neighbors had known or ever heard anything from the Blake house. Interestingly, when Josie had asked Marion if any of the neighborhood women had known Mary Clare, he'd shrugged. "They never met her, but they sure are interested in sticking it to the neighborhood association." With a neighborhood like this in which the nearest house was a quarter mile away through twisty roads, Mary Clare would have been extremely isolated by even more than the sheer size of her house. Kind of a sad state of affairs if she'd had troubles.

"Let's just check upstairs before we go," Lizzie said, sensing Josie's thirst for adventure had been a bit deflated by Marion's general kookiness.

"You're right. We're here. We came this far. We have to keep going. I want to hit every room if we can." Josie needed to pull herself together and stay focused.

She paused in the foyer at the bottom of the stairs to take a quick look at her phone. It was 12:48 am. Her signal bars were still low and flickering, but her phone had managed to pick up one short text message from Drew. It said he was back at the hotel and was going to sleep, but that he wanted her to wake him up when she returned to let him know she was safe. Which made her feel conflictingly loved and incredibly guilty at the same time, but she couldn't stop to have a case of the feels right now. She had work to do.

"Are you coming?" Lizzie hissed down the stairs.

Josie jogged up the Errol *Flynn* steps with one hand on the wrought iron railing. The landing at the top was covered in a thick piled carpet, and as she stepped onto it, she was sucked into a cocoon of silence as if she'd stepped into a super lush library. Hallways led to the left and right. Ahead of her, a massive great room with a pool table overlooked the foyer. The flat screen TV mounted on the wall ahead of them had to have been at least six feet across, the size of a tall man. This part of the house, at least, was thoroughly modern, considering Billy didn't live here. At least, according to what DJ had told her.

She didn't get it. Who was decorating this place and keeping it up-to-date?

"Which way?" Lizzie asked her. She held her detector up as if it were her compass. She was a Ghostbusting Girl Scout, plus mascara.

Despite the weirdness of the situation, Josie was still creeped out by the size of the house and its tomblike silence. How many people living here would it take to breathe some life into this place? Maybe thirty-five kindergarteners with cymbals and snare drums. The last time she'd broken into a building of this size was her high school to extract revenge on a petty and vindictive teacher. She'd almost gotten caught and most likely expelled, but the gods of idiotic adolescents had been looking out for her that day…and pretty much ever since then, too.

"Maybe we could turn on the lights?" she asked. "I mean, the neighbors know Marion is here. They wouldn't call the cops on us, I don't think."

"Nooo. You'll ward off the spirits," Lizzie hissed, handing her a second flashlight that she dug out of her bag.

Josie was sure her rampant skepticism had already done that. But whatever.

"Maybe we should split up. We'll cover more ground faster."

Josie had more than one reason for suggesting they divide and conquer the house. Searching through this amount of square footage was going to be a challenge if they wanted to get of here before dawn. Also, she was going to hit the first light switch she came across. She'd been weighing the pros and cons of sticking with her companion, but decided she'd had enough of stumbling around in the dark. And yeah, the semi-darkness was getting on her nerves in a way that might be making her on the verge of panic.

"I'll take the left," Lizzie said. "Another word for left is 'sinister,' and I like the sound of that." She hitched her bag up on her shoulder and gave Josie an excited grin. It seemed Lizzie had gained her ghost hunting legs. She was ready to give it another try. After stumbling across Marion's gaunt face in the dark, Josie wasn't sure how much scarier the real thing could get.

"You go, girl." Josie gave her a lame salute and took off in the opposite direction.

Down this part—the un-sinister side, or so she hoped—of the hallway, she could make out three doorways before the hallway ended. She tried the first handle in mild hopes that it might lead to a restroom. Though she'd spilled most of her root beer on the boombox in the hotel room, the rest of it had made its way through her. While it wasn't urgent, she wasn't opposed to finding a bathroom even if it had to occur in a possibly haunted mansion. An event to remember for sure, she thought, mentally rolling her eyes at herself.

She turned the heavy handle and pushed open the door, noting that it seemed as solid and stately as everything else in the house did, also adding to its tomblike silence. The door closed behind her, shutting out all sounds except the faint hum of air circulating through the house's ducts. The heat was on, she assumed, but now that she thought about it, the entire house had seemed to be one steady temperature—unlike her small apartment in Boston, which ranged from tropical to frigid zones all in one tiny space.

Must be nice living in a constant state of 72 degrees. How much does it cost to heat and cool this mansion? Especially when no one is living here?

It didn't make any sense.

As soon as the door closed behind her, she slapped the wall next to it until she found a switch. Searing brightness flooded the room and she squinted in shock, not only from the assault of the light, but from the attack of floral patterns. Big flowers. Little flowers. Tropical orchids. English country roses. Pink, pink, and more pink.

Her eyes watered as she counted the bedroom's numerous and bold competing fabrics. One—the vertical striped pink mess on the walls.

159

Two—the pink chintz of the bed comforter. Three—a circular dark pink area rug that covered a good part of the large room, its large blossoms gaping at her like multiplying monsters from the Little Shop of Horrors. Four—pink ceiling-to-floor sheers on the windows.

Holy heck. Someone bought out the pink section at the designer fabric store.

Another door stood across the room, and Josie hesitated a beat or two before making her way across the florid carpet to investigate. She guessed it was a closet, but she was scared to see the pink chaos sprawl into another room. However, if this had been a room that Mary Clare had lived in, Josie *needed* to see if any of her belongings were inside.

She opened the door and wasn't half wrong. While it was a closet, it was also a bathroom. Also horribly pink. *Ugh.* She felt a little woozy.

For all the times Josie had been sick to her stomach, lying on her own bathroom floor, becoming intimately acquainted with the small black and white tiles on the floor and larger tiles on her walls, she had never been as grateful for their simplicity as she was now. Because, holy Pepto Bismol. And after this, she would need some.

Pink shower curtain. Pink countertop, toilet, and bathtub. Pink tiles on the floor and the walls—and pink rosettes inlaid throughout. A large picture mirror over the counter did nothing to alleviate the unrelenting pinkness. Josie felt like someone had shined a light inside her small intestine—a place she had never wanted to visit. Whose room was this? Either a demented little girl like the Willy Wonka kid or else a crazy old lady. Either one fit the bill.

The bathroom—which was the size of Josie's bedroom at home—had an attached walk-in closet, but the shelves and floor were as empty as the pantry downstairs. The clothing rod didn't even hold an empty hanger or two. Nothing. No personal effects anywhere, including the medicine cabinet, which Josie opened with the side of her pinky finger.

Her urge to leave this bathroom as quickly as possible had overruled her need to use it, so at that, Josie turned on her heel and made her way out, pausing to check the drawer of the bedside table and the space under the bed before she left. They were both also empty, which led her to believe the room had been intended either as a guest room for an extremely unfortunate guest…or perhaps a mother-in-law. She flipped off the light on her way out.

Back in the hall, Josie took a deep breath. Amazing how color and pattern could be just as oppressive as a physical force.

Because geeze, how could anyone stand to stay in there?

The next door yielded a restroom, bland compared to the last one she'd entered. Breathing a sigh of relief that it wasn't pink, she used it quickly, opting to dry her hands on her shirt rather than leave DNA on the pristine white hand towel hanging on the rod by the sink. As she stood in the hall after closing the bathroom door behind her, she wondered how on earth Lizzie's cousin was going to sell the house with the pink bed and bath. She'd have to re-do that whole mess or else negotiate a price with a fixing-up allowance including. Because, yuck. That tile and those fixtures…

Facing down the last door in the hallway, Josie braced herself for anything, not sure what to expect. This end of the corridor didn't have a window at the end as she would have expected, so it was even creepier than the rest, but she braced herself and forged on.

Without Lizzie, she felt vulnerable—she had known she would. It wasn't as if her new friend could offer much in the way of protection, but having a buddy and even Lizzie's goofy "in like flint" thing helped ward off her quakes of anxiety. On her own, Josie felt a little…sweaty, which was definitely a sign of nerves in this perfectly climate-controlled monstrosity of a house.

She took a deep breath as she reached for the last door knob on this end of the hallway only to discover it was locked. She pressed her ear against the wood, feeling the cool grain of it on her cheek. Maybe it was a utility closet. She didn't hear any water or loud air flow, though. Could this be an electricity…thing way up here? Seemed unlikely.

A shiver ran through her and she couldn't tell if this end of the hall was actually colder or if she was just freaking out. Though it was darker here, she realized her eyes were open wide and she was blinking more rapidly, along with her elevated heart rate.

Okay, deep breath. I'm in Austin. This is Texas, not Arizona. I haven't been dragged and left for dead out in the desert. I'm okay. Keep breathing.

Her lungs filled with the recirculated air of the house, not the sweet smell of creosote and mesquite where she'd had the incident that still affected her nerves. Was it her imagination or was this end of the hall also slightly more stale-smelling than the rest?

She tried the door handle again, as if this time it would magically open. Too bad she hadn't brought her new lock picks with her, but she hadn't thought they'd be necessary on vacation...or if they'd even get through airport security. She put her ear against the door one more time, frowning when she thought she heard a whisper of faint footsteps.

"Hey, you'll never guess what I found," Lizzie said at full volume directly into her exposed ear. She fought a gasp of terror and had to blink a couple of times before the spots cleared from her vision.

"I found an elevator. Isn't that the coolest thing ever? Can you even imagine having one in your house? If I had one, my grandmother could live upstairs with the rest of us instead of having to change the living room into a bedroom. That would be awesome. Then I could've had more friends over and hung out and grand-*mami* could have more privacy."

"Yeah. So cool," Josie managed to say even though her heart was still trying to pound its way out of her throat. "Want to know what I found? A locked door."

"Aw, that's too bad." Lizzie set her bag down by her feet.

"Yeah, it's the last door on this floor. Maybe even the last place in the house we haven't checked out yet."

"I mean, it's too bad I have this set of lock picks, but I haven't learned how to use them yet." She showed Josie the small leather case she'd dug out of her bag.

CHAPTER 27

The last thing in the world Josie thought she would be doing at one o'clock in the morning in a mansion in Texas was giving a tutorial on how to pick a lock to a Goth ghost hunter. However, here she was, talking about tumblers and pins—to an apt pupil, too.

"Okay, you got this. Shake out your fingers and try again. Just go slow."

Lizzie, on her knees in the thick carpet, had fumbled her first two attempts, dropping her tools in the thick, plush carpet, so Josie coached her to try again. Lizzie muttered the steps to herself, her words muffled by the pick she held between her lips.

"Insert the tension thingy into the bottom of the hole, using a little pressure."

"Excellent use of the technical term *thingy*," Josie said. She'd taught her that.

"Insert the pick into the top of the hole," Lizzie repeated from memory.

"Yep. Now the slightly tricky part. Nice and easy. Slow and steady wins the race."

Truth be told, Josie was feeling slap-happy from alternating fatigue and adrenal overload thanks to her constant state of jumpiness. Right now, she probably couldn't rush even if monsters were chasing her.

"Use a slight torque pressure on the first thingy, and move the second thingy back and forth until the pins set..." Lizzie's face wrinkled up in concentration, her perfectly symmetrical eyebrows coming down in curled twin awnings over her eyes.

The lock shifted and the door swung open into blackness.

"Hey, you did it! Good job."

A waft of stale air, smelling of dust and mold, drifted across their faces. Josie froze in the middle of offering Lizzie a high-five as a feeling of dread—no other way to describe it came over her. Kind of like she'd bitten into a raspberry filled donut only to discover the filling was gray with mold. Revulsion at a visceral level.

"Uh, I got the door open. You can go in first," Lizzie said, stepping backward, her rounded shoulders even more sloped as she scuttled out of the way.

"Yeah. Sure." Josie tried to sound ballsy and not as reluctant as she felt. She dug deep for some false bravado, as if she'd actually done anything to earn the P.I. license in her wallet. How bad could it be? It was just a room, right?

Deep breath. I got this.

As with the atrocious pink bedroom, she stepped in and felt with her hand along the inside of the wall, searching for a light switch. The wall, as with the room, seemed colder than the hall, but her wrist suddenly sparked and burned right where her new beaded bracelet wrapped around it. The accompanying zapping noise reminded her of a mosquito porch light, except in this case, she was the bug. And that charred smell was not good. Kind of like roasted pork.

"Son of...!" Josie clutched her wrist where the coin on her bracelet had fried her skin.

"Holy *chet*. What was that?" Lizzie asked from out in the hall. She poked her head in. "Is something on fire?"

"I think it's me. I just got shocked."

"By what?"

"No clue, but *ouch*."

"Here, take my flashlight." Lizzie handed her the red "ghost light," and Josie shined it on the wall she'd been touching.

Where the wall switch should have been was a gaping hole with a couple of frayed wires jutting out, completely uncovered and dangerous. Any unsuspecting fool could come along and—well, she now knew how easily that could happen.

"That is definitely not going to pass the buyer's inspection," she said, her wrist still tingling, but not as bad now. "Looks like someone is in the middle of remodel—"

Swinging the light around to the rest of the room, she was unable to finish her thought.

If she were going to design a living space for a shut-in…or a dead, mummified mother, this room would have exactly matched that dark and twisted vision. With Lizzie all but plastered against her back, she scanned the room, slowly sweeping the red light from side to side.

Rocking chair in the corner — check. Dressmaker's mannequin by the wall — check. Antique birdcage large enough to hold a small child or…a velociraptor — check. Stacks and stacks of old magazines and newspapers, enough to make a hoarder feel at home if not crush her to death — check. Apparently this enormous mansion didn't have an attic because this room was a catch-all for the family's weird and nightmare inducing cast-offs.

And that smell…*ugh*. What was that dank, fetid odor, and how had a single closed door managed to trap the smell in this room?

"Phew!" Lizzie waved a manicured hand in front of her face. Then she grabbed Josie's arm in excitement. "I think it's a paranormal smell. Oh my God, my first ghostly odor. I should take a selfie or something. Oh, well, maybe not a picture."

"Huh?" Josie wasn't too sure about that. Something could have died in here — easily — and stayed undiscovered for years.

"And that disgusting burning smell on top of it. This is amazing."

Josie looked at her with narrowed eyes. Lizzie looked like she was about to enter a state of rapture.

"That disgusting smell would be my burnt flesh."

She held up her wrist, a bit afraid to remove the bracelet to see what kind of damage her skin had suffered. She had Schrödinger's arm burn, just like the famous cat in a box paradox. Her wrist was both burned and unburned as long as she didn't look underneath.

"Oh. Right. Sorry." Then Lizzie gaped at Josie's wrist. "Oh my God, that bracelet totally protected you. You could have been shocked to death."

"Huh?"

She stared at the black sparkling beads wrapped around her bony wrist joint. Now that she thought about it, it kind of looked like a Victorian version of one of Wonder Woman's Amazonian cuffs that she used to block flying bullets.

Well, sure. If it's a love charm and also a deflector of evil, I'll take it. It's not like I'm going to say no just because I'm stuck in a skeptical frame of mind.

Josie edged further into the room. The red flashlight was less than inadequate in warding off not only the inky darkness, but the willies that zinged up and down Josie's spine. She didn't sense any other people in the room — *living people,* that was — no crouching bad guy waiting to spring out at her.

Josie swung the flashlight again, and Lizzie shrieked, making Josie flinch and nearly fling the light out of her hand. She cursed her jumpiness, which she knew wasn't normal, at least not for her. Her stupid adrenal glands were in constant hyperdrive.

I need to get a frickin' grip.

"Oh my God, I just saw a face," Lizzie said, her voice high with either excitement or fear — or a combo of the two. She'd also dropped her device when she screamed and ducked down to snatch it back up from the floor. Waving it in front of her again, she stared at the lights, which weren't moving, giving a cry of frustration when she couldn't get her machine to work.

"Yes, it's okay. You really did see a face," Josie said, shining the light around the room again. This time, she let it come to rest on a framed portrait leaning against the wall. "A whole bunch of them."

The painting was one of those posed family deals, with the father seated and the rest of the family clustered around him, patriarchal and pretty stuffy-looking. From the clothing and hairstyles, she thought the portrait had been taken in the early 80's, maybe. Mom and daughter had donned matching Laura Ashley floral dresses with wide, white Peter Pan collars. The three boys were stiff and unsmiling in matching gray suit coats and red ties, like miniature Republican senators. Mary Clare's family portrait. Josie stared with morbid curiosity at the girlhood face of the dead woman and at her family's faces as well.

In the portrait, Mary Clare was pretty, in a starched and artificial way. She'd been brunette back before Miss Clairol had gotten ahold of her.

166

Her expression wasn't exactly a smile—more like facial rictus. Her lips had either been glossed with pale pink lipstick or she'd been later painted that way. Too perfect, too plastic, like some of the other poor little rich girls Josie had known and felt sorry for in her life.

She located a Tiffany lamp against the wall and reached under the shade to turn it on, hoping it was plugged in and properly wired, unlike the wall switch. With a twist of her wrist, the bulb came on, and the entire room was bathed in red, bloody light.

"Hey, what do you know? A red lampshade. That's *much* better," Josie said.

"Red-rum," Lizzie blurted out with a nervous giggle.

"What is this place?"

Now that she could see better, she turned in a circle, taking in the rest of the room, and discovered a couch and a fully made-up bed with a ratty quilt and pillows. A bedside table was littered with papers and tissues, a plastic drinking tumbler, and medicine.

"Was someone…living here?" Lizzie asked.

CHAPTER 28

"Someone definitely could have stayed here. There's a bed. A bookshelf. No kitchen or fridge. No windows." Lizzie turned in a slow circle.

She was right. This weird...cell was a temporary bedroom, a barely livable room for a person with a real penchant for the solitary life. Basically they were in a storage room with a bed. Or...a prison cell? With a really weird selection of books—a leather-bound, embossed Children's Bible and what looked to be a full shelf of hardback Nancy Drew mysteries, the older ones with the yellow covers. The first six Harry Potter books, but not the last and final one.

Maybe this is hell.

With a sour taste in her mouth, Josie went back to the door to check for a lock, but no, other than the standard lock on the handle, there were no special deadbolts to indicate imprisonment. No fingernail scratches on the inside of the door. No tally marks counting off the days like a prison wall etching. No bars on the bed. No handcuffs either, fuzzy or otherwise.

Okay, *whew.* At least that was one question answered. This room was no torture chamber or freaky playroom. But why, if a person lived in a mansion like this, would they stay in a windowless, dank-smelling monk's cell even for a few days?

"Oh, and here's the source of that rotten stench." Josie picked out a wooden walking stick from a canister by the door and poked it into a heap of something furry—which she prayed was dead—on the floor, partially obstructing the heating duct. The fur, which turned out to be some kind of stole, maybe sable if she had to guess, was like the kind which elderly ladies used to wear around just their shoulders with a tie in the front. It fell into two pieces as she tried to pick it up with the end of her stick. As it disintegrated, it released another cloud of gamey, rotten stink which had Josie breathing through her mouth.

Ew. Burnt fur and skin. So nasty.

Lizzie said, "Did you know that when you smell something—a good smell like fresh bread or a horrible smell like dead skunk—that you're actually inhaling tiny particles of whatever it is that you smell? That's what makes a public toilet or a latrine extra disgusting. I mean, you're actually breathing in other people's feces. Or like when you're driving in your car and you get stuck behind a really slow garbage truck on a hot day..."

"Thanks. I didn't know that." Josie yanked the collar of her t-shirt up over her nose, wishing she had a face mask. She hadn't even considered the possibility of something actually toxic having been stored in this room, and she had Lizzie's safety to consider as well, not just that of her own foolhardy self.

A freestanding rack of clothes stood along the opposite wall. The bar of it had nearly buckled with the weight of coats and dresses, all women's clothes and some of which looked suitable even for a formal evening in Dallas. A mass of iridescent sequins glowed in the dim, red light from her flashlight. On the floor below, matching shoes made a front line at a debutante's battle. The foot soldiers. Josie snorted to herself at her horrible pun.

Josie crossed the room and squatted down to examine the prescription bottles on the bedside table without touching them. Clozapine. Prozac. Lorazepam. Xanax. Bottles all prescribed to a Janet Martinez with handwritten labels in Spanish and no dates, which was shady as heck. Not even expiration dates, never mind when they had been filled. Okay, then. Fake prescriptions. Fake identity for anonymity. Real drugs—a major pill stash, with weeks' worth of doses just sitting here in the dust.

She did a double-take—not at the pill bottles, but at the layers of dust on the table and on everything else in the room. Unlike the rest of the house, which had been well-kept and spotless, this room was a dump, grimy and foul-smelling. But how long had it been this way? She went the nearest pile of newspapers and took the first one off the stack. If the very top paper was dated September 28, 1995, she'd consider this a closed case, job done. To her mind, a newspaper dated the very day Mary Clare had disappeared would more or less confirm that this room had belonged to her at some point in her troubled existence.

Josie scanned the top of the front page, then found the date under the *Legislator* title bar.

"October 10, 2005."

What the heck? This newspaper was much too recent to have been here while Mary Clare was alive. Unless…

"Sorry, what did you say?" Lizzie had finished making a full circuit of the room with her unblinking gadget and tossed it back in her bag, where it clanked against some of the other junk she had in there.

"This newspaper is from 2005. Mary Clare disappeared ten years before that. There's no way she could have put this on the stack of papers here when the last day anyone heard from her was September 28, 1995."

"Maybe someone else put it in here, like as a storage space. Maybe they wanted to save all the newspapers in case she ever showed back up again. You know, so she could read about everything she missed. I mean, look at all this junk…" Lizzie's voice tapered off tiredly after that. In the red light of the room she looked tired, even under all of her makeup. The actual mental cataloging of clues didn't seem to be her thing after the initial discovery of the room.

Don't give up now, girl. We're almost onto something.

The thrill of the chase, on the other hand, had awoken Josie. Or maybe that was just another gush of adrenaline from her overtaxed glands. She knew she was headed for burn-out, but that was a worry for another day. After this was over, she could lie on the couch for a month. But for now, they were just so close to…something. She could almost smell it.

"Listen, do you hear something?" Lizzie was clutching Josie's arm again.

"Hear wha—"

"Shhh."

Josie frowned as Lizzie shushed her. Of all the nerve. Miss Scaredycat Ghosts-in-Theory was telling her to be quiet—

A police siren wailed outside, and Josie executed a mental about-face, taking back her uncharitable thoughts.

"Seriously? Someone called the cops on us? I thought the neighbors liked Marion. I can't believe they turned on him like that! Bunch of two-faced liberals-just-for-show. Oh, it's all fine and good until a trans-skimpily-vestited hobo lives next door to them. Then the claws come out. Not in my backyard. Not on my...hard-scrabble, gravel composite front yard."

"We need to hide," Lizzie insisted, looking wild-eyed in the red gloom. A pulse visibly pounded in the girl's neck. Josie recognized a burst of fear-fueled energy when she saw one. But no way was she going to get trapped in this godforsaken Miss Havisham-esque dungeon of bad memories and creepy cast-offs. No, thank you. She had no idea if the police were going to have to search each room while they crouched and cowered in here for hours. One night in this monastic cell of misery was one night too long. No way, no how.

"Hit the lights. We're getting out of here," she told Lizzie as she clicked the feeble flashlight on again. After they had both stepped back out into the hallway, Josie made sure Lizzie still had her shoulder bag and that nothing had been left on the dirty floor in the room. She didn't want any trace of them left behind, especially since she was going to tell Skip everything she knew at the soonest opportunity. She locked the door behind them and they went down the hall the way they'd come.

Lizzie gave a moan so long, drawn-out, and full of dread it actually made Josie feel like the place might be haunted after all.

"We don't know why the police are here," Josie said, trying to mollify her as she led them back down the spiral staircase—granted, at a much faster clip than they'd ascended. "It could be just a routine security check."

With siren blaring and turbo-charged engine roaring up the street.

If they ignored Lizzie's SUV parked in driveway by the front door.

"And even if they do want to ask us a few questions, we haven't done anything wrong."

Other than criminal trespassing. But hey, we hadn't broken anything, other than nearly frying my skin in the hell hole upstairs. It will most likely be classified as a misdemeanor and not prosecuted as a felony. If we're lucky.

"Hold it right there. Keep your hands where I can see them."

"Oh, chet," Lizzie said, yelping her mixed English-Spanish curse again. She dropped her bag at the foot of the stairs with a thunk and raised her hands sky-high in light of the service firearm pointed at them.

Part 4: Inferno

In Dante's *Inferno*, Hell is made up of nine concentric circles of suffering—the usual peccadilloes: Limbo, Lust, Gluttony, Greed, Wrath, Heresy, Violence, Fraud, and Treachery.

I know what you're thinking: *What is she talking about?* After all, you didn't come to a food blog for lessons on ancient allegory. You want to know how long to smoke a pork butt or what's my go-to classic Sonoran style rub recipe. You want to know how long you can keep a Santa Fe Green Chile Chicken Casserole in the freezer.

You want me to stick to the recipes, to the facts, to be a predictable commodity. A service without interruption and of consistent, high quality. I have a brand, a recognizable name.

I should never explode with unexpected emotion or rage in a fiery, confusing ball of pointless classical references about antiquated notions of sin and passion.

Like Bruce Banner combusting into The Hulk when trapped and cornered. *Josie angry. Josie smash.*

—Josie Tucker, discarded blog post entry

CHAPTER 29

"Keep your hands where I can see them," the officer said, causing Lizzie to squeak again, even though the guy seemed pretty relaxed for a cop. "Just stay where you are."

"Yes," she said. "I understand. I speak English and I'm a U.S. citizen. Although my grandma isn't—well, never mind. Yes. Hands up."

Josie sighed and also put up her hands, feeling resigned—signed, sealed, and...stupid.

This evening could have gone so, so much better.

While the police officer holstered his weapon and radioed in his situation, she contemplated her life. Up to this point, she'd been fairly lucky for someone whose life could have gone downhill quickly, given her circumstances. Her great-aunt and uncle had taken her in and saved her from an uncertain future in the foster system. She'd gotten a solid college education and stumbled into a potentially great career as a blogger. Lucky breaks, one after another. Solid and much appreciated gifts from the universe, the powers that be...fate. So the question was, why did she continue to squander her good luck by putting herself into these risky situations?

Crap, crap, crappity crap. Drew was going to kill her.

No, not *literally* murder her, like whatever horrible thing had happened to Mary Clare, but absolutely slay her the way he always did by being incredibly understanding about her constant ability to get herself into a jam. He was going to kill her with his kindness. Oh, no doubt about it, he would be angry and blast her poor judgment for a while, but then he'd admit that it was a part of her. Then he would accept it. Somewhere deep in her heart, his compassion would pierce her to the core and remind her what it was like to feel like a disappointment again and again.

"Do you two have I.D.?" the officer asked, his shoulder radio chirping. He reached up to turn it down a notch or two. His mellow tone and loose stance suggested he didn't consider either of them a risk. That was a good start, because she was *so* not a threat.

"In my back pocket," Josie said. "Can I reach my hand in and get it out?" She spoke slowly and explicitly, as if she were talking to a preschooler. Not to be condescending. Just in case. Hey, she'd seen the stories on the news. One bad cop didn't spoil the barrel, but it did make a person pretty darned cautious, especially if that person happened to be caught perpetrating some alleged suspicious activity. In the middle of the night.

He seemed to be considering her jeans, not for any level of attractiveness or to determine if anything came between her and her...Levis, but as to whether she could be hiding a weapon in them or, more likely, how he could avoid a sexual harassment lawsuit while trying to retrieve her driver's license.

"Go ahead," he said finally, though he watched her closely.

Lizzie had already found her wallet—a big purple velvet thing with zippers and snaps—in the outside pocket of her shoulder bag and had thrust it at him. He shined his flashlight on it, squinting at her information. He took out her license and handed the rest back to her without comment.

Josie, however, knew her I.D. was going to cause a few questions. Shaking her head at herself, she swept a finger in the inner pocket of her wallet, handing him the ridiculous piece of paper that said she was a private detective as well as her Massachusetts driver's license.

Before he could look at it very closely, however, the overhead light flooded on and the entire foyer was filled with bright, almost-blinding light. As they blinked and squinted at each other, Josie shifted her eyes toward the monstrous chandelier above them. It was a multi-tiered fixture with innumerable cascading, twinkling crystals, like a sparkly Venetian fountain of diamonds. A monstrous display of wealth. A thousand stars in the darkness.

"Whoa," she said. "Check that out."

The others looked up and admired the crystal masterpiece, then together as one, swiveled toward the kitchen at the *clip-clop* of unsteady footsteps in high heels. Marion emerged from the kitchen in all his splendor. In his gravity-defying wedges and fresh coral-pink lipstick, he held a pitcher in one hand, the emaciated fingers of his other wrapped around the stems of two glasses. He'd taken the time to draw on some eyebrows as well as perch his tiara atop his greasy gray locks.

"Hey, girls, the next batch of sangria's done. Sorry it took so long. Almost lost my buzz. Y'all ready for freshies?"

While Josie appreciated the effort he took in his appearance and his commitment to making his performance believable — that he'd even go out on a limb for them — she wished he'd gotten his butt out here sooner and saved her the near-heart-attack.

"Well hello, Officer Gorgeous," he said to the cop and shifted his weight to one bony hip.

The officer put his hands on his hips below his service belt. Kind of an aw-shucks move, except he was armed, bullet-proof vested, and had a utility belt more packed than Batman's.

"Marion, what in the heck are you doing out in this neck of the woods? Aren't you usually at the Front Steps shelter over on 7th?"

He wasn't crossing his arms, Josie thought. From all of her past dealings with the guys in blue, all the way back to the juvie officers in her past life, the crossed-arms stance was her least favorite. She knew what crossed arms meant, so this casual buddy-buddy act made her wary. Unfamiliar territory, so to speak.

"Well, long story, Officer, but I'm living here now. And these are my girls." Marion gave them a Vanna White wave, making Josie feel like a new washer-dryer combo on a display pedestal.

"Is that so?"

The police officer looked at her and Lizzie with a heavy dose of skepticism.

Waitaminute. What did he think Marion meant when he said they were "his girls?" Like, girls for hire kind of girls? Because Josie was a lot of things in life, including a lame burlesque dancer and a person who would consider flirting just to borrow a research file, *but she was no hooker.* She almost shouted for him to take that look back but figured, against her first instinct, that silence was still her best course of action if she wanted any hope of seeing her hotel room and not-yet-fiancé within the next 24 hours.

"As a matter of fact, I do have a signed and notarized lease out in my suitcase by the pool. That's my patio bedroom, if you'd like to come into it." Marion lowered his voice suggestively, and even Josie, who was normally okay with other people's public displays of affection, had to look away.

"If you wouldn't mind," the officer said, playing into Marion's scene. "Ladies," he said, handing Josie back her I.D., "it's been a pleasure. Apparently the neighbors got a little trigger happy calling us out tonight during your book club, scrapbooking, or whatever it is you're doing here. Since it's late, you're going to want to get home now." His comment was neither a question nor a suggestion, but a command he expected them to heed.

No problem whatsoever with that plan, as far as she was concerned.

As the officer followed Marion out to the patio and his poolside room with a view, Josie heard him asking their transvestite savior of the evening whether he'd been getting enough to eat lately.

"This was both the best evening of my life and the worst," Lizzie told her.

"That's very Dickensian," Josie said, her words slurring with exhaustion. Her eyes had stopped focusing. Her lids had decided earth's gravity was inferior to Jupiter's and were acting accordingly, and she could no longer hold them up. From behind her mostly closed eyelids, she could see the faint glow of the passing streetlights, rhythmic and soothing.

They were just minutes from Josie's hotel. She didn't know what time it was, but she thought the sky was starting to lighten. She stubbornly refused to acknowledge it was a new day until she'd been asleep for a while.

Her mind should have been flooded with images of what they'd seen that night, but her thoughts were pretty much a flatline of nothingness, which meant she needed a pillow under her head. Preferably within the next ten minutes, or else she was just going to sleep standing up in the elevator, or here in Lizzie's car.

Lizzie, on the other hand, seemed ready for more adventuring. Her voice was extra loud in the chilly darkness of the car, too loud for Josie's dwindling ability to concentrate. And luckily at this hour, the streets were empty, because Lizzie had started gesturing with her hands and swerving a bit, or at least she seemed to be as far as Josie could tell with her eyes now fully closed.

"I mean, we didn't collect any conclusive evidence pointing to the infestation or even presence of spirits in the Blake house," she said, cutting across two lanes. "But I was able to use most of my equipment in the field. I'm not a field virgin anymore! High-five me."

Josie opened an eye and dutifully smacked the hand Lizzie held up. Her side of the celebration was more of a listless brush, but Lizzie didn't seem to mind.

"I think I could really do this," she said.

"You might have trouble making a living off hunting ghosts," she told Lizzie, murmuring more than actually talking. "I don't know how you could monetize that unless you sold t-shirts or had some kind of Etsy storefront. Branding would be really tricky. I'm sure there's a copyright on that Ghostbusters red circle with a slash through it...I don't know what that's called, but I think it has a name. Something weird like umlaut..."

The next thing she knew, Lizzie was shaking her awake and telling her to go into the hotel.

CHAPTER 30

The door to her darkened hotel room opened before she could get her card key out from her pocket, and Drew peered out into the bright hallway at her. She didn't comprehend his explanation of how he knew where she was. Something about an app on her phone and GPS. Technology was amazing as long as she didn't have to understand it right now. And even though she said she was fine, just tired, he insisted on pulling her into the room and lightly checking her over until he was satisfied she hadn't been beaten or stabbed or clonked on the head.

That last one, she appreciated.

And also that he didn't seem to be mad at her. Why had she thought he'd be upset? Was that all in her own mind? If so, she had more issues than *People* magazine. Had Mary Clare ever been written up in *People* magazine? The Ramsey family sure had. Josie remembered reading some of those articles in the dentist's office.

"I really need to get some sleep. Did you already do that?" she asked him as she kicked off her shoes and unzipped her jeans.

"Yeah, a few hours until I realized you weren't back yet," he said, guiding her to bed. "Do you need a drink of water?"

"No," she said, eyes already closing, "Haven't been out drinking...just ghost hunting."

She dropped her pants on the floor and crawled into bed. Then she sat back up and removed her jacket, which also landed on the floor.

"What's up with this bracelet on your wrist? It looks black."

Her head hit the pillow. At freaking last. "It's supposed to be black," she said. "It's a Victorian death charm. I mean a Romany love charm. Gypsies. Whatever."

Also, she needed to ask him something, but she couldn't remember what it was. She traced back through the evening in her mind.

Aha. Now she remembered.

"Hey, want to get some barbecue tomorrow?" she asked, but she fell asleep before he answered.

When she woke up some hours later, arms and legs sprawled in an X across the bed, Drew was gone, but he'd left a handwritten note on the pillow next to her. Though she was much more awake now, she stared at it for several minutes trying to decipher what he'd said. Freaking doctor's penmanship. The cliché was alive and well. Fortunately, the door clicked open while she was still sitting there in bed.

"Hey, you're awake." He set a takeaway paper cup and a granola bar for her on the table next to the bed. "What are we doing today? While you were asleep, you said something about barbecue, a smoke house on fire, and Mr. Rochester."

Talking in her sleep? That didn't sound good. She had a lot of crap in her head that would be better off staying in there.

The opening of the cup had some foam puffing through it. She sniffed the drink and discovered it was a chai latte, but it was too hot to drink, so she ripped into the granola package as she considered where to start. Luckily she didn't have to go into the plot of *Jane Eyre*. She'd proofread his paper on that book during their undergrad years, so she knew he'd read it. But the Mary Clare part, she needed to start at the beginning on that.

"I saw your file on the desk here. I hope you don't mind I read some of it while you were sleeping. I saw the boombox, too, but I didn't want to wake you up. I'm guessing the tape has something interesting on it." He looked embarrassed and a little...nervous?...as he pushed a hand through his hair.

She, on the other hand, experienced a curious warmth building in the center of her chest. If she weren't such a general crabapple, she'd say it was pleasure. Yeah, that had to be happiness. Or something.

She slid off the bed in her t-shirt and undies and headed over to her Guy Friday where he sat at the desk, shifting papers around. "Excellent. I'm glad you did." She slung her arms around his shoulders from behind. "I've been to Smiley's already, but I think we need to go back. If not for answers, then at least so you can try their amazing beans."

"That's the weirdest proposal I ever heard," he said, and she nearly choked. "So, what? Are we going for lunch or dinner?"

"I don't even know what time it is. And I need a shower." She kissed the side of his neck.

"We've got time for a shower," he said with that half smile she liked so much.

Later, Josie tracked down Gary on their way to the lobby and returned the boombox, which she had gone over with a washcloth one more time to make sure it wasn't sticky. After fiddling with the buttons and inner gears a little more, she was relieved to get Rewind to work.

Thank you, Samsung.

She tidied up the Mary Clare file and slipped the cassette inside the folder in case they had time to return it to Skip after lunch.

As they headed out of the hotel lobby on their way to the rental car, the baby-faced bartender stopped them. Today he wore trendy skinny jeans, along with some goofy leather driving gloves that left his fingertips exposed, as if he had a Formula One car waiting for him outside with his pit crew. With his height and slight build, he would have made a better jockey for horse racing, she thought. They stood practically eye-to-eye—and she was short, *yes, she could admit it in this case,* for a woman.

"Hey, Ryan," Drew said to him, momentarily confusing both Josie and the boy, who was apparently named Ryan, unbeknownst to her. Some P.I. she was.

"Oh, hey, I didn't realize you two were here together." He looked wary, like he didn't know how to proceed. "Look, can I talk to you for just a minute?" he asked Josie, still darting his glance back to Drew. "Is it okay if—?"

"Yeah, he knows what's going on," Josie said, though Drew didn't exactly know every single detail, including this part, probably.

Ryan the bartender led them to a more secluded seating area behind a bank of planters filled with big leafy plants. A big leaf smacked Ryan in the head when he sat down, and he jumped like he'd been goosed. Josie took a seat next to him on a couch and Drew picked a chair opposite them.

"Look, I didn't know who you were when you asked me questions before. Later I kind of...saw your name on your credit card receipt and I looked you up on the Internet. I mean, you're not a cop, but you're kind of a reporter, right? Or cook or something. So if I tell you this, like give you some information, you'll do the right thing with it? At least, that's what I'm hoping. I mean, I can't really keep going with what I know and not telling anyone."

The circles under his eyes were more pronounced than before, but Josie had just chocked it up to his fair skin and unfortunate babyface—and maybe a habit of late-night partying or playing video games or sculpting his goatee. Whatever extracurricular activities he was into.

"The thing is," he said, picking at his nails, "I wasn't fired from Smiley's. I quit." He lowered his voice. "I didn't want to work for a murderer. That's not the kind of place I can stay in. I just didn't feel good there."

Josie stared straight into his eyes. "How do you know he's a murderer?" She'd been working on him—on Ryan—for only a couple days, and now he had come to her willingly with information. She'd *known* there had been more to his story. She was so close to plucking the info out of him, she could almost taste it.

He had turned fidgety though and was squirming in his seat.

Wait. No, what's he doing?

He'd reached into his jeans back pocket and pulled out a...plastic baggy. Which he handed to her without a word.

"What is this?" she asked as she took the mystery object between her thumb and forefinger through the plastic. Turning it this way and that, she tried to figure out what it was.

It was pink and...*good lord, were those teeth?*

CHAPTER 31

She gave the bag to Drew.

Okay, that was an understatement. Her jerky hand-off was like her tossing a hot potato, more of an underhand fling.

"Dental bridge," Drew said without hesitation, probably to calm her if her face was showing half as much disgust as she felt. At least they weren't real teeth and gums.

A wave of queasiness had come over her, but it passed as realization dawned. Skip had had several of Mary Clare's receipts in his file and more than one of them had been for dental services—that unpronounceable name on the invoice that Josie was going to look up online later was no doubt a bridge.

"It was hers," Ryan said. "I *know* it was Mary Clare Blake's. Those things have serial numbers on them. You can look that stuff up."

True enough.

She gestured at the bag that Drew was still holding up, examining it in the sunlight, as it were. "Where did you get this?"

"I found it when I was working at Smiley's, like ten years ago. I used to bus tables, scrub floors, wash dishes—all the crap jobs. But I mean, I was in high school and I was kind of an asocial bastard. Didn't have any friends or manners. I was sixteen. I was lucky they even gave me a job I could walk to, you know? I didn't have a car and it was close to my mom's house.

"I got there one day after school—the restaurant was closed up on Mondays—to do ash duty. That's when we shoveled out most of the ash from the fire pit. I was all into helping out because I thought maybe if I stuck around and did an amazing job, I could get moved up to the waitstaff or maybe bartend like I do now. I could start getting some tips and make some real money because I wanted to buy a car. Get my own transportation. So I was real thorough, you know. I cleaned that pit like you wouldn't believe. And down in the bottom under all those layers, this popped up. It wasn't even melted. I don't know how it wasn't. Maybe it was insulated under all that ash, like the ash was a blanket."

"And you kept it this long without telling anyone?"

Josie had trouble believing he could have just pushed such a gruesome discovery out of his mind like that until now. It had been a decade, for crying out loud. Who keeps a filthy dental bridge in a keepsake box for ten years? Rabbit's foot. Scout badges. Old journal. School pictures. But a dental bridge of a high-profile missing woman?

Not unless he's been planning to blackmail someone.

"At first, I didn't know what to make of it. I mean, it was gross and I almost threw it out. I cleaned if off and put it in this box of stuff I have at home. I tried not to think about it for a while, but it was always in the back of my mind. It had to have been hers, right? I mean, by the time I was working there, she'd been missing for, like, ten years or something. People weren't out searching for her anymore. It didn't seem that urgent."

Not unless you're a mother waiting for a sign that her child is still alive...

"I actually did forget about it for a long time—until you mentioned it the other night. So it's kind of your fault. I mean, because of you. If you hadn't really pushed me about why I quit, I probably wouldn't have started thinking about it again. But then I remembered I had this in that box in my closet...Could it even last that long in the fire pit? I mean, would it melt or something?"

"I don't know how much heat one of those can take," Josie said. She looked at Drew for his opinion.

"It's probably porcelain fused to metal," he said, holding the baggie closer to his face so he could examine it.

Gag. So gross.

His face was alight with pure, intellectual curiosity. "The center part looks like two whole fake teeth—I think those are called pontic teeth, or dummy teeth—and they're attached to crowns on either side that would hold the whole thing in place permanently. Not one of those bridges you could just pop out like a denture, but one that was fixed in place like any other crown." He held it at arm's length. "And it kind of looks like upper front teeth, if I had to guess. Just by the size, shape, and uniformity. I'm no dentist, though. We'd need an expert to confirm all that."

Okay, then.

Mary Clare, the former beauty queen, had a dental bridge for her upper front teeth? In what kind of tussle does a socialite get her teeth knocked out? Josie's mind flew to all kinds of dark speculation. A DUI, perhaps. Or a fight? Or maybe passing out while on medication…

She stared at the baggie. She was absolutely willing to believe, based on the dental receipts and coincidence of finding the bridge in the ashes of the fire pit at Smiley's, that these were Mary Clare's front teeth. She knew that when she eventually gave the bridge to Skip Richmond, he would be able to track down the serial number on the piece of dental work and tie it back to whoever made it.

She needed to know the very specific course of events that had led to the bridge ending up there. A person wouldn't wander around without it. How had Mary Clare lost her bridge in the pit? How had she lost her real teeth in the first place?

Billy Blake would be the person to ask. If only she weren't dreading talking to him.

After Ryan left them to go clock in on his shift, walking with a lighter step, she and Drew got into their rental car and turned north toward Leandro. Drew rode shotgun because this was her second time going to Smiley's—if she didn't count the return trip she'd taken with Officer Louis, Leandro's finest boy in blue—so she knew where they were headed.

He'd turned on the public radio station and found an old recording of *Austin City Limits* with Johnny Cash singing about walking the line for his beloved, which made her think of that passionate conversation she'd heard on the voicemail tape, about how devoted Billy had sounded as he tried to help his troubled wife. And how very distraught Mary Clare had been. Out of nowhere, Josie's eyes filled up, and she blinked rapidly.

Somehow, that weight Ryan had been carrying around with him had been transferred to Josie's shoulders, and she felt the heaviness all the way in the pit of her stomach, almost as if she'd eaten something bad. She knew it was emotional, something she was over-wrought with these days. She wasn't sleeping well, she assumed Drew would be upset with her when he wasn't, and she jumped at shadows, especially when she was alone. If it hadn't been for Lizzie, venturing into the Blake house would have been a fiasco. Speaking of which...

"You should have seen this house last night," she told Drew as she merged onto the freeway. "It was amazing. It was all beautiful stone, symmetrical structure with a chandelier that would fit in Buckingham Palace, a massive spiral staircase, and this huge round part of it that went up through the center. Like a tower with a round roof."

"What, like a pergola?"

She squinted at him. "A pergola is type of covered patio."

"Oh, so a cupola?"

"Yes! Oh, my God, yes. A cupola." Her heart gave a warm thump.

"Were you scoping out our retirement home?"

She gave a rueful laugh. "Only if we have an extra five or six million lying around by then."

He whistled and turned down the radio. "Yikes. Pretty nice, then?"

"It had an elevator."

"Well that's perfect for when we're old and decrepit."

Her jaw went a little slack.

Well, crap. Leave it to the doctor and his aging clientele to think of that.

"That's exactly what it was for." She banged on the steering wheel, causing an accidental honk. Ahead, the woman in the minivan with the Coexist bumper sticker glared in her side mirror at them and flipped her middle finger.

"What?"

She rubbed her wrist where the black beaded bracelet chafed. She still hadn't taken it off to look underneath despite having showered. Talk about being in denial.

"The elevator at the house was for an older resident. That, combined with this horrible pink room I found—seriously, you would have barfed at all of the flower patterns—and the floral patterns of hers and Mary

190

Clare's dresses in the family portrait. That was Bunny's fashion sense, no doubt about it. I think they were planning for Mary Clare's mother to live with them."

"Wait, you're talking about Bunny Rogers, that crazy woman in the interview transcript?"

She gave him a sidelong glance. "You're a fast reader."

"You were asleep for a long time."

"Okay. Fair enough."

She slowed the car as the brake lights ahead of them all went red. They ended up neck and neck, inching forward with the woman who had flipped them off just miles earlier. She pointedly refused to look at them.

"So, they made a mother-in-law suite. Is that so bad?"

"That's not the only room they made. There was a freaky Jane Eyre room as well."

"What do you mean, a hidden ex-wife in the attic?"

"Hidden, yes. But not an ex-wife, just a wife. I think Mary Clare lived in that storage room. Maybe even all those years she was supposedly missing. There were prescriptions in there and newspapers dated years after she had supposedly vanished. I don't think it was against her will. There weren't any big locks or bars. It just seemed like someone's crazy old reclusive aunt had lived there."

"I don't get it," Drew said. "If so many people were out looking for her, why would she hide?"

Because she was sick? Depressed? Agoraphobic?

"That's a darned good question."

CHAPTER 32

On the rest of the way to Smiley's, Josie filled in Drew with the rest of what she'd found out so far, including Marion's rental agreement and hanging out with Lizzie, the newly minted ghost hunter.

"Ghosts, huh?" he said.

Josie shrugged. "I never saw any last night, but that doesn't mean they weren't there."

"Really," he said, totally deadpanning. "You, of all people, are going to be optimistic and open-minded about the existence of ghosts?"

"What do you mean, me of all people? I *am* open-minded. Well, more about trying interesting food combinations or an unknown wine label. But, heck, even though the existence of spirits that walk the earth seems far-fetched and, I might say, kind of ridiculous, who am I to deny the excitement of a person who's really into it? Just because I don't have proof of it doesn't mean I'm going to roll my eyes and snark at other people."

She scratched her wrist where her bracelet had started up a fierce itch, like it was a lie detector that had caught her telling a doozy. Great, just what she needed. An accessory that was a moral watchdog.

So, fine, she still didn't believe in ghosts. But she did believe in karma. And if Billy had killed Mary Clare, possibly in the restaurant by the fire pit...*or in the fire pit....* Ew. She shivered and rubbed her wrist again.

"What's going on with your arm there? I saw it was kind of black last night."

She stared at where she rested it on top of the steering wheel. Other than the making her want to scratch like a dog with a hot-spot, it seemed normal to her. At least it didn't sting anymore.

"Huh. That's funny. It doesn't hurt, but I must have burned it worse that I thought." She hung it over her other arm so he could see it better while she kept her eyes on the road. "Can you take it off and look at what's underneath?"

Dating a doctor had its advantages, like checking out her bumps and bruises without that annoying co-pay. That, and constantly reminding her not to Google her ailments because, wow, that was a quick trip to Crazytown on the Hypochondria Bullet Train.

He fumbled with the bracelet's tiny clasp and slid it off. She was busy for a minute or two, changing lanes to avoid a slow truck, but then had to wait to maneuver around a clump of cars all going the exact same speed across all three lanes of traffic. She paused to grumble at them, "What we have here is a failure to communicate." It took her a while to realize he was still silently examining her wrist.

"What?" she asked, casting him a quick glance out of the corner of her eye.

He didn't answer, so she twisted her bare wrist so she could see it.

On the outside of her wrist, like a watch face, was the burned impression of the coin from the bracelet. She now had the red outline of a Romany, or gypsy, love charm on her skin. She'd been branded. Permanently.

Guess I don't need to buy a souvenir from this trip.

"Hey, little missy, you came back," DJ said, greeting Josie at the counter at Smiley's. "You come in one more day this week and you're gonna have a permanent spot over there next to Lefty Braunfels."

A grouchy old geezer in overalls, bald but for some nearly transparent white fuzz on his head, waved at her to a chorus of cackles at his table. She wasn't certain, but Lefty might've had fewer teeth than Marion, and she wondered how he was fairing with the pile of ribs on his plate. He shouted, "She's more than welcome anytime—she's a darn sight prettier than you, that's for sure."

"Yeah, thanks for that, old man," DJ said, taking off his cap and wiping the sweat off his pink forehead. "Keep 'em coming. Iron-clad ego over here."

"Good, 'cuz you're going to need it with that face," one of Lefty's cohorts shouted to more hooting from his table mates.

"Is this your fella?" DJ asked her.

Maybe it was her imagination, but his smile didn't quite reach his eyes as he looked Drew over. Then they did that male aggressively hearty handshake thing over the counter while she tried not to roll her eyes.

"We came here to eat. I've been chatting up the beans. Hard to get them out of your mind when you start craving them. I can't tell if it's the brown sugar or the bacon, but they're addictive. And I was also wondering if Billy Blake would be open to talking with me. I'll be respectful, of course. Just wanted to check and see."

She had to inhale a bit before she said that last part. The previous time she'd stood in this spot and encountered Billy, she ended up with black spots floating in front of her eyes. Her heart rate was already jacked up into hypertensive range. She was going to need a geriatric prescription from Drew. If Billy was in a temper today, she might be better off avoiding him, although her time here was running out. If she wanted to confront him, she needed to do it now.

And by "confront," I mean ask a couple questions and then hightail it out of here. Maybe even leave the state.

"Sorry to say, he went out of town for a couple days. He's on a road trip." DJ looked at her with a slight question in his expression, one fair eyebrow hiked up just a tad. "Something I can help you with?"

"Was this a planned trip?" It seemed weird to take off on the spur of the moment when he'd just been so angry about the vandalism painted on the side of the restaurant. But maybe he'd had an itinerary set before that had happened. She noted, also, that she breathed a little more steadily now that she knew he wasn't in the building.

What a wussy. When had this happened to her?

Actually, she knew the answer to that.

"Nah, sometimes he just likes to drive to blow off some steam. Eat some good food in other cities where people don't know him or his history too well."

DJ hadn't been around during the time in question when Mary Clare had vanished, but maybe he did have some insight about his boss. She might be able to finesse some details out of him—she glanced at Drew, who was looking at Smiley's GM with suspicion — if she could get the dogs to call off their pissing match.

"What do you say?" she asked DJ. "You want to sit for a while and have lunch with us?"

He seemed to think about it for a minute as he eyed Drew.

"Let me grab a pitcher of Bud."

CHAPTER 33

"We met someone who used to work here. A guy named Ryan," Josie said with what she hoped was nonchalance.

They'd settled in at a corner table with a platter of pulled pork, slices of that ubiquitous doughy white bread, and a side of beans. She took a sip of her beer while she waited for him to answer. Budweiser was never at the top of her list of things to drink, but she was being polite. Plus, it was draft, which made it a little more palatable. Drew was playing the part of her silent bodyguard, though the eye daggers he shot at DJ spoke volumes.

Seriously. She wanted to kick him under the table, but she also needed to concentrate.

"Hmm. Doesn't ring a bell. Maybe it was before my time here."

She wasn't absolutely sure, but there might have been a slight hesitation before he'd replied, so she pressed the matter.

"He's a shorter blond guy. Kinda artsy. Wears weird stuff like leather wristbands or sometimes gloves. He would've been a kid when he worked here. After school bus boy type of worker." When DJ shrugged again, she said, "I guess he wasn't here long. How many years have you worked here?"

"Ah, Billy and I go way back. I've been here and there over the years."

"Way back, like back-back?" she asked.

Was it possible he'd *actually* been around while Mary Clare was alive?

He cleared his throat and swiped a hand across the back of his neck. "What is it you want to know?"

Her brain was churning, probably giving off smoke from her ears as she raked over the details that had come across her path the last couple of days. But there were still a few things that didn't make sense...like who

DJ was and where he'd come from. She hadn't missed his evasion of her question.

"I'm sorry if this is rude," she said, "but what does 'DJ' stand for?" She figured she'd look him up when she got back to the hotel. Maybe even ask Skip Richmond to work his research magic and see what he could find out. Surely DJ was on a few public registers somewhere. Maybe even Facebook or Instagram…though he didn't exactly seem the social media type.

"It doesn't stand for anything. It just says 'DJ' on my driver's license. That's the God's honest truth."

"Your parents gave you just initials that weren't short for anything?"

He gave a humorless grin. "Well, now, I didn't say that, did I?"

More evasion, cloaked in cockiness. Red flags were fully flying in her mind. His attitude was all swagger and none of the friendliness from before when it had just been her. She wanted to get back to that easy rapport they'd had previously, but she didn't think it was possible while Drew was there glowering at him.

Now she kicked him under the table. When he jumped and rubbed his shin, she tipped her head toward the door, hoping he'd get the hint and go take a stroll outside. He frowned at her, then at the door, but stayed put, adding a confused shrug.

Darn it.

"Seriously, you weren't even named after anyone? Just DJ?" she asked, wondering if it was a country thing. "Does it go better with your last name or something?"

"Nah," he said, and now the grin came back, the cocky bastard, "but it does keep 'em guessing."

"Hey, DJ," the guy who'd taken over the front counter hollered. "Phone for you."

"Pardon me," he told them. He tapped their table with two knuckles before he walked away, saying over his shoulder, "You two enjoy your meal. Don't forget, it's on me."

Well, if that wasn't a dismissal, Josie didn't know what was.

She hadn't touched her beer after the first sociable sip she'd taken while DJ was sitting with them. Staring at her plate, she couldn't muster up the desire to take a bite, though it looked the same as it had the other day when she'd enjoyed it. Just as she was debating how to ask Drew, politely, to take a walk, DJ's voice rose up over the lunchtime din of the restaurant.

"What in hell are you talking about?" he shouted into the phone.

Her eyebrows shot up as she turned to look. The entire restaurant had fallen silent. Even the table of old-timers had put down their beers and listened with heads tilted, exchanging glances with each other.

His side of the conversation consisted mostly of cursing and *whats* and *whens*. Then he slammed down the phone and stood there staring at it with his hands on his hips. His face was a mask of tension, and a florid pink flush had taken over his entire neck and face up into his fair hair line. One of his large meaty hands swept across his mouth as he visibly tried to gather himself.

"What's going on?" Josie approached the counter.

He shook his head. "I don't even know where to begin. The Sheriff says Billy's house burned down this morning. Not much left standing of the west side. Major damage to the rest. They're questioning some bum about it, but the guy was so beaten up they took him to the hospital. And now they're looking for Billy—but I know for a fact Billy is out of town. He called me from El Paso early this morning. That's about an eight hour drive."

Josie's heart sank. Sweet, sassy, vulnerable Marion beaten up? How could anyone want to hurt someone so painfully vulnerable? And Billy's big, beautiful mansion charred and in ruins? No more Errol Flynn staircase and crystal chandelier. She wanted to cry. Or cuss a blue streak and hit someone.

Not good. Not good at all.

"Why are we going to the hospital instead of the house?" Drew asked. "I mean, yes, I'm concerned about the well-being of the person who got hurt—doctor here, obviously. I just want to know why *you're* more concerned about him than any potential clues at the fire."

He has a point. This diversion off my single-minded track must seem out of character to him. Fair, but ouch.

He was driving now that this was a new neighborhood for both of them and she had wanted to call Skip. She held up a finger as his voicemail picked up. "Just a sec."

"Hi, it's Josie," she said. "You probably already heard about the fire at the Blake house this morning, but also there was a man…person at the house who was badly beaten." She went on to explain, as best as she could, who Marion was and what he was doing at the house. It was possible Skip already knew about Marion, or at least had either seen or heard of him before, since he was hard to miss tooling around downtown on his bicycle in his string bikini.

After she hung up, she explained to Drew, "Marion saved my bacon the other night. He could've let the cop take us in, but he didn't. That's a code of honor I can only hope to understand one day. I'm not even going to attempt to emulate it. I just want to see if I can do something, if he needs any help."

Seriously. The guy was homeless, *literally* homeless, again now that the fire had probably burned up his lounge chair. Going to the hospital to see how he was doing was the very least she could do. Maybe he needed something that she could help with. She just pictured him there, all bruised and bandaged, attached to beeping machines, and something in her cold, shriveled chest felt like it cracked.

"I think you may have a heart after all," Drew said. He said it as if he were joking, and the side of his mouth crooked upward, but she took his words as truth. She wasn't entirely sure what the state of her insides was underneath her crusty, hard shell. Maybe she was soft and squishy—sentimental—on the inside. All she knew was that she couldn't bear it if Marion were lying alone and broken in a hospital bed with no shoulder to cry on.

Her phone rang while she was trying to gather back together her soft, nougat center.

"Josie," a voice who was not Skip said.

"Greta," Josie said, stalling while she tried to remember whether she'd actually called the woman when she'd been thinking about it before.

No. No, I did not. This proves she has ESP. I should think more quietly next time.

"When you return to Boston, I have a favor to ask of you. Normally, I wouldn't bother you, but I didn't want you to come home and immediately make arrangements for another trip. I know your blogging career allows you to move about easily."

That was the most Josie had ever heard her employer say in any one stretch.

"You miss me, don't you?" Josie asked.

Greta was silent. It was possible the woman didn't know how to respond to an open statement of affection, not having experienced it much in her life. On the other hand, she probably thought Josie was being sarcastic, which she might have been. Even she didn't know.

"Incidentally," Josie continued, "I have a question for you."

"Yes?" Greta sounded a little too eager to enter back into the normal parameters of their relationship. Namely, to get back to talking about work instead of *feelings*. Josie was on board with that. However, it was fun to taunt someone even more out of touch with herself than she was.

"Do you know of a Houstonite named Bunny Rogers? She'd be in her sixties—"

"Yes."

"Yes?"

"I met her once in person at an American Red Cross function in Washington, D.C. in the early 1990's. We were seated at the same table, so we conversed for some time. I thought she was a very cold woman, though she behaved perfectly sociably."

Dang. Anyone the ice queen Greta Williams assessed to be cold had to be sub-zero.

"She had three sons and a daughter," Josie said, intending to ask if Bunny had been more of a Patsy Ramsey questionably murderous mother or a Carrie Fisher stage mother extreme.

Greta paused. "I heard about the misfortune with her daughter some years later. I now feel a certain empathy for her."

Now it was Josie's turn to pause awkwardly.

"Sorry I can't be much more help than that. I met her only one time."

"Of course," Josie said. "And I'll text you as soon as I'm back in town."

"Thank you. I prefer that to phone calls."

And that is why we get along so well.

"She sounds good," Drew said, not meaning it. He put on his signal to turn into the hospital parking lot.

Josie had to snort as she rested her chin on her chest for a minute. Though she didn't actually know if she were laughing at herself or Greta.

Hospitals used to give her the willies, but her frequent, sometimes unplanned visits to them were helping her get over her fears. She guessed it was a kind of immersion therapy of an unplanned nature. All the same, her heart rate hardly ticked up as she caught the attention of the receptionist.

"I'm looking for Marion, the beating victim from the Billy Blake house fire over in Bee Caves," she said, realizing she didn't know Marion's last name or if he even had one. He could've been one of those one-name people like Cher, Madonna, or RuPaul—or was that two names?

"Are you a reporter?" the woman asked. She had a sticky note stuck to her sleeve and her hand on her desk telephone, probably to call security, before Josie could speak.

Oh crap. Was this one of those family-only situations? Was Josie going to have to lie to get in to see Marion? Or was she going to have to pull out her P.I. license again? She cleared her throat, ready to spread some kind of ferocious B.S. all over the woman's desk.

"Excuse me," Drew said, "I'm Dr. Hornsby. I've been called in as an independent consultant by the victim's doctor." He had come up behind Josie. He pulled out his hospital badge from home and flashed it at the woman.

"Oh!" she said. Flustered, she reached for a pen lodged behind her ear. "This is highly unusual. You're supposed to check in down the hall. I'm just a hospital volunteer, not a Human Resources officer. I'm not really equipped to handle consultants."

Though she still looked hassled, with gray curls escaping the clip on the crown of her head, she batted her eyes at Drew in appreciation. Josie felt a spike of annoyance.

Oh, how the tables have turned.

"It's all right. Just point us in the right direction and I'll find the right people to talk to and the forms I need to sign," he said, his voice ringing with an authority that made even Josie want to eat a more balanced diet and cut back on caffeine.

He continued to bluff until the poor woman directed them to the nurses' station upstairs. They followed color coded stripes on the wall around the corner and located the elevator bank. She pressed the button for the second floor, and they waited in silence.

"Dr. Hornsby?" she asked as the steel doors slid shut.

"Sorry. *Mandolin Rain* was playing in the lobby. Bruce Hornsby. It was the first thing I could think of under pressure. I'm not good at this— I've never lied like that before. I could lose my license to practice medicine if someone finds out." He paused. "If I get fired, can I be your professional sidekick?"

"It really doesn't pay." She listened to the bing-bong of the elevator passing the second floor. "Can you actually play the mandolin?"

"No, but I know all the words to *Mandolin Rain*."

"First chance we get, we are getting you drunk and doing karaoke."

On the third floor, they followed more color stripes on the walls to the nurses' desk, where Skip Richmond was talking to two police officers.

"Josie," he said, a thin smile on his wrinkled face, when he spotted her. "I got your message, but I was already here. Figured I'd run into you."

"Hey, I know you," one of the cops said. "Josie Tucker. From last night."

She recognized him as the officer who had come to the Blake house in the middle of the night. So, he had read her I.D. after all, the sneaky bastard with his aw-shucks attitude. She'd been right to be wary of him.

"Uh, hi," she said, not quite sure if he was about to arrest her for assault and battery, or possibly arson.

To her surprise, he gestured to a nearby room with a tip of his chin. "Marion's over there. He mentioned he was hoping you'd come visit him. Honestly, I wasn't sure where you were staying until Skip here saved me the trouble of tracking you down. For an out-of-towner, you sure do get around."

She thanked him and finally thought to read his name tag, which said, "Handsome."

CHAPTER 34

Marion was frail and plain without his makeup and finery. Propped up on a mountain of pillows with a nurse swabbing his arm with an alcohol wipe, he looked as dainty as a baby chick in a nest. Even a decorated war vet could look vulnerable clothed in nothing but a paper-thin hospital johnny. Josie knew all too well the feeling of having nothing but threadbare cotton ties between her and flashing a full moon to a room of strangers. Despite his beaten and bruised face and looking like someone's malnourished granddad, Marion was still full of sass.

"Sorry, girly," he told the nurse, lisping even worse than before. "My veins on that side are shot, plain and simple, even though I've been clean for years. Tell me a homophobic joke and make the angry ones on my forehead pop out. That'll help ya."

The nurse chortled and switched arms, getting his IV changed out in a matter of minutes.

"Honey, baby," he cried when he noticed Josie. "I've missed you."

Both of his eyes were almost swollen shut and already purple. The right one had a pool of red in it that probably looked worse than it felt — at least, she hoped so, because it looked disgusting. One of his cheeks had a trail of stitches high up on the bone. He had a bandage on his forehead, lips so swollen a Kardashian would be jealous, a torn earlobe, and bandages wrapped around his entire rib cage that made him look like he was wearing a tube top under his front-opening johnny.

"Oh, Marion," she said, her chest tight with regret, almost to the point of pain, as she pulled up a chair next to his bedside. "What happened to you?"

"You will never believe it. About an hour or so after you two and Officer Gorgeous vamoosed, I was sound asleep in my chair having probably the best dream ever — shoe shopping at a store that didn't want my money—when this stunted Nazi skinhead shows up and starts beating the ever lovin' stuffing out of me. I didn't know what to think. I'll tell you *what I did think*. I was back living on the streets in Tulsa again, that's what. My dream turned into a nightmare real quick." The word *stuffing* came out sounding like *th'tuffin*.

Josie bit her lip. If she and Lizzie had stayed just an hour longer, they might have prevented this from happening. Three against one, even if the three were woefully unqualified to defend themselves, were better odds than Marion had faced.

"Did you get a look at the guy?"

"He was short and blond, like one of those baby Nazis they used to put in Nazi school before they could be real soldiers. That's all I know. After that, all I saw were his fists."

Short? That ruled out both Billy Blake and DJ. The two of them were both giants compared to Josie, and shortness wasn't a characteristic a person could fake.

"Did he say anything to you?" she asked.

"Just the usual stuff," Marion hedged, smoothing his bed sheet.

"What do you mean?" She wasn't sure what he meant, but she had a rough idea.

"He said *eff you* a million times and insulted my sexual orientation," Marion said. "Not like we were swapping secrets and having a sleepover. He just assumed I'm gay. *Who does that* anymore? This isn't the Don't Ask, Don't Tell Dark Ages. If he wanted to know that bad, he could have just asked me. At least then he'd know whether he was assaulting the right type of person."

Was Marion gay? She didn't know either. Whatever. It didn't matter to her. "How did you get away?"

"I started throwing things at him—that jerk broke my tiara, too. My beautiful crown. I could almost cry. But then I got mad and hit him with my acrylic platforms. *Pow*. Right in the head. He was coming after me *for real* after I did that. I thought it was worse than that other time—long story short, I thought I might as well kiss my butt goodbye. Then there was a big boom. The house shook like a tornado was coming through. We saw smoke and the patio roof started to fall over. He got scared and ran."

Josie glanced behind her, glad to find both Drew and the police officer standing in the doorway. By their expressions, they had heard Marion's statement as well. She turned back to him. "Is there anything else you can remember about the guy? You said he was short and had fair hair? About how old was he?"

"Young, young, young. So young, I don't even remember being that age."

Josie got a bad feeling in the pit of her stomach. "Like, how old would you say?"

"Barely old enough to grow a beard, though he was trying." His own beard was even more rumpled than before and still had some blood in it.

"So he had some facial hair?"

"Yeah, one of those little fake looking goatees. But you could barely see it because it was almost invisible. It almost looked like crotch hair, if you know what I'm saying."

She nodded. Unfortunately, she knew exactly what he was describing. *And who.*

"Anything unusual about his hands?"

"No, not that I can remember, other than his knuckles connecting with my face."

Hmm, Josie hadn't been expecting that. The last time she'd seen Ryan, he'd had black fingernail polish, but maybe it was a smashed nail from working with his steel sculptures. Nevertheless, she was pretty certain Marion's attacker had been him.

"Is there anything you need that I can help you with?"

Where would he go after this? Who would take care of him if he needed help?

"Aw, you're a sweetheart" — *thweehar* — "but as long as I'm here, I get some good meals and cable TV. I'm all set for now. And believe me, girly, this isn't the worse shape I've ever been in."

"You get all that?" Josie asked the cop as they exited the room and lingered in the wide hospital hallway, the squeaky clean floors shining up at them like a white, MRSA-filled river. She could feel a strong case of the hospital willies coming on. She'd need a gallon of hand soap and a 30-minute Silkwood shower at this rate.

Hospitals. Yuck, man.

Skip hung back to ask Marion a couple more questions before his painkillers kicked in. He'd refused opiates, so Josie didn't know what they were giving him. Every tiny thing she learned about him made her like him just a bit more.

"Go ahead and fill in some of the blanks for me, would you?" the cop that Marion—and now Josie—had taken a shine to asked her. She made a mental note to ask him where Marion could find some people to lean on after the hospital kicked him out. He'd mentioned some kind of shelter the night before. Maybe they had a place for Marion. She just couldn't handle picturing him living on a street corner, wounded, after seeing his setup poolside at Billy's mansion.

"It was Ryan who attacked him, wasn't it?" Drew asked. "We were just talking to that little creep this morning."

"I think so." She turned to the cop to explain. "We suspect the bartender from the Omni downtown has a grudge against Billy for firing him. He also gave us this tooth bridge this morning, claiming he found it at Smiley's in the fire pit when he was working there almost a decade ago." Josie handed the dental appliance over, relieved to be rid of it. The thing was disgusting, even though it was possibly the closest piece of evidence of the missing woman so far. It carried a lot of bad mojo as far as Josie was concerned—which wasn't the same thing as being haunted. It just felt...nasty.

The cop took the baggie and also wrote down a few things in a notepad. Josie felt confident he'd follow up on some of the leads they gave him, not only judging by his attentiveness, but by the way he'd treated Marion the previous night, as if he were a human being. As wary as she'd been of cops in the past, she found that she was extremely in favor of this particular one.

Josie neglected to mention the tooth bridge to Skip when he eventually came out of Marion's room. She figured his possessiveness with the file was enough to put him over the top when it came to something that came directly from the victim's mouth. She didn't want to witness that kind of enthusiasm over something so nauseating and personal a possession as that. But she did feel bad about it since Skip had trusted her with so much information.

"I don't get it," Skip said. "Why would someone beat up our beauty queen in there and then fire bomb the Blake house? Or...did he set the explosion to go off and then accidentally discover Marion sleeping next to the pool?"

Josie had a million questions herself. *Had Ryan been working alone? Did someone hire him?* All of this violence and destruction couldn't have been the result of a simple vendetta against Billy for firing him.

"Crap," she said as another mini-realization struck. "Ryan had black paint on his fingers. I'd bet you a million bucks he was the one who painted the graffiti on the side of the restaurant."

CHAPTER 35

"Who *is* this kid and why is he suddenly behind everything about this case?" Skip asked, his normally dry, wrinkled brow furrowing even more. He had a Styrofoam cup of coffee in his hand.

He had a reason to be confused. Ryan probably hadn't even been born yet while Skip had been busy assembling his beloved case file about Mary Clare. Ryan wasn't even a blip on Skip's radar, so there was no way he could have factored him into the puzzle of Billy Blake's messed up life.

"Ryan was a busboy at Smiley's a long time ago. He quit."

"And…?" Skip asked.

"And nothing," Josie said. "He was just a busboy. Product of a single-parent household. Currently works as a bartender downtown while he creates ironic steel sculptures."

"That makes no sense. Why would he graffiti the restaurant, act like a homophobic skinhead and beat up Marion, and set the house on fire—and do all of this decades later?"

"I don't know."

Even with the added evidence of Ryan possessing the dental bridge and possibly resenting Billy Blake for having anger issues—and Josie stirring up the subject while chatting with him in the hotel restaurant—there didn't seem to be enough that was trigger-worthy to set him off all these years later.

It made *absolutely no sense.*

Unless…something else was motivating him. What would a young starving artist want? A showing in a gallery. Connections in the art world. Cold, hard cash. All definitely possibilities. And all ones that could be traced in time, through money trails or sudden and unexpected success in Ryan's future. However, Josie didn't have time for that. Two days remained in her Texas vacation. Her clock was ticking down, and fast.

She turned to Drew. "How about we go check out the house now?"

Any evidence left at the house might help another piece of the puzzle fall into place. Right now, however, it seemed like she might never find the missing parts.

The drive through the twisted roads of Billy's neighborhood was just as challenging in daylight as it had been the night before, mainly because Josie had been a passenger in Lizzie's car the first time. But what made it difficult were the lack of road markers and recognizable landmarks. Every gnarled live oak tree looked the same as the last.

Skip followed their rental car in his ancient Datsun truck, which looked like it was about to be eaten through by rust. She'd offered him a ride with them, but he'd declined, saying he needed to run errands afterward. As she glanced in her review mirror at him, she wondered what he did in his spare time. Hot yoga, maybe. That would dry a body out faster than he could say, "Namaste, electrolytes."

She rounded the last corner, expecting to see nothing but the burned out husk of the house, like Thornfield Hall in *Jane Eyre*. Instead, nothing seemed out of place from the front view of the house. The tower thingy — cupola — was still intact, flanked on either side by the stone wings of the house. Other than yellow police tape winding around the entire front perimeter, it didn't look any different than before.

"Didn't DJ say the house was pretty much destroyed? He said the west side was almost entirely gone and — oh."

She was cut off in mid-sentence as they followed the slightly rounded curve of the driveway and she saw the front of the house was nearly all that was left other than the garage. Charred half-walls stood in a shaky semblance of the house's former footprint. The pristine landscaping had been stomped, chopped, and otherwise demolished by both debris and, Josie assumed, firefighters, people doing their darnedest to try to save the structure.

"Wow," she said as they climbed out to join Skip beside their cars. They stood in silence, mouths hanging open. *Now* she was seeing ghosts —

the specter of the majestic house in her mind's eye as it had stood in its full glory just the night before.

The smell of smoke and damp ash still hung in the air, along with a weird chemical odor she hadn't been expecting. What was that? Insulation? Fibers from inside the house? She'd never been on the scene of a structure fire, and all she knew was that it definitely didn't smell like a barbecue smokehouse — which was savory spices, meat, and clean wood fire. No, this was…ruin. Destruction. *Entropy*. Chaos and disorder.

"We shouldn't go any closer," Drew, the voice of reason, said.

Skip raised his eyebrow at Josie as if to say, *Is this Nervous Nelly for real?*

True, the last thing she wanted to do was to interfere with any potential investigation, or get arrested for once again trespassing. Not only was this the site of a possible arson, it was also where Marion had been attacked. Ryan might have left evidence in that matter as well.

But she was here now. And the authorities weren't, at least for the moment.

She took a step toward the house, but Drew laid a hand on her arm.

"It's not about clues or evidence," he said. "It's about your personal safety."

And now would have been a great time to start listening to him, to begin taking his loving advice. Yes, *loving*. But, man, she really wanted to explore the wreckage of the house.

She took one more step with his hand still on her arm.

Behind them, engine noise grew louder as another vehicle pulled up the driveway.

CHAPTER 36

"What in the hell are y'all doing here?" DJ yelled as he climbed out of his truck.

In the passenger seat, Billy Blake sat staring at the ruins of his house, rendered dumb with what Josie took for shock.

"I thought you said Billy was in El Paso," Josie countered, ignoring his question. Obviously, she didn't want to answer his question because they were snooping where they didn't belong.

DJ strode toward them after a cursory glance at his boss. "He was in El Paso this morning. It's an eight-hour drive, but only an hour and a half flight. He left his truck there and caught a flight home after I called him and told him what happened. I just picked him up at the airport. He's kinda shellshocked. Speaking of which—Jesus, Mary, and Joseph." He swept off his baseball cap as he looked at the house. "This is...this is crazy."

She had to agree. Just last night she'd been traipsing around inside of the place with Lizzie, imagining Errol Flynn on the staircase, for crying out loud. *How ridiculous was that?*

"I don't even know what to say," he said. "I mean..."

Billy still sat in the car. He rubbed a hand over his face and paused, covering his mouth, as he blankly stared at the ruins of his mansion. As he slowly got out of the truck, Josie watched the frozen numbness turn him into a statue as he stood on the blacktop of the driveway looking at the wreckage.

Skip had turned away and was speaking to someone on his cell phone. He'd already snapped a few pictures, but it struck Josie as being ghoulish to capture this particular moment in time, though the sun was shining. The bright blue sky made the burnt house stand out in stark relief, conflicting emotions of happy daylight and dead dreams clashing harshly.

After all, Billy and Mary Clare had built this behemoth together, and had at one point moved in with the optimism of newlyweds. Or so Josie imagined. Time and troubles had worn away its newness. Addiction or rifts of the psyche had taken its toll on the couple, whichever problem it had been. But now, it was nothing but a façade barely hiding a life in shambles.

Drew had released his hold on her arm, and she took a couple of cautious steps to the side for a better look at the garage, which seemed mostly untouched. DJ walked with her and Drew paced behind, his steps sharp and tight, tension rolling off him.

She realized how precarious the carved out stone walls of the house were without the rest of their support beams, and she wasn't about to go spelunking through the cavelike blackened timbers in back. She just wanted to peek in the side window of the garage to see if Mary Clare's car was still inside. Though she had poked around inside it by flashlight, she thought maybe, just maybe, she had overlooked something…

Behind them, yet another car pulled into the drive. Officer Gorgeous, this time. He parked his patrol car behind DJ's truck. She could see him through the windshield swiveling his head side to side, warily assessing all them behind his dark sunglasses. She could only imagine what he was telling the dispatcher over his two-way radio. As he exited his vehicle, yet another car pulled up behind his, effectively blocking them all in as if they'd gathered for a backyard wedding…or a funeral procession.

"It's a regular Tupperware party here," DJ said, his voice taut with stress.

This most recent car was a sleek black Lincoln with a livery license plate, the type of car driven by a private limo service. Josie's gut reaction was to wonder what in the world Greta Williams, her sometimes-boss, was doing here at this burned out house in Texas. The woman who got out from the car in her oversized bug-eye sunglasses, however, wasn't Greta.

Well-coifed white hair in what Josie thought resembled a newscaster's hairdo—a solid state, with not a hair out of place—emerged first, followed by the big, round movie star eyewear. The rest of the woman was a woolen, plaid fortress, accessorized by pearls, hose, and black pumps. Despite what Josie thought were balmy late-fall temperatures, this woman was committed to her November attire, body and soul. Make no mistake, though, she was no frumpy matron. She exuded wealth and conservative sensibilities.

Next to Josie, DJ swore. "What's she doing here?"

"Who is that?" Drew asked, confusion evident in his one-eyed squint of suspicion.

But Josie knew—it could only be one person. "It's Bunny Rogers."

DJ stalked toward the older woman and met her just as she caught up to Billy Blake. Josie lightly whacked Skip's arm with the back of her hand as she stared at the trio next to Bunny Rogers's limo. Seeing them together, Josie suddenly knew who he was and why his name, his initials, stood for nothing. Though Billy was taller and broader, the physical resemblance between the two of them was undeniable.

Why didn't I realize it sooner?

Both stood over six feet tall. Though DJ wore his customary farmer's cap, Josie had seen how fair his hair was at the restaurant when he'd swept his hand through it. Billy's hair, though almost white, was also fair. Both men had ruddy skin that tended to turn pinker when they were upset or otherwise riled up. Standing beefy shoulder to beefy shoulder now, they had almost identical posture.

"I don't know what DJ's last name is, but I bet you ten-to-one it's Ruby. How could they not be cousins? Just look at them," she said to Skip. "I think he's Levar Ruby, Billy's first cousin who started Smiley's with him. They had some kind of fight. He up and quit for a while to work in San Antonio."

Josie had learned that whole story earlier in the week from her pink-lipsticked friend, Georgia, who worked at Ruby's, the local barbecue rival of Smiley's. She hadn't been kidding when she'd warned Josie that all the local smokehouses were interrelated. The smokehouses themselves were cousins, in fact.

"Oh for crap's sake," Skip said. "He worked in a club as a deejay. And he calls himself DJ now. Why did I not see it?"

"Well, just look at them. They could be freaking descendants of Thor. I didn't figure it out until just now."

The fact of the matter was, Billy's sheer size and explosive temper intimidated her—enough to the point that she had avoided speaking directly to him. DJ, with his awshucks manner and blond farmer charisma, on the other hand, was friendly and easy to approach. Flirtatious, even. She hadn't had the tiniest blip on her fear radar from him. The difference in their personalities had temporarily blinded her. They were night and day.

This discovery of their familial relationship, however, put a whole new spin on things. If DJ was involved in this latest arson and beating, maybe he was a whole lot more than just Billy's general manager. Maybe he was also his confidante and was privy to exactly what Billy had done with Mary Clare.

As Josie watched the two men and Bunny Rogers a little bit more, she wondered suddenly why the ground was moving. She looked down, catching a weird, undulating feeling of standing in the ocean waves, like a tide was rolling in.

Oh crap, she realized, as the black spots suddenly came into her vision. She was about to pass out.

Not a good time for this. Such an inconvenient moment for panicking.

She looked back at the trio and realized that she'd subconsciously transformed them in her mind into two brothers she'd known in the past—the Williams brothers who had nearly killed her before. In Josie's panic-stricken mind, Bunny had become Greta Williams. While Greta was an ally now, she'd been an imposing matriarch when Josie had first met her.

Take a deep breath. Hold it. Count to twelve. Let it out.

She did her in-and-out breathing trick for two cycles of breaths, but the black spots were still dancing in and out of her vision. Only when she felt Drew's hand on the back of her neck did they start to subside.

"Geeze, I gotta get this taken care of," she muttered, as if her PTSD were the Check Engine light coming on in her car. As if it were that easy.

"You will," he said.

Her doctor. Her life coach. Her best friend. Though she hadn't spoken much about it, he totally knew what she was going through. And he had patiently waited for her to realize she needed to talk with someone and sort her head out. Well, she was ready to get that help now.

Except, just as she had that thought, an explosion ripped through the garage.

Part 5: Ashes

Sometimes when you cook, the magic occurs after the flames die down. Not every piece of meat requires an open flame to achieve tasty perfection.

A traditional Hawaiian pig roast requires that you dig a big hole in the ground and fill it with river rocks, which turn white-hot from the heat. A banana leaf cover locks the heat in until you have a succulent, roasted delicacy.

Carcinogens aside, many cultures have also been known to cook with ash, from South Americans cooking meat or fish in large pits like the Hawaiians. Native Americans used to add some ash to the water when they cooked corn. And it's even used in making cheese.

You could say that ash, in some cases, has the unique quality of giving life after death.

—Josie Tucker, *Will Blog for Food*

CHAPTER 37

Debris rained down around them. The garage—what was left of it—was burning. A plume of dirty smoke blew out sideways from the garage and was taken westward by the wind toward the lake. The side of Josie's face, from temple to jawline, was mashed against the gritty blacktop of the circular drive. Her ears had blown out—temporarily, she hoped—but her eyes were fine. In fact, she'd seen a lot more than she had realized right before the explosion.

"Are you all right?" Drew asked her, though she could barely hear him. He pulled himself up from where he'd been pressed on top of her.

"Did you just…throw yourself on top of me?"

"Yeah, sorry about that. Did I squish you?" He helped her up and brushed some gravel off her cheekbone.

"No, I'm fine." He'd just put himself between her and an exploding building. Like freaking Superman.

"Stay here. I'm going to check on them," he said, heading toward Billy and the others. The police officer was also jogging toward them.

How could he hear anything? Officer Handsome appeared to be barking orders at them, but all she could see was a pantomime of him telling them to stay back—no sound filtered through. She stretched her jaw to try to get some sound to filter through what felt like cotton stuffed in her ears. While she yawned and tugged on an earlobe, she turned to see the charred remains of the garage.

The back wall still stood, which made sense because it was the most reinforced and had previously been attached to the house. However, the front three sides had been fairly well blown out. What was left of Mary Clare's car was a smoldering white-gray pile of bent metal and tires. Half of a blackened silk flower from the heart-shaped wreath fluttered to the ground next to Josie.

The thought crossed her mind in a spine-shriveling sweep that she'd been going over the garage, digging into the toolbox, and dropping her bottom right into the seat of Mary Clare's car. She and Lizzie could have been blown to bits if the bomb had already been planted by then.

"I think I'm having a Gulf War flashback," Skip said, next to her, in a raspy whisper.

She eyed him, looking for the signs of PTSD with which she was personally familiar. Was he seeing the spots in front of his eyes right now? Was his throat closing up? Did his chest feel like he was having a heart attack?

"Are you okay?"

He seemed to consider it, his leathery face taut with worry. Kind of like he was Columbo, mentally patting his trench coat pockets not for his lost keys, but for his emotional stability. Then he relaxed. "Yeah. False alarm. I'm good."

Dang. She knew how that felt, too. Like walking on eggshells around her own frickin' psyche. "What do you know about bombs?"

"Not much. They're violent and noisy and have made it so I haven't gotten a full night of sleep since 1991. This one was for damage, not injury. No nails or projectiles. Maybe an improvised car bomb? If something looks like a bomb and sounds like a bomb, I'm thinking it's not a gas leak or a propane tank blowing up. I'm no expert. Just guessing."

Sounded like some educated guesses to her. Maybe he'd tell her more about that later, but for now, she had something more pressing on her mind. When the explosion had occurred, she'd had her back to the garage. She'd been in prime position to watch the reactions of not only Billy and DJ, but also of Bunny Rogers.

The moment the garage had blown up—the very instant the first rumble had occurred—Billy Blake had lunged toward the garage, only to be held back by DJ, who'd grabbed the big man and enfolded him in his arms, blocking the explosion from his sight. On just the other side of them, a very composed Bunny Rogers had opened her car door and slid back inside.

Before anyone could stop Josie and before her common sense could kick in, she marched over to the limo and rapped on the window. With charred bits of the garage and its contents littering the ground around them, she mashed her fists on her hips and watched the glass slowly lower with a silken whirr.

Her lack of forethought, fueled by anger, made her somewhat blunter than was probably wise when she blurted out, "What the hell do you think you're doing?"

"I beg your pardon. Who are you?"

While Bunny may have matched Josie's boss, Greta Williams, in social stature and dress, the similarities ended there. True, Greta had witnessed some horrible things in her lifetime which should have turned her into an angry and bitter woman. Instead, however, she'd moved forward with her life and put her vast fortune to good use while also meddling in Josie's life as well.

Bunny Rogers seemed to have taken her grief to heart. Her expression was hard and unyielding, a certain meanness reflecting out from her cloudy blue eyes before she lowered her sunglasses over them.

"I'm a private investigator," Josie said. Not that she expected her job to have any sway with this woman.

"How very fine for you."

Granted, the woman had probably conversed with tens, if not hundreds, of reporters and detectives over the decades...all the same, a little decorum would have been appreciated. Then again, Josie had stomped over here and been rude as well.

"Listen, lady, I just saw you turn away from a freaking explosion and nonchalantly check your watch like you suddenly remembered you had a prior dinner engagement at the Driskill Hotel. Normal people don't act like that in the face of something shocking."

Josie felt a hand on her shoulder.

"Do normal people make such angry accusations in the face of violence?" Drew said gently.

She blinked. He thought she was having a PTSD episode because of the explosion? She wasn't the war vet here. She'd survived a shovel attack out in the Arizona desert, not a roadside IED in Kandahar.

Brushing off his hand, she said to Bunny Rogers, "What do you know about this explosion? Do you know who set it? Because you act like maybe you do."

The woman, eyes covered again by her enormous, dark lenses, turned her head away from Josie. Still not quite looking at the smoldering remains of the garage, she stared at the back of the limo driver's head. He certainly was well-trained. Like an automaton, he sat ready for his employer's next command. If Josie had been in his position, she would have had her cell phone out, snapping pictures—especially of her icy-hearted and suspiciously behaved employer. *Screw the job.*

"What about Marion, the homeless man you allowed to sleep here on the patio? Did you have him beaten? Did you purposely endanger his life?"

The slightest of indentations creased Bunny Rogers's forehead. Confusion. Thank goodness the woman hadn't Botoxed recently or her forehead wouldn't be moving, even as minutely as it was now.

So, she didn't know about Marion? Then who paid him to live here?

"And what about selling the house? Was it you who called Cookie Casteñada, the real estate lady, and not Billy?"

Bunny didn't answer, but her lack of surprise on that point confirmed Josie's suspicions. Contrary to outward appearances, it had been Bunny who'd wanted to sell the house, not Billy.

Because Bunny's limo had been the last to arrive, it had a free and clear passageway to the street. As Bunny tapped on the back of the driver's seat and indicated that she wanted to leave, Josie jogged behind the back bumper of the car and blocked its way, smacking her hands on its trunk to make sure the driver—and Bunny—know she was there.

"What are you doing?" Drew asked. He looked as if he wanted to shove her out of harm's way.

"She knows what happened just now. I was staring right at her when the garage blew up. She didn't react. No surprise. No flinch. Nothing."

"Well..." Drew started. "Maybe she's on medication."

Yeah, thanks for that vote of confidence, she thought with a grimace. Was her judgment that unreliable to him thanks to her panic attacks?

Skip came alongside Josie at the back of the limo. "I got this," he said. "Go get her." He stood with his thin arms crossed over his chest, glaring at the driver of the limo in the rearview mirror. Before she could resume her interrogation of Mary Clare's mother, Officer Gorgeous called out to them.

"Hey now," he said, still calm and authoritative as ever, but with a slight edge to his tone. He'd been radioing in for help and now he was, well, policing them. "Ma'am, I need you to step out of the car. You've just witnessed a possible crime and I'll need to get a statement from you."

Perhaps Bunny's Texas-born fatal flaw was an unwavering respect for the uniform. For whatever reason, she obeyed the police officer and opened the door.

Josie sighed with relief. She really had no desire to be run over by a car today. Not even a limo.

CHAPTER 38

Josie relinquished her mental claim on Bunny Rogers and handed her over to the police, figuring that no matter how much she tried to cajole the woman into telling her the truth, Bunny would never cave. After all, she'd had decades to develop her story about her missing daughter and her own alibi.

"Don't get me wrong," Josie said out loud as she picked her way around the debris to DJ and Billy Blake, "I don't think Bunny set up the garage to explode all on her own. Can you imagine her on her hands and knees planting it on the undercarriage? Nah, neither can I. But I *do believe* she hired someone to do it. Probably that kid, Ryan."

The two men stared down at her from their distinct height advantage wearing mirror expressions of wariness and disgust, their fair-skinned faces both scowling at her. Her steps stuttered until she could screw up her courage to resume approaching them.

These are not the Williams brothers. I have too many witnesses. I have a police officer. They won't attack me.

After a deep breath, she pushed forward, hoping no one noticed her hesitation. It probably hadn't been that obvious. Much.

Stay focused on the task at hand.

Billy's added expression of abject misery had her doing a double-take. He rubbed a hand over his face, and Josie wondered if it was possible he'd had that much emotional investment in his wife's car to be this upset. After all, he'd chosen the garage for the location of his shrine to her.

"Why'd she do it?" he asked no one in particular, his voice sounding hoarse and muffled.

"I don't know, Billy," DJ said. And now he looked done in. However, he wasn't looking at the house but at his friend and boss.

"I have to get in there and see what's left," Billy said.

But DJ wouldn't let go of him. "No, you're not going anywhere."

Was Billy *that attached* to his dead wife's car? She'd known people who were car aficionados, but in light of the complete and frighteningly expensive destruction in front of them—the house in utter ruins—the car seemed like it should have been the lesser worry. Wouldn't he have a photo or a smaller memento to remind him of Mary Clare?

DJ said, "It had to have been that little jack-off, Ryan, we had to fire. She got ahold of him somehow and got him to blow it up. Now he's her odd-jobs man."

Holy crap. DJ knew about Ryan? He'd told them he didn't even know who the kid was. How much else was he lying about?

"You're Conrad's son. You're Levar Ruby," she blurted out. She was tired of pussyfooting around what she'd been suspecting for a while now. DJ could avoid her questions all he wanted, but she would get to the bottom of it. His ruddy look, which was so similar to Billy's and, even more so, his dogged loyalty marked him as Billy's cousin.

However, it wasn't DJ who confirmed her suspicions.

"Yes. That was his given name," Billy said, finally looking at her instead of the ruins of his estate. His face was drawn and, well, just *wrecked*. "He's my cousin, but he's closer to me than a brother ever could be. All the things we've been through together."

All what *things?* She wanted an enumerated list. A spreadsheet. A thesis with footnotes and photographic support.

"You asked why she'd do this," she said to Billy. "Why do you think? Why would your mother-in-law lure Marion into staying here and then try to kill him?"

"What are you talking about?" Billy frowned. She noticed he didn't ask who Marion was. "I hired him to live here. I had a bunch of rental forms left over from one of her other properties. She wanted to sell the place, but I didn't. I was willing to do anything to stop her, even hire some crazy guy to stay here. But I guess that wasn't going to stop her from burning the place down. All my memories are in there…or they were."

Well. Thanks to Bunny's signature on the lease form, she hadn't seen that kink in her theory coming. But it did clear a few things up.

"*You* hired Marion?" she said again, just to make sure she was hearing Billy correctly.

"Yeah, he's an icon around town. Well-recognized with his shoes and bikinis and whatnot. Having him stay here at the house would make it tough for anyone to sell it, especially in this snotty neighborhood."

Josie didn't bother to mention bunco night and how the neighbors had taken a shine to Billy's tenant, contrary to his plan. "And your mother-in-law is so intent on getting rid of the house that she'd rather see it burned to the ground than let you keep it?"

None of this made sense. Billy *wanted* his house. Bunny Rogers burned it to the ground, most likely using Ryan the bartender as her go-to firebug.

Unless...

"Oh my God." She couldn't keep the words from slipping out of her mouth.

Thunderbolt brainstorm. Big time.

"What is it?" Skip said, walking up behind her. "You figured something out, didn't you? I knew you would. My instincts are rarely wrong and I knew this about you."

Staring at her, Billy had turned pale, his pinkish skin draining of its usual color. DJ, on the other hand, looked grim for once. Gone was his charismatic lopsided smile that had drawn her into conversation over the counter at Smiley's. In its place was a downturned mouth and a furrowed brow as threatening as any stormy sky. As she glanced back and forth between them, the details sorted themselves out in her head.

Mary Clare was here.

Not alive. Not in the well-searched house or car, which had both been thoroughly gone over by investigators at the time, including the creepy storage room with the bad smell. They could have searched that room for days and never found any clues of foul play. Nothing violent had probably occurred in the room. Nevertheless, Mary Clare was here somewhere.

And Bunny had tried to burn the place down. She either wanted to destroy what she thought was evidence of a crime—Billy's crime—or else she simply didn't think Billy would let go and allow her to sell the house. She was right about that part. He was irrationally attached to a massive mansion that he didn't live in. In fact, he was probably the person insisting on its upkeep and periodic modernization. *He was clinging to a reality that didn't exist.*

Whether Bunny knew what happened to Mary Clare or not wasn't clear to Josie yet. All she knew was that Bunny had wanted to burn the place down to the ground, and when the job hadn't been completed last night, she'd gotten someone to come back and finish the garage today. By blowing it up.

How close did Lizzie and I come to being blown up with it?

Meanwhile, Billy was obsessed enough with keeping a house that was much too big for him alone—which wasn't even *owned solely by him*—that he was willing to hire Marion to squat there. Not the most rational, well-thought-out, or effective plan, rather like Billy himself. And why was he so concerned about the house? Why couldn't he let it go?

For what reason?

Josie stared at the smoldering remains of the garage. Curls of smoke rose upward. The only thing left under all the debris was probably the cement slab.

Evidence? They were looking right at it.

CHAPTER 39

"Mary Clare is *in the garage*," she said.

In her mind she pictured the skeletal remains of the woman encased in the cold cement of the garage floor. Mary Clare's Acura was a steel and fossil fuel monument, marking her tomb with her gravesite portrait and silk flowers hanging on the wall overlooking her.

Chills went down her neck as if someone's icy fingers had run across it. Josie swept a hand over her hair to brush off some half-lit ashy debris that had landed on her. The last thing she needed was to catch on fire thanks to an errant ember. The gray flakes caught on her beaded bracelet and she shook them off.

"But that garage has been searched a million times, including that blasted car he's obsessed with," Skip blurted out. "There's no way they could have missed her. Hundreds of people have been in and out of there. All over it with their fingerprint dust and Luminol checking for latent bloodstains. You're telling me they overlooked her?"

But neither Billy nor DJ looked surprised at her statement. She was on the right track. She knew it. No wonder the man—the gentle giant from the secret tape recording—had never unloaded this monster of a mansion. It was his wife's tomb.

"Is it the floor? Is she buried in the cement under the car?" she asked them. She needed some kind of confirmation. She watched their eyes for any signs, any tells.

Mary Clare's final resting place could have been behind the wall right where Billy had constructed his memorial to her, but that didn't seem like a safe enough place for her body to stay hidden all this time. No, a cement floor would be more permanent and marked by a two-ton steel gravestone, namely her Acura. She would be preserved forever. As long as Billy kept the house.

Billy sighed, but DJ looked like a storm cloud gathering, ready to unleash a torrent of...something. Her heart rate took off toward the stratosphere and she started breathing harder. She took a step backward and bumped into Skip, who was holding up his cell phone, capturing the whole exchange.

Okay, good. She had a video recording of all this if she were about to be pummeled to a bloody pulp. She hoped it was a good quality video so a jury wouldn't have any reasonable doubts.

"You don't know what you're talking about," DJ said, his shoulders expanding and filling up her line of vision.

Yeah, she needed a quick panic level check. Her perception was going wonky again, and her hearing was momentarily blocked out by the rush of blood to her head.

"I think I might," she said, though maybe not as bold as before.

"You're making some wild accusations that are going to make you need an army of lawyers. You got that kind of backup ready?" DJ looked livid, and now it was Billy who held him back instead of the other way around. From where he stood by Bunny Rogers, Officer Gorgeous threw them a concerned glanced. To be fair, they were giving him more than one officer could handle.

Drew had joined them again. Josie felt more emboldened, so she demanded to know, "Was this the primary crime scene, too? Did she die here or did you bring her body here later, after it was done?"

With the tooth bridge from the fire pit—if Ryan's story could still be trusted—Josie was fairly certain that Mary Clare's life had ended at Smiley's. The thing was, the timeline didn't match up. She'd been missing since the mid-90s, but Smiley's had burned down in 2007.

Brain flash. Aha, I got it now.

"*Yes,* the house and the garage were searched at the time," she told them, explaining it now to Skip. "But Mary Clare wasn't in the garage in 1995 or even 1998, for that matter. That whole timeline doesn't even matter."

Bunny Rogers had left the cold comfort of her cushy limo and approached them with the deliberate steps of a queen entertaining filthy foreigners on her lawn. Officer Handsome had her chauffeur back the limo out of the drive to make room for first responder vehicles that would no doubt arrive shortly. On cue, just down the street, a siren wailed.

"Young woman, just what are you implying?" Bunny asked. Her face was pulled down so tightly with condescension and disgust, one fatal pull and she probably could have rolled her face up like a window shade.

"I don't know. What are you inferring?" Josie couldn't help but snap back.

Another squeeze on her shoulder made her take a deep breath and start over.

"Look," Josie addressed Billy in full sight of the others, "I know why you were reluctant to file a missing person's report on your wife. And probably only did so under pressure from the local authorities…and her." She tipped her chin toward Bunny. "It's because your wife wasn't missing."

Next to her, only Skip and Drew looked surprised, which was very telling of the rest of them, including DJ. He just looked angry, like an avenging angel about to take out his sword and …

"Ridiculous," Bunny announced, crossing her plaid-covered arms, splaying out her fingers and displaying a deep red manicure. "You just accused him of hiding her body in the garage. Now you're saying she's alive?"

"You're purposefully misunderstanding me. So if you'd like to keep interfering with my theory, by all means, go ahead. Just don't be alarmed if I haul off and punch you in the throat," Josie told her. She could feel her shoulders tightening as if she were spoiling for a fight. Anger flooded through her system and it felt…good. Really frickin' good.

"Josie," Drew said in a tone she couldn't quite identify. Not exactly calm, but kind of. Maybe studiously stern and collected.

Huh. She didn't really like his tone. She brushed him off and proceeded with her magnificent tirade, her Hercule Poirot parlor-room, big-reveal moment. She was in charge now and she hadn't felt this good *in months.*

"The fact is, she *was* alive, at least for the next few years. Tell me, Mrs. Rogers. Why did she choose to live in that strange little room upstairs? The one with all the children's books and old clothes? Did you keep her prisoner up there with your rudimentary nursing knowledge? Did you live down the hallway from her in that terrible pink room so you could act as her caretaker while you kept her heavily sedated, heavily medicated day in and day out? Why did you keep your daughter like that? People don't lobotomize their rebellious daughters anymore. Like Rosemarie Kennedy. Like your aunt. There's not the same stigma against mental illness as there used to be."

"You have no idea what you're talking about," Bunny Rogers told her through a jaw so tightly clenched only her lips moved as she spoke.

"Well, enlighten me, then," Josie said, not entirely in control of her mouth, taunting the woman into action. "Why did you keep your daughter in that room upstairs?"

While she and Bunny exchanged words, she failed to notice DJ approaching from the side. He had left Billy's side and stalked across the drive to them. By the time she realized he was still headed her direction, it was too late.

His fist hauled back and slammed into the side of her head.

CHAPTER 40

The world spun. As Josie's cheek hit the pavement, she thought again about TBI. Traumatic brain injury. If she eventually lost her mind due to all the times she'd been whacked on the head, she'd have to rent the room next to her mother in the dementia care home. Or maybe they could be roommates.

Please don't let me have a concussion. I meant it when I said I don't have the brain cells to spare.

All around her were shouted voices of outrage on her behalf—thank goodness for that. It proved she hadn't been a complete a-hole through the events leading up to the punch. Through her wooziness, she saw Officer Handsome sprint up the drive toward them. Now that her adrenaline had faded, she realized how much she had screwed up. Not about Mary Clare—she was right about her—but in allowing her panic to turn into anger, letting it feed on itself until she'd felt nothing but aggression and rage.

So yeah, she needed to talk to someone about her problems before this got any worse. She knew it without a doubt now. And she would get on it, just as soon as she scraped herself off the ground.

"Don't move yet," Drew said from somewhere above her. "Give yourself a minute. Easy does it."

Aha, there was his soothing hand on her back. Maybe he didn't hate her after all, even though she was a complete jerk.

Off to the side, she heard smacking and the sounds of a scuffle in the dirt. Slowly, checking for dizziness and nausea, she let Drew help her into a seated position from which she saw DJ and Billy going at it in a churning, punching heap on the ground.

"Brother, that woman lost her mind and you know it," DJ said right before he took a hit to the jaw. Apparently he was more used to it than she was because he barely flinched before adding an uppercut to Billy's ribs.

"They're brothers?" Skip asked. He'd squatted beside her to see how she was doing.

"I think it's just a term of affection," she said, testing out her jaw, which seemed to be fine. Her cheek, on the other hand... "Like 'bro.'"

"Aha. Got it."

But what woman were the cousins talking about? Surely not her, but Mary Clare.

"You don't hurt women," Billy shouted at him, and tackled DJ back to the dirt. The two of them rolled again, someone landing a punch to the kidneys. She couldn't tell who.

He was definitely talking about Josie now. Or was he?

"We're blood. I'll get anyone who threatens you. I don't go back on my promises."

Officer Handsome shouted at them to break it up. Luckily for them, he was a calm kind of fellow and hadn't drawn his firearm, though he was threatening to do so now. His patience paid off, however, because after three more punches apiece, the cousins fell apart on the ground, panting hard with no collateral damage to the officer. Josie was glad—she'd taken a shine to the man in blue, although if he had to hit DJ once or twice, she wouldn't really mind because, *ow*, her head hurt.

"Mr. Ruby, I'm going to have to take you in for assaulting this woman," he said, and DJ groaned, though it wasn't clear whether it was from that or the walloping Billy had just given him.

"Damn straight you are," Drew said, anger turning his voice into a growl.

"Why'd you hit me, you ham-fisted Hulk? I'm, like, half your size," Josie yelled, still wobbly, from where she sat across the driveway to DJ. Her anger was gone now, though she felt twice as mouthy. Getting punched in the head had pressed her Reset button.

And to think she'd liked chatting with him over the counter at Smiley's. Man, was she ticked off. She hated being wrong about a person, especially so badly.

DJ sighed, hanging his head between his knees. One of his cheekbones was red and swelling up. She realized she probably looked the same thanks to him.

"Mary Clare was out of her damn mind half the time," he said, and Billy made a noise somewhere between denial and a whimper. "She had schizophrenia. It didn't blow up until after they got married. And it was getting worse and worse. Hallucinations. Voices in her head. Everything you hear about. You see it on TV, but I didn't even know it could be that bad until I saw it happen to her."

"We were controlling it with medication," Bunny Rogers said tightly.

"No you were not," DJ said. "She needed more care than you could provide. I knew it. Billy knew it. We all knew it. She needed to be in a hospital with medical professionals, not in that miserable room upstairs, all because you wanted to save her reputation—and yours."

"She loved her house. She wanted to stay here with Billy," Bunny yelled.

DJ's voice rose, too. "She wouldn't let him live his life. He couldn't live like a normal person. What kind of existence is it, wondering whether she was going to kill herself or you or him at any point?"

Billy groaned, cradling his head in his hands. "She was my wife."

DJ said, "I know, buddy. I'm sorry."

"When did she die?" Josie asked, talking across the driveway at Billy.

By now she had a pretty good idea, so when no one answered her, she guessed. "Was it 2007 when Smiley's burned down? Did she live for twelve years in that room upstairs until you killed her? Why did you keep her around so long only to murder her after so much time? After so many wasted hours of investigation and volunteers searching for her and all the pain and anguish of the people who really cared about what happened to her?"

Drew put a hand on hers. She realized she sounded as if she were about to lose her temper again, but this time, she was perfectly in control. She needed a confession from Billy to confirm her suspicions, so she kept goading him, hoping neither he nor his cousin had enough steam left to come across the pavement at her again. Officer Handsome hadn't pulled out the zip-ties yet, so she was fair game until they were trussed up.

Even Skip had been rendered speechless at this point. He'd gone so far as to take a step back from her as if to avoid any fallout damage, but he still held his phone up, capturing the video of her meltdown.

Billy had made another anguished sound of protest during her last verbal attack, so she thought she might be getting closer to cracking him. The sirens were getting closer, so she knew her time was running out. As soon as more cops arrived, they'd all be carted off for questioning or shooed away, if they were lucky.

"What did you do to her at the restaurant that got her teeth—her tooth bridge—knocked out? We found it in the fire pit. A person doesn't just walk around like nothing happened after something like that. Were you going to burn her body in the restaurant fire? The wife you'd imprisoned after more than a decade of her life?"

She was purposely making false accusations at this point. She didn't think Billy had kept Mary Clare imprisoned—Josie had seen the room herself. And she did think that he had sincerely loved his wife, at least truly *had loved* her.

"Are you going to allow this to happen to Billy, DJ? The less he talks, the harder it's going to be for him. I have enough evidence to nail him to the wall now. The restaurant will go down the tubes. It'll have to be shut down. Everything he's worked for his whole life—and you, too, right alongside him—it'll all be for nothing. Bankruptcy. Ruin. And forgotten forever. Are you going to let this happen to him? You've been protecting him your whole life. Are you just going to let him fall now?"

"Don't say a darned word, DJ," Billy said. "I'll take my chances with a lawyer. And she's going down with me." He cocked his chin toward his mother-in-law. "This is all her fault from the way she dealt with it from day one."

Josie smacked her hands together with a loud crack to get DJ's attention back. "You listen to me, DJ. This has gone far enough. Tell me how Mary Clare got hurt. Did she hit her head? You tell me now."

Officer Handsome had gotten behind the two men where they sat on the ground and had trussed their hands up with zip ties behind their backs. As soon as DJ's wrists were tightened behind him, the last of the fight seemed to drain right out of him.

"Tell me," Josie said again.

And then he began to talk.

CHAPTER 41

"She hit her head on the fire pit," DJ said, without meeting her eyes. "She fell and hit it. That's how she lost her tooth bridge. She hit her mouth on the edge."

Billy made that strangled animal noise again, but DJ didn't seem to hear him this time. He was locked in his own memories.

"Was it a fight?" Josie asked. "Did you hit her?"

"No. I was stopping her. She'd set the kitchen on fire. Smiley's was burning. She had a can of gas." His voice became calm and fell to a quiet monotone.

"Why didn't the gas show up in the two fire investigations? If there was an accelerant, it would have shown up during the investigations."

"I don't know," he said. "That's something you need to ask *her*." He tipped his chin toward Bunny Roger's car, where she sat with the door open exactly where Officer Handsome had asked her to wait.

Interesting. Had Bunny Rogers paid off both investigators to cover up the arson? That meant not only did she know her daughter was alive in 2007, but she very well may have been the reason Smiley's had burned down.

"So you're saying not only was Mary Clare alive in 2007, but she was at Smiley's. How did she get there?"

"She drove herself in her car. She didn't go out anymore, but she knew where the keys were, so she just took herself over there. We had to drive it back to the house."

"What do you mean? You drove it back to the house when? After she was dead?"

He stared dully at the pavement between them. "Yeah, afterward, because she was dead."

"And who hit her—sorry, I mean, who shoved her when she was lighting the restaurant on fire? Was it Billy?"

"No, I did it," DJ said. "I shoved her."

"And she hit her face on the pit?"

"Yeah."

"And this was 2007 when the restaurant burned down?"

"Yeah," he said again.

"So Mary Clare wasn't missing the whole time?" She realized she was repeating herself, but she wanted to see what other details she could coax out of him while he was in this weird almost-fugue state.

"She was living at the house. Her mother was giving her medication. It was supposed to keep her from…losing control of herself. She had hallucinations. Right, Billy?"

Billy didn't answer. He sat on the edge of the pavement, dumbly, face pale and blank.

"She had a lot of problems," DJ continued. "That's how she lost her teeth in the first place a bunch of years before. Blacked out on medication. Pills and drink together."

Josie shuddered thinking about the kind of life the woman had lived. The hand she'd been dealt. Was any of it her fault? She'd been sick. And she'd suffered twice over for it.

"Where is Mary Clare right now?"

His gaze briefly flicked toward the house. "Over there in the floor of the garage, just like you said."

"And did Billy do this?" She looked at Billy, but he remained face downcast, no longer responsive, as if he'd just given up.

"Yeah. He wanted to keep her at the house. Close to him."

"And that's why he doesn't want to sell the house?"

DJ nodded.

"And where does Bunny think Mary Clare is?"

"We told her she swam out into the lake one day and didn't come back in."

"And did she believe you?"

DJ shrugged. "I guess she believed what she wanted to."

Josie glanced over at the woman, sitting in her car staring straight forward at nothing. Icy, perhaps, or maybe just unable to face the hand that life had dealt *her*.

Officer Handsome helped DJ haul himself up to his feet just as two more squad cars rounded the bend and pulled into the driveway.

"Doggone, Josie. You're every bit as impressive as Greta Williams says you are," Skip told her, to her surprise. He gave her a hand up.

For one thing, she felt as if she'd been holding on to her sanity by a hair's breadth. None of her interrogation techniques had been skill. For another...*that Greta.* Although by now, Josie shouldn't have been surprised that Skip had tracked her down and quizzed her about Josie. The woman seemed to be behind everything everywhere Josie turned. At this point, she'd be expecting Greta to be the tooth fairy. Although the tooth fairy probably didn't scare little kids as much as Greta.

As the squad cars parked, Josie could see that in the backseat of the nearest car sat Ryan the bartender, looking worse for the wear. His face was black and blue and blood streamed from both nostrils.

She moved closer so she could overhear the newly arrived officers tell Officer Handsome, "Found this guy trespassing on a lady's property about a mile down the street. She was beating the crap out of him with a Swiffer, shouting at the top of her lungs about Bunco and Marilyn Monroe, I think. No idea what that's about, but I figured he had something to do with y'all's mess over here."

One of Marion's Bunco girls, Josie realized. She wondered if she could get in a few minutes alone with Ryan, too. In fact, she was currently exercising all of her self-control—what little she had left—in restraining herself from beating on his window and flipping him the bird.

"Right now, he's our primary bombing and arson suspect. You can see burns on his hands. And his knuckles are all torn up. Nice job on the collar," Officer Handsome told him. "We gotta take him in and swab his hands. Maybe Mrs. Rogers over there would like to come with us and perhaps throw him under the bus."

"Let's hope so," the other guy said.

CHAPTER 42

Josie and Drew stood outside the perimeter of the police tape at the house with the third remaining cop, waiting for what would most likely be a parade of crime scene processors. They'd have to come and check for remaining explosives. Then they'd have to dig Mary Clare up, process her, and eventually release her to the family for a proper burial. Whatever family was left.

Josie tried to say goodbye to Skip because she thought she might not see him again. He planned to follow the parade of cop cars and livery downtown to the police station to watch them all get processed and, presumably, to lawyer up. Plus, he had the video recording on his phone that he wanted to transfer to a flash drive as soon as possible. When she approached him, he refused to accept her goodbyes.

"I'm sure I'll see you around," he said, and she left it at that. Would she meet up with him again? Maybe in Boston, if he ever got up that way. She and Drew were leaving Austin for San Antonio in the morning, so she wouldn't be running into Skip again this trip. However in her experience, people had a habit of turning up at the weirdest times.

"We should get you some ice for that eye," Drew said, and the tone of his voice made Josie cringe. Gone was the over-wrought, angry-on-her-behalf boyfriend. Here was the fed-up-with-her guy who had put up with too much of her crap even before this trip.

She took a deep breath. If she was going to make an honest go at this whole engagement thing, she needed to grow a proverbial pair and face her problems.

"I really lost it back there," she said. As good a place to start as any.

His eyes widened as he turned to face her in front of the burned out house fire. "Are you kidding me?"

Uh-oh.

He said, "You were totally out of control. I've never seen you like that before. You were raging like the Hulk, like you were going to do a flying leap and jump that guy." He flapped his hand as if to imitate her in flight over the driveway.

"Yeah, about that…"

"I've never seen anything so damn magnificent in my life. You lost it, but you reigned it back in, and then you totally nailed that guy to the wall." He did a fist pump. "I could watch that a million times and never get sick of it. Do you think Skip is going to send you the video soon?"

They checked out of the Omni the next day and made it to their hotel in San Antonio in about an hour and a half. The drive south was pretty easy despite the crush of traffic and rainy skies. The Saturday morning crowd seemed to be less hell-bent on getting ahead of itself than on the average Austin weekday. Josie slept part of the way down while Drew drove.

Josie's phone woke her up about halfway there.

"Hey, did you see the newspaper before you left town?" Skip asked.

"I grabbed it on the way out of our room, but I haven't read it yet." She unbuckled her seatbelt so she could reach into the backseat for the paper. "Here it is. Ah, nice front page over the fold. You must have burned the midnight oil for this."

He'd gotten the top story of the day with a headline that screamed:

KILLER CONFESSES IN MARY CLARE MURDER CASE

Skip bragged, "In bed by ten, lights out at eleven. Slept a solid nine hours for the first time in decades."

She skimmed the article and was relieved not to find her name mentioned. She didn't need or want that kind of notoriety.

"Nice job," she told him. "How's it feel to close the file after all these years?"

"Pretty good, but I'm still hoping to cover the court days if it drags out into a trial. We're probably going to have three separate ones after Billy, DJ, and Bunny lawyer up. Unless someone decides to take a deal."

"What do you think is going to happen to the restaurant?"

Skip exhaled on the other end of the line. "It will probably close up, I'm sorry to say. I blame you for that, but it couldn't really be helped. That's the real reason I kept your name out of the article. Didn't want you getting death threats over it."

"Well, I appreciate it."

"How's your eye?"

"Puffy and tender, and it woke me up every time I tried to sleep on it last night. But it'll heal. No concussion at least. That's the good news."

"Good to hear."

"Hey, I have a favor to ask you."

"What's that?"

"As soon as you know where Marion ends up, can you pick up something I bought for him and deliver it to him? Kind of a pain, sorry about that, but I didn't know if he was heading to the shelter next or what."

"Sure, what is it?"

"It's a tiara I had made for him by the bead lady downtown. You know, that bead store off Congress? She'll have it ready for him in about a week. It's under his name."

He chuckled. "No problem. Writing it on my calendar now. Listen, I gotta go. There's a press conference in an hour. Next time you're in town, I owe you a cup of tea."

"And a muffin that's not undead."

"You got it."

CHAPTER 43

Despite Drew's enthusiasm for her inner She-Hulk, she intended to go see her friend-slash-therapist, Victor, to ask what advice he might have about her panic attacks. As soon as they got home, she'd pay him a visit. Living with unexpected bouts of anxiety was a pain in the rear, to put it mildly, so if there was anything she could do to make them stop, she was willing to try it.

Including talking to someone about my feelings. Which I really suck at.

Speaking of which, she still had Drew's ring, and now it was in her pocket instead of her suitcase. She just needed the right moment.

They'd just finished eating dinner at the restaurant recommended to her by a friend—and he'd called ahead to let his cousin know she was coming, which meant they'd been treated to a whole tableful of dishes they couldn't possibly eat by themselves, including the best chicken *molé* she'd ever had in her life. She could wax on about it for her blog later. Right now, she had other things on her mind.

With a pleasantly full belly, she was enjoying a stroll along the River Walk, holding Drew's hand.

"Wanna ride in one of those boat thingies down the river?" she asked him.

"I kind of like walking," he said.

The sun was setting. The rain had cleared up, but the cobblestones along the edge were still shiny and a little bit slick.

"Just don't fall into the water," she said. "I saw they have pub crawls here. I wonder how often people topple over into the river. Or get pushed."

He stared at her. "You're a little bit demented sometimes."

"That's why you like me."

"Probably." He squeezed her hand.

"Also, I have a black eye, so you'd better be nice to me or people will think you're a bad, bad man."

"Hush, you." He pulled her in for a gentle kiss. When they broke apart, he said, "Got any room for dessert? There's a chocolatier right there."

Ha. As if he had to ask.

They went inside, and she spent a good ten minutes poring over the sparkling display cases and rows and rows of chocolate truffles nestled in their ruffled paper cups. Drew waited patiently at a bistro table by the window sipping an espresso while she picked out four truffles. Silver tongs used with medical precision extracted the chocolately delights from their positions and packed into a small cardboard box with tissues and tied up with a gold string. "It's lovely," she had told the chocolatier, not bothering to explain that the packaging would not survive the next ten minutes.

"That looks fancy," Drew said when she slid into the chair across from him.

"It is, just like me."

He laughed. They both knew it was the opposite of the truth.

She toyed with the gold bow on the box. In her pocket, she slipped his ring on her thumb. The indestructible tungsten ring that Lizzie had sold her. Surely that was symbolic of their relationship, right?

"Aren't you going to eat them?" he asked, looking at the box of truffles between them.

"Why? Do you want one?" She laughed at his hopeful expression and pulled the box apart, his ring still on her thumb. "I got coconut—sorry, I know you hate that—but I also have a double chocolate, a salted caramel, and a blood orange. Do you want the double chocolate?"

She stripped off the top layer of tissue paper. It seemed the chocolatier had added a couple more while she wasn't looking. She lifted the last layer of paper and found...a ring.

Wow.

"What do you think?" he asked. "It's an antique. It was my grandmother's. It's not very ornate, but I think it'll go well with, you know, a t-shirt or whatever."

Wow again.

252

The ring was a delicate thin band of white gold with a hexagon-shaped setting for a diamond. She thought the sides were elegant with their art deco styling. Also, she wasn't wearing her usual t-shirt this evening, but a cowl-necked burgundy sweater with her nicest jeans, just for the occasion. And yes, she'd combed her unruly hair nicely.

"I love it," she said, feeling the smile spread across her face. She gave him a thumbs up with the ring she'd picked out for him.

NOTES FROM THE AUTHOR

- Lizzie's full name, Lizabeta Del Valle Del Jabalí, translates roughly to Lizzie of the Valley of Boars. Kind of weird, but the surname Borden is Old English for "boar" and "valley." Her name, just as a tongue-in-cheek joke is Lizzie Borden, after the famous axe murderer.

- The character, Marion, is based loosely on a famous Austin icon, Leslie Cochran, a mostly homeless cross-dresser, who ran for mayor several times. In 2009, he was badly beaten allegedly by a group of people whom he tried to talk to about drug abuse. Sadly, he died in 2012, most likely as a result of his 2009 injuries. March 8, the day of his death, is Leslie Day in Austin, TX.

- The minor character, Yvonne, who competed against Mary Clare in beauty pageants, has the surname, Lugnar, which is similar to the German word, *Lügner*, which means "liar."

- Austin has a ton of amazing barbecue places, naturally. None of the places in this book resemble the ones I've visited there although the made-up names in this book are in homage of several of them, like Rudy's and The Salt Lick.

DID YOU ENJOY THIS BOOK?

Please leave a review on Amazon or Goodreads.
It would mean *the world* to Emily.
Even better, tell a friend.

ABOUT THE AUTHOR

EM Kaplan grew up in Tucson, Arizona, and later lived for almost a decade in Austin, TX, where she worked as a technical writer and ate a metric ton of barbecue. She lives in Illinois with her husband, author JD Kaplan, their two kids, and their dog, Max, a.k.a. the officemate.

Visit www.JustTheEmWords.com to discover her social media hangouts and blog, sign up for her newsletter, and see upcoming events.

OTHER BOOKS BY EM KAPLAN

Josie Tucker Un-Cozy Un-Culinary Mysteries
The Bride Wore Dead
Dim Sum, Dead Some
Dead Man on Campus

Rise of the Masks, Fantasy Trilogy
Unmasked (Book 1)
Unbroken (Book 2)
Undone (Book 3, coming soon)

Made in the USA
Monee, IL
02 June 2021